A HARVEST OF BLOOD

AN OMEGA THRILLER

BLAKE BANNER

R

RIGHTHOUSE

ISBN-13: 978-1-63696-337-2

ISBN-10: 1-63696-337-4

Cover design by: Damonza

Printed in the United States of America

www.righthouse.com

www.instagram.com/righthousebooks

www.facebook.com/righthousebooks

twitter.com/righthousebooks

ONE

Is revenge any part of justice? It's a question lawyers and philosophers agonize about in the abstract, usually over a fine malt, or a cognac, and a Havana cigar. But ask a mother whose daughter has been taken from her, raped and murdered, and she'll tell you justice is revenge. They are the same thing.

Marni had stayed six months. Omega had left us alone. They had their hands full dealing with the press and the media, and above all, with a very aggressive select committee appointed to look into the UN fracas, and former President Hennessy's death[1]. It was still big news, and I figured it would be for years to come. I never watch TV or read the papers anymore, but even so, it was hard to get away from the debates, the investigations, and the conspiracy theories that had sprung from it. And all of that had Omega keeping a very low profile indeed.

---

1. See *The Hand of War*

So they had been six idyllic months at my house in Wyoming, in the remotest place in the western world. We'd hardly seen anyone from one week to the next, and that suited us fine. We walked in the hills, fished and hunted for our food, and spent the evenings in front of the open fire, reading, listening to music, talking, laughing; healing.

But we both knew our time was limited. Omega had not gone away, and it would not be long before they came looking for us. So, as November drew to a close, I locked up the house, she packed her things, and we headed for San Francisco. There she called Professor Gibbons at Green College in Oxford and gave him a coded message that she was going back. At International Departures, she gave me one last kiss and told me she'd be in touch. The fight against Omega would continue. And as long as it did, we could not be together. It made us too vulnerable.

And next thing she was gone, swallowed by the crowd beyond the security gate, and I was alone. Again.

After that, I had driven east on the I-80, into worsening weather conditions. A weather alert had been issued. An unseasonable freezing front had been reported coming down from the Arctic across Canada and into the northwestern states. There were severe blizzards reported in North Dakota, Montana, and Idaho. It had been cold in San Francisco, but the skies had been blue and I had not expected problems driving back to Wyoming.

East of Reno, I had made a pit stop at a service station. It was three in the afternoon and I noticed that the sky in the north was turning black, and a cold wind had whipped up. I debated staying at the motel across the road, but I was seven hundred miles from home, and I'd figured I'd try and make it that night. In the Zombie 222, my modified Mustang Fast-back, weather and cops permitting, I could make it in six hours and maybe beat the worst of the snow.

That was what I'd figured. So I stepped into the warm, noisy diner, found a table with a view of my car, ordered a steak sandwich and a large black coffee, and stared at the TV behind the bar. It was a current affairs talk show and Larry O'Connor was talking to Senator Cyndi McFarlane, who looked as though she was getting mad. She was leaning across the table, stabbing at the air with her finger.

"You know what makes me mad, Larry? I'll tell you. It makes me mad that Professor Gibbons has been publicly humiliated by the press and the media across this country, not because he lied, not because former President Hennessy proved him wrong, not because he was exposed—none of those things happened. He has been ridiculed because a bunch of hecklers made him look comical on stage. But everybody—and that includes you, Larry—everybody is carefully ignoring what he said. And everybody is ignoring the fact that today, in America, we have a select committee asking the question '*How the hell did an American-made nuclear device get into the hands of Islamic terrorists?*'"

Larry played it for the camera, which obligingly closed in on his face. He smirked and said, "I don't think everybody is ignoring it, Senator. It's just that he looked funny up there, getting excited like that. And let's face it, he *does* look like Bilbo Baggins!"

He got a laugh, but not from Cyndi McFarlane. She turned and surveyed the audience, waited for the laughter to die down a bit, and said, "Did any one of you lose somebody on 9/11?" The laughter died and Larry looked embarrassed.

She went on regardless. "Anyone here out of work, or can't afford medical care? Because let me tell you something, somebody put a nuclear device in the United Nations building. And they put it there, partly, to silence Professor Gibbons, the man you like to ridicule so much. And he was there to tell you that *successive* administrations, Democrat and Republican, have spent *seven trillion dollars* waging a war that only cost a few billion. Those seven trillion dollars are *interest*. Interest on money borrowed from financial institutions that belong to the friends, colleagues, and associates of the presidents in office during that war. That is not funny. You think that's funny? I don't. And I think it is very sad that you do."

Larry made a comical, chastened face for the camera, but only got a small, embarrassed laugh from the audience. They were with the Senator. He cleared his throat.

"So, moving on..."

"Who said we were moving on, Larry? I'm not ready to move on." Now she got the laugh, plus some applause. I smiled. I decided I liked her. "I am here to tell you," she said, "and America, something important. And neither you nor your network are going to silence me. There is a web of corruption in this nation of ours. It's a cancer that spreads clean across America, across the border into Mexico and across the sea into China and Russia in the East, and Europe and the U.K. in the west. And this corruption is controlled by a small group of men and women who will stop at nothing, and I mean *nothing*, to further their own corrupt ends. They have attempted to institute an unfettered government within the government and bend our democratic processes to allow them to rule supreme. But neither the legislature, nor the people, of this country, will allow that to happen!"

She got a lot of applause, whistles, and shouts of support, and Larry O'Connor was forced to join in. He was smiling, but you could see he was mad. I wondered if Ben and his cohorts at Omega were watching. I was pretty sure they were. Ben had told me once I could not hurt Omega. So far I had killed two of their senior members and right now I figured they were squirming in their padded leather chairs. But I wasn't kidding myself. They would manipulate the situation, and they would end up using it to their own ends. That was what they did best.

I paid my bill and stepped back into the parking lot. It had grown dark and I was surprised at how far the clouds had spread from the north. The wind had turned from cold to bitter and I shivered as I crossed to my car.

The Zombie 222 is the creation of a couple of crazy geniuses in Texas. The body is an original Mustang '68 Fastback. But under the hood she has twin lithium-fueled electric engines delivering eight hundred bhp, one thousand eight-hundred foot-pounds of torque direct to the back wheels. She'll go from 0 to 60 in one and a half seconds, with a top speed of 200 MPH. And she is totally silent.

I slipped out of the lot and headed west into the gathering dark. As I chased the amber funnels of my headlamps along the endless, straight thread of the blacktop, my mind reached back. The last thing that Marni and I had discussed was where we went from here. My own plan had been to hunt down the twenty-seven members of Omega, one by one, and assassinate them. It was simple and effective, and followed the most fundamental of rules in warfare: Cut off the head and the body will die. But she had dissuaded me and begged me to let her talk to Professor Gibbons, to use his contacts and bring in more allies. I wondered vaguely if Senator Cyndi McFarlane was one of those contacts. Either way, whether she was or not, for now there was nothing for me to do but wait.

Within half an hour, the sky had turned black and it had started to snow. Fifteen minutes after that, I passed the town of Lovelock. There was no traffic on the roads, the snow was beginning to stick and drift, and for the second time I thought maybe I should stop for the night. But fate had other plans for me.

Another fifteen minutes and I found myself in a blizzard, slamming on the brakes because I had realized at the last minute that I was plowing into a intersection that shouldn't have been there, and there was a truck bearing down on me fast from my left. I stopped with my hood three feet over the line and the truck passed within six inches of my headlamps. The blast of air rocked my car and a shower of snow, sucked up by the slipstream, smothered my windshield. The wipers cleared it, but suddenly I had no idea where I was, or how I had got there. Hindsight got busy telling me I should have stopped at a motel in Lovelock, and I was now inclined to agree with it. But hindsight wasn't telling me how I could get back to Lovelock. I knew straight ahead would take me deeper into the storm. The intersection gave me no left turn, so I turned right and hoped for the best.

The road got dark and the snow grew heavier. I began to worry. I would soon need to recharge the lithium batteries, and if I got stranded out here in this snow I would not last long. I told myself that sooner or later I must find a service station, a motel, or even just a house. But hard as I looked, I could see no sign of life. I could see nothing at all except the blackness and the glow of the deepening snow in my headlamps.

From cruising at 120 MPH I was now down to crawling at little more than 20, and if the snow got much deeper I wouldn't even be crawling. I'd be stuck and buried.

Eventually, after maybe half an hour or a little more, I began to see flickering lights on my right. I figured the road would eventually turn that way, but as I crawled on, the lights seemed to stay parallel. That told me there must be a turn off, an intersection, which might be hidden by the snow. But I could not afford to miss it. I needed to get to those lights. It would be ironic, I thought without much of a smile, if having survived ten years in the SAS, the worst that the Sinaloa cartel, FARC, ISIS and the Mujahidin could throw at me in hostile territory all over the world, I were finally to be killed at home, in Nevada, by a snow drift.

Ahead, the glow of my lamps picked out an irregularity on the roadside; a couple of signs, maybe a rest area, a row of mail-boxes, a fallen tree trunk... I slowed, stopped, and climbed out of the car. A million tiny knives of ice tore through my skin. I tramped unsteadily, ankle deep in snow, and saw it was a turn off that led through a blanket of darkness to the small cluster of lights flickering in the distance. There was a wooden sign by the road and I could just make out the name 'Independence' written on it.

I turned back to the car and saw again what I had taken to be a fallen tree trunk. It wasn't a tree. I walked over and hunkered down, wiping the snow from the body. It was a girl, maybe fifteen years old. Her skin was white and her lips were blue. I felt for a pulse. It was hard to tell because my own hands were freezing, but I thought I felt a flutter. I opened the passenger door, picked her up, and placed her with difficulty in the seat. I had a couple of rugs and blankets in the trunk from where Marni and I had gone on picnics. I grabbed them and wrapped her as warmly as I could. Then I closed the door, got behind the wheel, and turned down the track toward Independence.

TWO

It was about two and a half miles of unpaved track. The snow was settling deep and several times I almost got stuck. Eventually, after five or ten minutes, we slowly slithered and ground our way in to a kind of town square, which was actually little more than a broadening of the road. On the right, there was a row of houses, with warm light creeping around heavy drapes to touch the heaped snow on the front lawns. On the left, there was a wooden fence with a gate. Through the gate I could make out a small orchard, a path, and a large wooden building with a sign over the door that read 'Pioneer Guesthouse'. But opposite, as an extension to the terrace of houses, there was a saloon bar that looked something like a large cottage. There were several trucks parked outside.

I left the Zombie by the gate to the guesthouse, opened the passenger door, and lifted the girl out, still swathed in rugs and blankets. She looked dead, but when I put my ear to her nose and mouth I could feel the soft, frail brush of her breath. I carried her across the small square, through the heavy fall of flakes, to the door of the saloon. I opened it with my foot and as I maneuvered myself through I shouted above the hum of voices, "*I have a wounded girl here! I need a doctor! Fast! I think she's dying!*"

Absolute silence fell on the room. Maybe a dozen faces stared at me. A man and a woman behind the bar, three men in their thirties standing at that bar, two tables occupied by middle-aged couples: twelve faces, staring, silent. I roared, "*A doctor! Now!*" An elderly man stood. I ignored him and turned to the nearest occupied table. "*You! Put two tables together!*" They jumped and started moving tables. To the couple behind the bar, I bellowed, "*Pillows! Cushions! Warm water!*"

It was like a chicken coop when Mr. Fox drops in for a visit. There were people all over the place trying to look busy. The two couples I'd shouted at had jumped up and pushed two tables together to form a make-shift bed. One of the men had pulled off his tweed jacket and folded it to make a pillow for her head. I laid her gently down and started rubbing her hands. I noticed the elderly guy who'd stood up was taking off her shoes and rubbing her feet. He shouted suddenly, "*Abi! That water! Hurry! Not too hot! Warm! Tepid even!*"

"You the doc?"

"I am." He glanced around. "Where is Sammy? *Sammy!*" A young man in his mid-twenties stepped up, looking apologetic.

"Yes, Doctor Graham."

"Take over from this man! Keep rubbing her extremities.

Get some warmth into her... You." This last was directed at me. "Get a hot drink inside you!"

But I was looking at Sammy. He had his mouth open and he was staring at the girl's face. I looked at the other people who had by now formed a circle around us. They all had the same expression as he had. I said to him, "Get a grip, Sammy. Start rubbing."

I pushed through the small crowd and went to lean on the bar. I felt suddenly very tired and very cold. I saw Abi bustle out of the kitchen with a pan of warm water and make for the table. There were three men leaning against the bar next to me, watching the proceedings, and as I put my elbows on the counter, they gave me the once over. They weren't hostile, but I got the feeling they reserved the right to turn that way. The guy behind the bar came over.

"What can I get you, mister?"

"Hot coffee, and a double whiskey. You can leave the bottle."

He poured me a generous measure and left the bottle, then went to the kitchen to make coffee. Outside, the wind rattled the windows, whistled, and rose briefly to shriek before settling again to groaning and moaning. I drained the glass and refilled it. The guy standing next to me said, "Passing through?"

I glanced at him. He was six foot, had balding, sandy hair and pale blue eyes. He was bull-necked, had strong arms and a barrel chest. I shook my head. "Nope. I got lost in the storm. I turned right somewhere after Lovelock."

"Where you headed?"

For a moment I thought of asking him why he wanted to know. Instead, I said, "Wyoming."

He gave his head a small twitch to the side. "You're four hundred mile from Wyoming. Reckon you turned south a Mill City." He smiled. It wasn't friendly. "Nobody ever comes to Independence on purpose."

Behind me, I heard the doctor say they needed to get the girl to a warm bed, and to bring some hot water bottles for her. Then there was a bustle of movement and I saw them carry her into the kitchen. I figured there must be stairs there to the upper floors. I watched them go and turned back to the big guy who'd been talking to me. "Where's your sheriff?"

His eyes seemed to half-close for a moment. "Over in Lovelock. He don't never come out this way. We got a whole mountain range between us and Lovelock. What you want the sheriff for?"

I wondered again whether to answer him or not. I took another drink and said, "I found her by the side of the road. I was wondering how she got there. I thought maybe the sheriff would wonder that too."

He didn't answer. He just stared at me with no expression. The young guy came out with my coffee and poured me a cup. I said, "You got any food?"

He looked momentarily astonished. Maybe that was the big thing in this town, being astonished by everything. After a moment of astonishment, he said, "Yuh! Sure! We have beef and red beans?"

I nodded. "Good, and some bread. And give me a beer."

I took my beer and my whiskey to a table and sat. My friend at the bar got the hint and turned his back on me, started talking to his pals. Eventually, the woman called Abi came out of the kitchen with a large bowl of beans and stewing steak, and a basket of bread and butter. She placed them in front of me and sat. I was surprised and told her so with my face.

"Excuse me." She looked distressed. I studied her for a moment. She was very attractive in an un-affected kind of way. She was maybe thirty-six or -seven, wholesome, blonde, blue-eyed; very much a woman. "I just wanted to thank you."

"For what?"

"Peggy. She would surely have died."

"Is that her name? Peggy?"

"Peggy-Sue Martin. Where on Earth did you find her? What happened?"

I was aware that the men at the bar had gone silent and turned to face us. I ignored them.

"I took a wrong turn 'round about Mill City. I was looking for a motel, or somewhere to stay the night. I stopped when I saw the signpost for Independence. Luckily I got out of my car to read the sign. At first I thought it was a tree-stump. Then I saw it was a girl."

She was staring at me like I was talking Klingon, and she didn't speak Klingon. "At the junction? With Bloody Creek?"

I shrugged. "The main road where you have your mail boxes."

"What in the name of the Good Lord was she doing there?"

I shrugged again, this time with my eyebrows, and shoveled a spoonful of meat and beans into my mouth. It was good. I spoke through a full mouth. "I was wondering the same thing."

She turned and stared at the men at the bar. It was hard to read anybody's expression. I said, "Is there somewhere I can stay till the storm passes?"

She turned back to me. "Of course. I have the guesthouse across the way. I'll fix you a room there."

I continued eating. She was about to stand but I asked her, "What about her parents?"

She didn't answer straight away, which made me look up from my food. Then, she said, "They live up the road."

"Is somebody going to tell them?" She didn't answer and I leaned back in my chair. "They didn't alert anybody that she was missing?"

She shook her head.

I drained my beer. "Tell me where they live. I'll go and get them."

My talkative friend at the bar spoke up. "You're a regular good Samaritan, friend. Take it easy. I'm going that way. I'll deliver the news and I'm sure they'll be down to thank you." As he walked past, he put his hand on Abi's shoulder. "Good night, Abi. Be seeing you."

I heard the door open behind me. There was a blast of cold air and the shriek and moan of the freezing wind in the trees. Then the door closed again, shutting out the night behind its fragile wood and glass.

"That's Earl," she said, as though she owed me an explanation, and an apology. "He works at the farm."

I should have let it go, but I could see Peggy's frozen white face, her blue lips and her fragile, childlike body huddled in the snow, and something made me say, "Farm?"

"Aloysius Groves' farm. Al. Most people 'round here

work for the farm. They'll probably be down in the morning."

I frowned.

She said, "Peggy's parents. They'll want to thank you."

"In the morning?"

"They won't want to come out in this..."

It was my turn to look astonished. I said brutally, "Let's hope she's still alive in the morning for them to see her."

She stood and went back to the kitchen. I finished my food and had another glass of whiskey. After that, I asked Abi to show me to my room. She pulled on a heavy coat and hat and I followed her out into the night. It was very dark and our breath billowed like cigar smoke in the freezing air. The flakes were dense and a fitful, gusting wind tossed them this way and that in swirls and flurries. Abi hunched into her shoulders and crunched across the snow, which was now five or six inches deep on the small square. She pushed through the wooden gate to the Pioneer and opened the door to the guesthouse.

It was warm and quiet inside. The walls were paneled in wood. The floors also were wood, and covered in thick, woven rugs. To the right there was a pine reception desk, and to the left a staircase, carpeted in deep green and illuminated by Victorian, glass-shaded lamps. Ahead, double doors stood closed. She opened them, revealing a comfortable living room with an open fire burning large logs. A girl, perhaps eighteen or nineteen, sat before it in a large armchair. Beyond her, a boy of perhaps thirteen lay stretched out on a sofa. They were both reading, but looked up when Abi opened the door.

"Primrose, we have a guest for the night. Will you show him to his room, please? Two B is made up."

Primrose stood and approached. She was more than pretty, but too demure and sweet to be stunning in the Hollywood supermodel sense. She wore jeans and a sweatshirt, but you felt she should be wearing a crinoline. She was the kind of girl a young man might fall seriously in love with, and spend all his time staring at the stars dreaming of rescuing her from evil-doers. She was a maiden, a damsel. She smiled at me and said a simple but pretty, "Hello."

I found a smile somewhere in my weary face and nodded. While Primrose got the key, Abi turned to me, wrapped in her coat and hat. "I must get back to the saloon. If you need anything, just call down to Primrose, she'll make sure you're taken care of..." She hesitated. "And...I don't even know your name..."

"Lacklan, Lacklan Walker."

"Mr. Walker, thank you so much for saving Peggy..."

Primrose turned to stare. I shook my head. "Anyone would have done the same."

She seemed about to say more, but turned and went back into the snowstorm, closing the door behind her.

Primrose led the way up the stairs through the dim light of the lamps. As we climbed, I realized they were oil. It was fortunate. Electricity would never have survived that storm. She opened a door at the far end of a broad corridor and showed me into a large, comfortable room, furnished in the style of the early twentieth century, with an en suite bathroom at the far end, by the window.

"I'll light the fire for you." She hunkered down and struck a match. As she put it to the kindling, she said, "The lamps are oil. We have no electricity or gas here. We're pretty much off grid."

"No phone?"

The flames caught and started to roar in the chimney. She shook her head and the flames danced amber on her face. She stood and turned to me. Her expression was oddly direct. "There's no line, and no coverage for a cell. No TV. No internet. We get some electricity from a generator."

"You're pretty isolated."

She nodded. "Especially in winter, when it snows."

"I guess you get what you need from Lovelock."

She smiled. It was an odd smile, part mischief, part irony. "The farm supplies us with basic necessities. Anything else we might need, we do without. What happened to Peggy?"

"I don't know. I'd like to know. I found her by the road-side, freezing to death."

She frowned and looked down at the floor. It was an expression of distress, but not surprise; not shock. "Was she..." She looked up into my face. "Did they...?"

"Who?"

She hesitated. "I mean, whoever..."

"Do you know what happened to Peggy, Primrose?"

"No! Of course not!" She turned. "I'd better go. Is there anything you need?"

I smiled and showed her the bottle of whiskey. "Just this and sleep."

She smiled, but it wasn't a happy smile. "Goodnight, Mr. Walker."

"Goodnight, Primrose."

She closed the door and I fell into an armchair in front of the warm, dancing fire. I poured myself a generous measure of whiskey and savored it without swallowing, watching the manic dance of the flames as they licked and consumed the dry logs. I told myself that in the morning I would fit the chains to my car, charge the batteries and, whatever the weather, I would head for home. There was a problem here in this town, that much was obvious, but it was not *my* problem, and I must not get involved.

But as I let the fierce amber liquid slip down my throat and warm my belly, I thought of Peggy, barely a child, left to die by the roadside, of cold and neglect. And it was not just the whiskey that warmed my belly, but anger.

THREE

I went for a run next morning at six. Abi and her two children were already up and about. Abi was at the reception desk and watched me come down the stairs.

"You're up late, Mr. Walker. Did you decide to have a lie in?"

She didn't exactly smile, but there was a glint of humor in her eyes that could have been mischievous. I considered her for a moment and then smiled. "I've been up for a couple of hours, Abi, but I thought I'd finish translating Genesis from the original proto-Aramaic before breakfast."

She raised an eyebrow. "Really? That is very worthy."

"Now I'm going for a run."

"Goodness. You'll find there is hot water in the shower when you get back, despite the weather."

"That will be a novel experience. Perhaps I'll give it a try. By the way, my name is Lacklan."

As I opened the door, she said, "You really are going for a run..."

I nodded. "I'll have plenty of time to sleep when I'm dead."

It was heavy going down the track. The snow had eased up, but it was a foot deep on the road and six to seven feet in the drifts. It was pitch dark, but above you could just make out a low, leaden ceiling of dense cloud. It was colder than I had expected, I guessed about 5 degrees F. I punched and dodged as I ran, did quick sprints to break up the pace and increase my heart rate and calorie burn.

After about half a mile, I became aware of some lights moving up ahead, and the sound of heavy diesel machinery. As I got closer, I saw there was a snow plow that had cleared a path to a structure about a hundred yards off the road, in the field. A large ten-wheeler truck, with a covered back, was pulling away from it, headed for the intersection. Once it got there, it turned right and moved south.

From what I could make out in the light of the plow and a couple of trucks parked thereby, the structure was some sort of pen, with a barn in the centre. It was big. The pen itself was at least a hundred and fifty yards by the same again square. And the barn was easily seventy feet long and fifty across. I saw Earl standing in the back of one of the trucks. He had a couple of friends with him. They all watched me run past. I ignored them and carried on as far as the road. By that time I had warmed up. I practiced a few kicks and some Tae Kwon Do patterns, and then ran back at a loose, relaxing pace.

In spite of my boast to Abi, I had a hot shower, dressed, and went down for breakfast at seven. She brought me bacon and fried bananas with a pot of coffee.

"There are pancakes and maple syrup if you're still

hungry after. Exercising in the snow will give you an appetite."

I smiled at her. "It did."

"Can I sit down?"

My mouth was full, so I gestured at the chair opposite me. She sat. She didn't say anything, just watched me. I swallowed, drank coffee, and asked her, "Any news on Peggy?"

She shook her head. "We moved her to the doc's house last night, where he can take care of her a bit better. Her temperature's up a bit, but she needs to get to a hospital."

"You want me to take her? I'll need a truck."

"No. There's heavy snow forecast. If you got stuck, she'd die."

She stared at the tabletop, like she was thinking about saying something but didn't know how to. Finally, I said, "What's on your mind, Abi?"

She looked surprised at the question, then said, for no apparent reason, "We're pretty isolated here, even when it doesn't snow. I've never known it to snow like this before. All we've got really is the farm."

"I saw them clearing the snow when I was out."

"At the depot?"

I shrugged. "Big barn off the track, with a fence around it."

"We call that the depot. It's where he stores his produce."

"Aloysius Groves?"

"He provides what work there is around here..."

I raised an eyebrow. "Is he the feudal lord?"

She laughed, but it sounded strained. "Something like that."

"What are you trying to tell me, Abi?"

She made a face like she was going to dismiss my question, then stopped herself and sighed.

I said, "OK, let me ask you something instead. Al Groves has a snow plow. He also has several trucks. Why isn't he either taking Peggy to a hospital or going for help?"

She took a while to answer. "I guess he has other priorities." She sighed again, heavily. "Mr... Lacklan, the weather is going to get worse before it gets better. It looks as though you may be stuck here for a couple of days. You may see or hear things that seem strange to you. It's just the way things are around here. Best if you don't get involved."

I drained my cup and sat back. "Does that include dumping children by the roadside, in the snow, to freeze to death?"

She didn't answer.

"Where is the doc's house, Abi?"

"Two down from the saloon. It has a blue door, and an arch over the gate."

"Thanks for breakfast, and for the advice."

I stood. She spoke in a rush, like she wanted to say it before it was too late, before I left, "It's not as simple as it might seem from the outside."

"I know, Abi. I've seen it before, many times, in Iraq, in Afghanistan, in the jungles in Colombia. You've told me all you need to tell me. I'm going to go and check on Peggy now."

There was a limpid gray light when I stepped outside. The clouds were low, thick and dark, and for the first time, I got a look at where I was. The village of Independence was tiny, and settled in the mouth of a steep canyon that rose to the west. To my right, the east, that canyon opened out into a flat plain that seemed to extend for miles. Right now it was blanketed in dense, luminous snow. Ahead and to my left, the terrain rose steeply into mountains, densely forested and shrouded, like the plain, in heavy snow. I raised my collar and crossed the road.

The doc's house was like something on a chocolate box, or a tin of Danish cookies. It was a cottage on two floors, with two chimneystacks and a black slate, gabled roof. It had a small front lawn enclosed by a stone wall, and a wooden arbor with a creeping rosebush over it, now dead and covered in frozen clumps of white.

I checked my watch as I pushed through the gate, and made my way to the shiny blue front door. It was ten minutes before eight, but I figured in this village people were early risers and I took hold of the brass knocker and rapped a couple of times. He opened the door almost immediately.

"Saw you out running earlier. Was going to call you in for breakfast..." He winked wolfishly, "But I figured you'd rather have coffee and bacon with Abi than me!"

I smiled. "I hope I am not too early."

"Too early? No such thing. Been up since five. Come on in. You'll have some coffee."

It wasn't a question. He led me through a small hallway with a narrow flight of stairs to a comfortable living room with wooden beams, a large open fire, and, arranged around it, leather armchairs and a sofa that looked at least a hundred years old. The walls were lined with books and there was an agreeable smell of pipe tobacco mixed with soot and freshly brewed coffee. A broad bow window overlooked his front lawn and the small square, and afforded a direct view of the guesthouse.

"In the summer," he said, as though he were answering a question, "we get the occasional weekend pioneer, with their luxury RVs and motor homes. But aside from that, I rarely get to talk to somebody from outside. Sit down." He said all this from the open doorway, then leaned back and shouted in a surprisingly big voice, "*Mrs. Entwhistle! Coffee for two!*" Then he closed the door. "She does for me. But I imagine you didn't come here for my sparkling conversation and amusing anecdotes. You came to inquire after Peggy."

I sat in one of his vast, cracked leather chairs by the fire. "How is she?"

He frowned, not at me, at the fire. "Know anything about medicine?"

I gave half a shrug. "First aid. I've seen a few cases of hypothermia, gunshot wounds..."

"You're a soldier."

I nodded. "I was."

He raised an eyebrow like an albino shrimp. "You still are. Believe me, I can tell. Her core temperature has risen. She should be recovering." He sighed. "But she should be in hospital. She has bruising..."

"Mind if I have a look?"

He gave a brief nod. "In a minute."

The door opened and a woman who looked remarkably like the doc, only less bushy, stepped in with a tray of coffee and biscuits. She smiled at me like the doc wasn't there and set the tray on the table by the window.

"Would you like me to pour, or do you think you can manage that?"

I smiled back. "I'm sure we can manage."

"Go away, Mrs. Entwhistle. Go back to the kitchen, where you belong."

She left.

"With a population of less than barely eighty people, you can't afford to sack somebody like Mrs. Entwhistle. Her ironing and cooking are second to none."

"I'm sure. She looks formidable. You were saying about Peggy."

He went and poured the coffee, handed me a cup with two biscuits, and sat in the other chair.

"Either she had a bad fall, or she was beaten. She may, of course, have been struck by a vehicle. Sometimes you get trucks coming this way, to the farm, then they go on down Independence Road, over the Humboldt Mountains." He shrugged and shook his head. "The long way around. I've never understood why."

I studied him a moment. "I found her at the junction, Doc. It's about as flat as it can get without your Mrs. Entwhistle taking an iron to it. How do you fall and get that kind of bruising, at her age, somewhere that flat?" He didn't answer, just stared at the flames in the fire. "There's something else, Doc. The bruising you get from a vehicle is different from the bruising you get from a fist, or a foot. I'm pretty sure you know that. I've seen my fair share of both. I'd like to have a look at Peggy's bruises."

He sighed. "I know. That's why you're here. Fact is, I'd like you to look at them too."

I carried on as though he hadn't spoken. "You see, I am having trouble understanding what a thirteen- or fourteen-year-old girl was doing three miles from her home in the middle of a blizzard, with no coat. So I am thinking that her bruises were not received where I found her. I think she got those bruises somewhere else, and was dumped."

He raised one of his Gandalf eyebrows at me. "You weren't a military policeman, were you?"

I raised a more modest eyebrow back. "Are you telling me you hadn't come to the same conclusion?"

He looked suddenly depressed. "No, I'm not telling you that. Come on, let's go and have a look."

He led me up the stairs I had seen earlier, to a landing with three bedrooms and a restroom. He opened one of the bedroom doors and I followed him in. There were two single beds and a broad window overlooking snowy hills, abundant pine trees and what seemed to be a frozen creek.

Peggy was lying in one of the beds. She had been bathed and her hair washed. I could see now that was blonde; a very pretty child. She had more color in her face and her lips were no longer blue, but she was still unconscious and had a large bruise on her right cheek. I felt a hot twist of anger in my belly and heard my own voice as though it were somebody else's.

"A year ago, she was probably still playing with dolls."

"You're not far wrong. She was just fifteen last month." He pulled back the covers. "She's in a coma, Mr. Walker. She is not aware of what I am doing."

He showed me her arms, and then her neck. There were deep purple marks consistent with having been gripped, possibly strangled. He pulled back her nightgown and on her ribs there was further bruising, consistent with having been punched. He put back her gown and pulled up the bedcovers, then stood staring at her for a moment.

"There could be internal bleeding, I can't tell. As I say, she should be in a hospital." He paused, hesitated a moment, then said, "I keep a rape kit. Nobody in the village knows that I do, but I do."

"Was she raped?"

Now he looked me straight in the eye. "You know that she was."

I frowned. "You saying you think I raped her?"

He smiled, shook his head and sighed. "No, of course not. The logistics alone would be impossible. Where? When? How did you get her there? No, Mr. Walker. I am saying that from the moment you found her by the side of the road, you have been thinking she'd probably been raped. The beating simply confirms it."

I nodded. "It was the only explanation that made sense." I studied his face a moment. "If this village has less than eighty people, plus a handful of men at the farm, and you keep a rape kit..." I shrugged. "That's telling me you have a fair idea who did this."

"Obviously. But I am not going to tell you."

I scowled. "Why not?"

His face became suddenly irritable. "Because it's more than my life is worth! That's why! Hell! I'm taking a risk just talking to you." He sighed again. "But there is something I want you to do."

"Name it."

"When you leave, soon, go back to Lovelock, tell the sheriff what you've seen here. Make them investigate."

I narrowed my eyes at him. "There have been other rapes of young girls..."

"I am not going to tell you another damn thing. You

come in here, throwing your weight around, demanding to see this poor child. You've seen what you've seen, now pack your things and get out of this town. Leave us be... You understand me?" He said it all without a trace of anger or feeling.

I nodded. "I understand, Doc. But there is worse weather on the way. I'm stuck here for at least another twenty-four hours."

"I know. Just keep a low profile, get out of here as soon as you can, and stay out of Joe Vasco's way."

. FOUR

WHEN I STEPPED OUT OF THE DOC'S COTTAGE, IT was just after eight forty-five. I glanced up at the saloon and saw there were two pickup trucks parked outside. They looked like the ones I'd seen earlier down at the depot. I thought of the doc's advice about keeping a low profile, and decided, with an ugly smile on my face, that the best way to do that was by blending in and having a morning coffee with some of the guys. Maybe they'd introduce me to Joe Vasco.

I pushed in and the door swung closed behind me. The place was empty but for four men standing at the bar. They all turned to look as I came in. Earl was one of them. Standing beside him was a tall, rangy man of about forty, with dark hair and dark eyes, wearing a white cowboy hat. Beside him were a swarthy, Mexican-looking man in red and black checked fleece, and an athletic blond with amused, cruel eyes. Behind the bar, looking worried, was Abi.

I smiled. "Good morning."

They didn't answer, so I went and leaned on the counter next to Earl. "I'll have a coffee, please, Abi."

She went to the kitchen without speaking. The tall guy in the hat spoke suddenly, with a voice that sounded like he was shoveling gravel. "You the feller who found Peggy at the crossroads?"

I turned to look at him before answering. "Yeah. That was me."

"Pretty lucky for her you were there. Almost a miracle."

I gave it a moment to let him know I understood where he was going. Then I asked, "You believe in miracles?" He drew breath to answer but I cut him short. "I don't. See, the unusual thing was not me being there. That might happen on a night like last night. A car traveling on the I-80, blinded by the snow, trying to get back to Lovelock. It could wind up at Independence. What is unusual is to find a young girl, without a coat, three miles from her home, lying in a snow drift by the side of the road. That's unusual. But it's not a miracle."

"You got quite a mouth there."

I didn't smile. "Again, I don't agree with you. Because, when you said it was almost a miracle, you were insinuating instead of coming out and saying what you really think. Now me? I'm talking straight. You? You're hinting and implying and suggesting. So to me, that gives you the mouth."

He stood and squared his shoulders.

I leaned my elbow on the bar and pointed at him. "Thing is, even if I did hit her with my car, you still have to ask yourself the question, what the hell was she doing at that crossroads at that time of night, in a blizzard? Shall I go on?"

Now he was frowning. His friends had turned back to the bar and were studying their cups. He said, "Who are you? You a cop?"

I smiled. Abi came out of the kitchen with my coffee and gave me a warning glance as she poured. When she was done, I looked back at the big man. "I'm just a man on his way to Wyoming, who happened to turn right instead of keeping on straight. Fortunately for Peggy I did." I took a sip and set my cup down again. "Forgive me if I came back a bit strong, but I find it best to nip that kind of insinuation in the bud. My name is Lacklan Walker, and I plan to be on my way as soon as the weather permits." I raised an eyebrow at him.

He was still frowning.

"I like to think that during my brief visit I did your town a good turn, and not a disservice."

He grunted and his three friends smiled at their cups.

"Name's Joe Vasco. I manage the farm." He indicated with his head in the direction of the crossroads. "I didn't mean no offense. Just..." He shrugged. "We're a small community here, Lacklan, and we all know each other. Naturally we are suspicious of strangers... It's hard to think of anyone 'round here doing anything to Peggy."

I nodded like I agreed. Then I asked, "Doing anything?"

His frown deepened. "Hurting her in some way."

I made a face that said I knew nothing. "I was under the impression she had been knocked down by a passing vehicle. I was confused at what she was doing out there in the snow, but I did not realize somebody had done something to her. What had they done, Joe?"

His friends had turned again to look at me and listen.

Joe's face had taken on some color around the cheeks. He'd stopped frowning and he looked mad.

"I only know what I been told."

"Oh." I nodded. "I thought maybe you talked to the doctor, or her parents. Have they been in yet?" I shook my head and sipped my coffee again. "They must be sick with worry wondering where their little girl is."

He stepped up close to me. "Yeah, well, that's the town's business, Lacklan. We're grateful for everything you've done an'all, but now maybe it's time for you to be getting along. I'm sure you've got folks in Wyoming who must be wondering about you."

I studied his face. I knew exactly the way he would fight. He'd think of himself as a dirty fighter, clever, devious, a cheat; but above all, he was a pack animal. He would depend on his friends to dominate his prey, before he moved in to claim the kill. I offered him a thin smile that told him I knew who, and what he was.

"That's awful thoughtful of you, Joe, but I haven't got anyone waiting for me at home. It's just me and my curious mind; nobody to worry about me, nobody to wonder where I am, nobody to report me missing."

He didn't answer for a moment. Then he said, "You have a safe trip, Lacklan." He turned to his boys. "C'mon boys, we got work to do."

They ducked out the door and let it slam behind them. I turned to Abi. She was watching me as she polished glasses behind the bar. She didn't look happy.

"That wasn't smart. I told you to stay out of things."

I made the face of innocence and showed it to her. "Me?

I was just hanging out with the guys, Abi. Where do Peggy's parents live?"

"Don't, please."

I smiled. "Shall I go and ask my new best friend, Joe?"

She sighed and let her hands drop by her side. "You're going to get yourself hurt, Lacklan. And you might get other people hurt in the process. Just *please* stay out of it!"

I leaned on the bar with both elbows. "Maybe you didn't notice, Abi, but somebody already got hurt. She was just fifteen. A child. You know what happens when something like this goes unpunished?" She bit her lip and looked away. I pressed on. "The person who did it begins to think he's above the law, he gets bolder and does it again, and then again. Maybe next time it will be you, or your daughter, Primrose. Let's face it, Abi, the selection here is not all that wide."

She picked up a glass and stared at it. Her voice was barely a whisper. "Please...stop..."

"Where do they live?"

She didn't look at me. "The Apple Orchard, a quarter of a mile up the road."

By the time I stepped outside again, an icy wind had whipped up and was lifting clouds of frozen flakes from the ground and trailing them, like giant ghosts playing tag across the plain below. I turned away from them, hunched into my shoulders, and made my way up the canyon, toward the dense woodlands, crunching shin-deep through the snow. But as I climbed, the snow grew more shallow, most of it having been caught by the canopy of trees above.

After about fifteen minutes' walk, the pine trees on my right began to thin and opened into farmland. There, set back some twelve or fifteen feet from the road, I found The Apple Orchard. It was a quaint farmhouse on two floors, with a paved path leading through a rose garden on the right, and an orchard on the left that, despite the name, seemed to be mainly cherry trees and plums; all now covered in icing, like a Christmas cake.

A dog began to bark as I pushed through the gate and made my way along the path. I noted that I was the first to disturb the snow. They hadn't left the house yet. I hammered on the door, and after a minute it was opened a few inches, and a woman peered out at me. She was in her mid-thirties with thick black hair pulled back into a bun. She had no make up on her face, and her clothes could have belonged to any decade from the 1930s to the present time: brogues, a tweed skirt, a plain blouse, and a knitted cardigan.

"Yes?"

"Good morning, ma'am, I am sorry to disturb you. Abi at the Pioneer Guesthouse said I could find you here. I have news about your daughter, Peggy…"

I heard the intake of breath. The fingers of her left hand went to her mouth. Tears sprang to her eyes, but she didn't say anything.

"It is extremely cold out here, ma'am. Do you think I might come in and get warm while I give you my news? I won't stay long."

She opened the door and let me in to a broad hallway. On the right there was a door. It stood open and there was a man in it, watching us. He was a little older than her, perhaps forty, though like his wife, he gave the impression of being older. He wore black pants and a black cardigan over a brown shirt. His black hair was slick and shiny as though he'd used brylcreem on it, and a thin, black moustache gave him a mournful look.

"What is it?" he asked.

I took off my jacket and, as she didn't offer to take it from me, I hung it on a peg on the wall. The man stood back and said, "You'd better come in, in front of the fire."

The room was not large, and had the same unhappy air as its owners. He returned to his chair, where he had a pipe and an ashtray on a small occasional table beside it. I noticed there was also a Bible with a marker in it. I wondered if it was Matthew 18:6. His wife sat on the sofa, leaving the other armchair for me. I sat and turned to the woman.

"Are you Mr. and Mrs. Martin, Peggy-Sue's parents?"

She nodded.

I glanced at him. He was staring at the fire, as though he was in some kind of horrific trance. "Mrs. Martin, Mr. Martin, I have some very bad news for you. I found your daughter last night..."

Before I could finish, she had covered her mouth with her hands, squeezed her eyes tight and let out a terrible, inhuman noise. Her whole body shuddered and she cried out, "*Oh God! Oh God, oh God, please help me...*"

I looked at him. He had gone gray and his bottom lip was quivering, though his eyes were still fixed on the fire.

"Mr. Martin, your daughter is *not* dead."

He turned to stare at me. It was an expression of shock, tortured hope and equal despair.

His wife cried out, "*What?*" and I felt her hands clawing at my arm.

I turned to face her, shaking my head. "She would have

died if I hadn't found her. But she is at the doctor's house now. She is very ill, badly hurt, but she is alive."

He collapsed in tears, curled forward onto his lap, his face buried in his hands. She dropped to her knees, half-hysterical, giving thanks to the Lord. For a moment, I felt like reminding them it was me who'd found and saved her, not their god, but it doesn't do to mess with people's faith. I gave them a while. Eventually, he stood and left the room. After a moment, I heard him noisily blowing his nose. She had a handkerchief up her sleeve. She used it and sat again on the sofa. For the first time then, she actually seemed to see me.

"You found her?"

I nodded and wondered if she was going to ask me where.

Instead she said, "Thank you so much. You were truly sent by the Good Lord."

I waited, watching her, but all she did was turn toward the fire and gaze at it. After a moment, he came back and sat down again. He looked at his pipe, like he was wondering if it was too soon to light up.

"Mr. Martin, I can't help noticing. Neither of you has asked me what happened, where I found her. You both seemed to be expecting this. Your fifteen-year-old daughter was out last night, without a coat, in a blizzard, and you didn't raise the alarm. What's going on here?"

He looked at his wife. Then he looked at me. "We knew," he said, "May God forgive us, we knew where she was and we knew she probably wouldn't be coming home."

FIVE

There was an unreal stillness in the room, broken only by the crackle of the fire. It is a strange fact that in life the most terrible things are often not awe-inspiring or momentous, but simply banal, and the more horrific for being mundane and unexceptional. I found myself wishing I could find what I had heard unbelievable, but the tragedy was that it was all too believable.

"You knew where she was?"

It was his wife who answered. "Who are you?"

I turned to her and there was bitterness in my voice. "You mean aside from somebody sent by the Good Lord?"

Her face tightened.

I went on. "My name is Lacklan Walker. I got lost in the blizzard last night. By pure chance I happened to see your daughter lying by the side of the road. She was barely alive. I got her to the saloon and the doctor was there. She is with him now, but she is still in a coma. I'd like you to tell me how she came to be lying at the side of the road, with no coat, at that time of night in a snowstorm."

Her face was still taut, but her gaze drifted away from me. "It is none of your concern. We are very grateful to you, and if you want money we will happily pay you, but it is not your place to ask impertinent questions."

I sat forward. "Impertinent questions?" I turned to him, but he wouldn't meet my eye. "*Impertinent questions?* Do you realize that somebody tried to murder your daughter last night?"

There was a hysterical edge to her voice as she repeated, "That is none of your *concern*, Mr. Walker!"

"I disagree, Mrs. Martin. Whose concern is it? You think maybe it's the sheriff's concern? Or the FBI's?" I reached over and grabbed the Bible he'd been reading. I slammed it on the floor at her feet. It made a loud bang, like a shotgun. "Doesn't your Bible say if anyone allows harm to come to a child, it would be better for them to have a millstone hung around their neck and drowned in the depths of the sea? If I find a child, beaten and strangled, and thrown in the snow to die, Mrs. Martin, I figure that's my concern. And if you two are too damned chicken-shit to protect your own daughter, well, then I figure it's doubly my concern. Because children need to be protected." I stood. "Especially from people like you." I pointed at him, then I pointed at her. "You went through hell last night and this morning, worrying about her. But let me tell you something. What you went through is nothing, *nothing*, compared to the horror she lived through while she was being beaten and strangled. And you willfully let her go through that. You are as culpable as whoever did it. You disgust me!"

I left their house and there was a hot rage in my belly as I walked back down the hill. The wind had picked up and was whipping tiny shards of ice into my face. The sky had grown leaden and it was starting to snow heavily again. But I didn't notice any of it. All I could see in my mind was Joe Vasco and Earl, out by the depot in their trucks.

When I got back to the saloon, I saw there was an old Jeep Cherokee parked out front. I went on a few paces till I had a clear view of the plain. I saw they were still down there, working. So I walked over to the Cherokee, tried the door and found it was open. The key was still in the ignition. God bless rural America. I climbed in and fired it up, then took off down the road, going too fast, slipping and sliding and raising a huge plume of powdered snow behind me.

I slowed as I approached the huge banks raised by the snow plow and turned into the field. Up close, I saw that the perimeter wall was a good eight feet tall. There was a large, double gate in the side which now stood open. Earl's red Toyota was parked in it and he came out to look as I approached. I stopped a few feet from the gate and swung out of the cab. Earl looked surprised when he saw who it was and turned back over his shoulder. I heard him shout, "Joe! We got a visitor!"

Joe Vasco and his other two pals came out past the Toyota. His eyes were bright with anger. "I thought I told you to get lost, Lacklan Walker."

I pointed back toward the town. "There is a child back there who needs a hospital. You've got trucks and you've got a snow plow. So you are going to help me get that child to a hospital. Now."

He almost smiled. He said simply, "God damn!" He

turned to Earl. "You hear that Earl? We're going to give Mr. Lacklan Walker here our snow plow and our trucks so he can get that sweet little girl to a hospital. Ain't that kind of touching?"

Earl and his two pals started laughing.

Joe said, "Get the hell out of here, Walker, before I get mad."

He turned to go.

I snarled, "What's the matter, Joe? You scared that if she comes out of that coma she might remember what happened? Tell me something, how did you know I'd found her at the crossroads?"

He stopped dead. Narrowed his eyes at me. The wind was starting to whistle in the cables by the road. The snow was falling heavier. He pointed at me. "You're the one who found her, Walker. You were the last one to see her alive..."

"She's not dead, Joe. And if I'd done this to her, would I have brought her in? Would I be this bent on getting her to a hospital?" I stepped toward him. "But you, why are you so reluctant to help, you son of a bitch? That child is dying! Is that what you want? You want her dead so she won't talk about what happened to her?"

He was exactly the kind of fighter I thought he'd be. He jerked his head at Earl and Earl, the big Mexican, and his athletic pal rushed me. Earl got to me first. There are a lot of fancy blocks in the martial arts. They all have their place, but nothing is as effective against a right cross as lunging inside your attacker's guard, with a rigid left arm at forty-five degrees, and a simultaneous right fist plunged into the solar plexus. Add a couple of megatons of rage and that mother won't get up. Earl dropped, retching, vomiting, and gasping for breath.

In the movies, multiple attackers are kind enough to come in one at a time. In the real world, they jump on you all at once, and try to take you to the ground. There, if you let them, they will pummel and kick you to death. As Earl went down, I had the big Mexican rushing me on my right, and the athletic blond reaching out to grab me with both hands on my left. I had no intention of going down. I grabbed his right wrist with my left hand and took a big step back, pulling him with me, right into the big Mexican's path. They collided and as he fell off balance, I took his wrist in both hands and twisted it savagely against the joint. I felt his shoulder pop and he screamed like a woman in a B horror movie. That left the big Mexican, who was struggling to stay upright in the snow. I took a big step up to him and smashed my right fist into his jaw. I followed up with my left and another right cross. He fell flat on his back.

I looked for Joe. He'd backed up a few paces and had what looked like a Glock 19 in his hand. I said, "Put that away or I'll kill you with it."

He shook his head. "Get out of here. Get in your Jeep and get the hell out of here."

"I'm not going anywhere, Joe. I don't know what's going on in this town, but I'll find out and I will make you pay. Count on it."

I knew I couldn't take him there, and I knew he wouldn't risk shooting me. He had to get his boys back to the farm, and by the time he did that, my body would be buried in snow. The risk of somebody finding me when the thaw came was too great. We had a stand off. I could hear

Sergeant Bradley's New Zealand accent growling at me out of the past, "Never get into a fight you are not sure you can win. Always fight on your own fuckin' terms, Captain!"

I turned and walked back to the Jeep. I'd been stupid to go there in the first place, but at least now they had three guys down who wouldn't be in a hurry to cross me in the future. I climbed in, slammed the door, and headed back toward Independence. The snow was heavy and visibility down to forty or fifty yards. As I ground my way back toward the saloon, I told myself I'd got something else out of the confrontation too. There was no doubt in my mind now, no doubt at all, that Joe Vasco was in some way behind what had happened to Peggy. I'd told him I'd make him pay, and by Odin I would..

I left the Jeep where I had found it and pushed into the saloon. There was a big guy in the middle of the floor staring at me. He looked mad. He growled, "You wanna tell me what in the hell you mean by takin' my truck without askin'?"

I scowled at him. "Are you one one of Joe Vasco's boys?"

"Yeah. What's it to you? I'm askin' you what you mean by takin' my truck?"

I looked past him and saw Abi, her face pleading, shaking her head. I sighed and looked back at the big gorilla. I said, "I'm sorry. It was an emergency. I wanted to try and get Peggy to a hospital before the snow set in."

He grunted and waved a finger like a sausage at me. "You should ask before you borrow a man's property. Remember that."

I pushed past him. "I will. I'll do that."

He went outside. The door slammed on the snow and

the wind, and he drove away, toward the farm. I leaned on the counter and looked hard at Abi.

"You need to tell me what's going on."

She shook her head. "Just leave it alone, Lacklan, please."

"I need to know."

"I'm closing up. There'll be no one in now till tomorrow."

She went into the kitchen. A moment later, the light went off and she came out wrapped in her coat, hat, and muffler. I followed her to the front door, took the keys from her and locked it. Then we ran across the road to the guest-house. It wasn't yet midday, but it had grown as dark as evening and the wind was howling and baying in the pine woods. Visibility had dropped further, to barely thirty yards. We pushed inside and closed the door behind us, with snow swirling around our feet..

Primrose came out of the living room. I could see the fire burning there. It looked good, warm and homey. She said, "Mom! I've never seen anything like it!"

"It's just a storm, Prim."

"It's insane! It's dark and it's not even night!" She turned to me. "Mr. Walker, you must come into the parlor, or the kitchen with us, where it's warm!"

Abi stared at her. "Prim?"

Primrose stared back at her mother and her cheeks colored with anger. "Mother! It is the very least we can do! On a day like this! And Mr. Walker saved Peggy's *life!*"

I wasn't going to argue. I looked at Abi and raised an eyebrow at her. She closed her eyes and took a deep breath. "Lacklan, of course it is the very least we can do. Would you care to join us?"

"I'd love to." I turned pointedly to Primrose, who was smiling but whose cheeks were still red. "Thank you."

I followed them both through what they called the parlor and into the kitchen. It was a large room. The floor was bare wooden boards, but it was covered in woven rugs and sheepskins. There was a blue iron range giving off warmth and a smell of baking pies and bread. There was also a heavy pine table, and sitting at it, watching me with an expression of awe, was the boy. Primrose said, "Sean, say hello to Mr. Walker. Mr. Walker, Lacklan, this is my brother, and nemesis, Sean. Please sit down, will you have some tea? Luncheon will be in about half an hour."

"Thank you."

Abi had set about washing vegetables and Primrose went to make some tea. I sat at the table and smiled at Sean. Both of the women had their backs to us, and he, with wide eyes, pointed at me and mouthed the words, "*I saw what you did!*"

SIX

I PUT MY FINGER TO MY LIPS AND SHOOK MY HEAD. He grinned, nodded and raised his thumb, then delivered a few silent punches to the air while mouthing the word 'pow'.

Abi put the vegetables on to boil, then she and Primrose came and sat at the table. Primrose brought with her a large, blue teapot and four cups, which she filled and distributed. I thanked her and looked at Abi, who was avoiding my eye.

"Abi, we are going to talk about what's happening in this town. It's not something that we can put off indefinitely."

Her mouth tightened and she sighed loudly through her nose. "How many times? I really wish you would leave it alone. This is none of your business."

I suppressed a flash of anger. "Murdering a little girl is *everybody's* business, Abi! We are not talking about your religious beliefs or your opinion on gay marriage! We are talking about a child, just a little older than your own son, who was beaten, raped, and strangled, and then thrown by the roadside to die of cold. And nobody in this village—not even her parents—gives a damn!" I frowned at her. She still wouldn't meet my eye, so I went on. "Well, I give a damn, and that makes it my business."

Primrose was looking at her tea like it had used foul language and blasphemed. She surprised me by saying, "And so do I, and so should you, Mom."

Abi's eyes flashed and her cheeks colored. She stared at her daughter but before she could say anything, Sean had spoken up. "Me too, Mom. It's not right."

"How dare you both be so impertinent!"

"Abi." Now she looked at me and her eyes were blazing, "It's an outrage for your children to tell you you should care that a child has been raped and almost killed in your village? But it is not an outrage to rape and strangle a fifteen-year-old girl?"

She had the decency to look embarrassed. She stared down at her cup and after a moment said, "That isn't fair..."

"What they said was not impertinent. It was very pertinent. Peggy's parents know who did this, but they are too scared to talk. I am willing to bet that you and the doc know who did it too, but *you're* too scared to talk. Just tell me one thing, have there been other cases?" She didn't say anything, but she didn't have to. Her face said everything. I nodded. "I thought so. How far does it have to go? How many little girls have to die? How bad does it have to get before you do something about it?"

She spoke in a flat, dead voice. "Please stop."

Primrose answered for me. "No."

Her mother glared at her. "Primrose, *enough!*"

"*No!* You think that because I've made it to nineteen, I

am safe? You think that because you're an adult *you* are safe! And Peggy was fifteen and blonde and pretty, so bad luck to her! Well, it's *wrong!* And *you* are wrong! Sooner or later he *will* come after us! And even if he doesn't, he hurts us as much by taking Peggy as though he had taken one of us!"

"Don't say that!"

"It's true!"

Abi's eyes filled with tears. She stared furiously at her daughter. "My job is to keep my children safe! My heart breaks for Peggy! But I will *not* put my children at risk!"

She turned to stare at me.

I said, "Abi, you are putting your daughter at risk by allowing him to continue. As long as he is out there, your daughter and every young girl in the district is at risk."

"And what do you expect me to do? Take a gun and go and *shoot* him?"

I gave a small shrug, "It's one option, but I wouldn't recommend it. You'd be better off telling me who he is, and what's going on."

She shook her head and buried her face in her hands. Primrose said, "We don't know who he is. He's one of the men on the farm. But they all stick together, like a clan. Anyone who has tried to do anything in the past has been beaten to within an inch of their lives."

Abi gave me a look and somehow I understood: the absence of a husband and a father in the house was no accident, but the kids didn't know. I gave a small nod that I got it and said, "Tell me what happened before."

Abi sighed and flopped back in her chair in a gesture of resignation. "Years ago. Two sisters, the Gordon girls, thirteen and fifteen. They went missing. They'd been visiting at the farm. They left to go home, but they never made it back. The whole village went out and searched for them. Eventually, their bodies were found up in the canyon. They'd been raped and strangled. It destroyed their parents. The story is they upped one day a couple of weeks later and left the town. They have never been seen or heard of since."

She paused, examining her tea as though wondering whether to drink it. Then she set it back down and continued talking.

"A year later, Sally Inigo was found out on the plain. She'd also been raped and strangled..."

I interrupted her. "Didn't anybody notify the sheriff's department?"

She looked at the backs of her hands, like she was regretting a bad choice and wished she'd picked nicer ones. "After the Gordon girls were killed, yes. But there was no evidence, no witnesses. They asked some questions and left. But after Sally was found, we had a meeting in the church hall. It was decided we were a very private community and we didn't want the papers and the TV crews coming in and prying into our business. In any case, the sheriff hadn't been able to do anything, so it was agreed we'd take care of it ourselves..."

"Take care of it? Take care of it how?"

"We didn't know. We all agreed it was best we didn't know."

"What are you talking about, Abi?"

"The men at the farm said they'd take care of it."

"Joe Vasco?"

She nodded.

I sighed. "Talk about asking turkeys to vote for Christmas!"

She shrugged. "There has been nothing since."

"Until now."

She nodded. "Yes, until now."

Primrose spoke suddenly. "It seems to me we have two problems. One is that whatever the men at the farm did five years ago, either the same rapist has come back, or we have a copycat. So it didn't solve the problem. The second, and more urgent, is that Peggy needs to get to a hospital."

I studied her face for a moment and decided I liked her. "That's absolutely correct." I turned back to Abi. "I talked to Joe Vasco and three of his men about half an hour ago, that's what I borrowed the Jeep for. I asked them to provide us with the snow plow and a truck to get Peggy to Lovelock. They tried to give me a hiding for my efforts, and Joe pulled a gun on me."

Sean grinned and drank his tea.

Abi said, "The only trucks capable of getting to Lovelock in this snow belong to the farm. And the way it is at the moment, without a snow plow we wouldn't stand a chance." She hesitated. "It could last days, perhaps a week."

I drummed my fingers on the table. "Peggy may not have a week. How far does the track go up the canyon?"

Sean sat up straight, his eyes bright and an expression of glee on his face. "It goes right the way through to the Rye Patch Truck Stop! And there are lots of houses around there. On a fine day, it takes no more than five hours to cross."

I said, "Nine or ten hours in this."

Abi's jaw dropped. "You cannot be serious. You'll never make it alive!"

"Is there another option? Whatever the consensus of this

village may be, Abi, I am not going to stand by and let that child die."

She closed her eyes. "You have made your point, Lacklan. But there is no point in going out there to die in the snow. You will *not* make it!"

I looked at the dark glass in the window, with the thick snow falling outside. There was a good chance she was right. "How far does the forest stretch? The trees are pretty dense on the slopes, they give some protection from the snow."

It was Sean who answered. "They follow the canyon about two-thirds of the way up, then they kind of stop. The top is bare."

I thought about it. "The wind is coming from the northeast, which means the far side will be protected, at least to some extent. It'll be a five hour climb, that'll be the hard bit. The worst part will be the top. The descent will be easier."

Abi shook her head. "You'll die."

"Not if you provide me with a couple of thermos of hot, sweet coffee, thermals, blankets. I'll need to stop twice on the way up. I'll make the descent in a single leg."

Primrose was watching me with narrowed eyes. "You've done this kind of thing before, haven't you?"

"In Afghanistan, in the mountains. It was worse than this." I turned back to Abi. "I'll try and arrange a chopper to come in and collect her. I'll notify the sheriff, and so will the doctors. There will be an investigation."

She closed her eyes. "I suppose it will be for the best. But if the investigation fails..."

"If there is no investigation, it will be worse, believe me."

We gazed at each other for a moment. She caught my

meaning and looked away. "I suppose I always knew this day would come, sooner or later. I think, unconsciously, I prayed for it."

I stared at her for a moment. "There are over fifteen thousand rape-murders in the States every year. And almost twenty thousand rapes without murder. I promise, the national TV and press are not going to swarm over Independence because a kid got raped by a redneck. And even if they do, that is not such a high price to pay to have this son of a bitch brought to justice."

She didn't look at me. "That was never my personal concern. But please, Lacklan, we don't cuss in this house."

"Then what is your concern?"

Primrose and Sean had gone quiet. Abi raised her eyes from the tabletop to look at me. "Isaac and Elsa Ibanez, Sally's parents. They also disappeared about three weeks after Sally was found. Word was they had moved away, like the Gordons. But, like the Gordons, nobody has ever heard from them since."

I leaned back in my chair. "You fear they were silenced as possible witnesses."

She nodded.

I added, "That's why Peggy's parents are so terrified."

"I imagine so. They are a very simple couple. The Lord knows how they are coping with this."

I grunted. "Not admirably."

"Don't judge them."

"Why not? Wake up, Abi. I never yet saw an angel arrest a killer, a rapist, or a drug dealer. And I never saw your Good Lord pass judgment on one. But I've seen plenty of cops and judges do it. I don't know anything about gods, heaven or hell. But I know a lot about this world. And in this world, we have to take responsibility for what happens to us, and the people around us. And while the Martins sat at home reading the Bible, their daughter was getting raped and strangled. I judge them to be poor, negligent parents, and so should you. Every judgment we fail to pass is an evil act that prospers."

A tense silence fell over the table. Outside, the wind rattled the glass in the windows. The gingham drapes moved in the frozen fingers of a hidden draft. After a moment, Abi said, "Are you quite finished lecturing me?"

"Yeah."

"Please have some lunch. Let's talk to the doctor and some of the other townsfolk, perhaps somebody can help you, drive you part of the way, give you some equipment..." She shrugged. "Make this something less of a suicide mission."

I nodded. "Thank you."

Sean was staring at his mother. "Mom, I should go, too. I know the way. I've done it plenty of times. Alone he might get lost, but together we can make it."

She was shaking her head long before he had finished. "Absolutely not, Sean! No! Out of the question."

He appealed to me with his eyes. I smiled and shook my head. "Thanks, pal. I think I have to do this one alone."

He sighed. "OK, I'll draw you a map."

"That would be helpful."

Primrose got up from the table and went and opened the oven. The smell of baking bread and hot steak pie invaded the kitchen. Outside, the wind howled and groaned, and for a moment it sounded like all the demons of Hell were baying for my life.

Maybe they were.

SEVEN

THE DOC, THE REVEREND, AND THE FEW NEIGHBORS Abi went to see could offer little in the way of help or advice —other than the eternal 'don't do it, stay out of it' refrain. The doc provided me with elasticized thermal long johns and socks, and the reverend gave me two extra thermos flasks, bringing my total to four. The doc told me not to drink alcohol, as it was a depressant and would make me more vulnerable to the cold. He then supplied me with a pint of whiskey and told me to drink it when I got there.

Nobody was willing to drive me up to the end of the woodlands. Nobody wanted to be seen helping me. I was going to have to make the whole journey on foot. I thought about using the Zombie, but I knew it would never make it. It would just get stuck in the snow.

Sean gave me a rucksack and Abi filled two of the flasks with hot chicken soup and the other two with hot, sweet coffee. That, a bar of chocolate, and a large slice of meat pie was my rations. Sean begged again to be allowed to come with me, but was promptly slapped down by both his mother and his sister. So he handed me a detailed, carefully drawn map which he had sealed in a plastic envelope, to keep it dry. He stood behind my shoulder as I sat at the kitchen table and explained it to me in the failing light of the afternoon.

"You just follow the road all the way to the end of the woods," he said. "As long as you're in the woods, the road is going to be easy to follow, and there won't be much snow. But once you get out of the trees and it levels off, it's going to be more difficult. It'll be dark for one thing, there won't be any stars or moon to guide you, and the road will by buried in snow." He reached in his pocket, pulled out a compass, and handed it to me. "Keep going west. But when you get to the top, you're going to see a big moth…" He glanced at his mother. "A big peak in front of you, so then you are going to go north, for about a thousand yards. See? That's here…"

He pointed at the map. I nodded. It was clear and well drawn. "Thanks, Sean, that's great."

"Wait! This is the next difficult bit where you could get lost. The canyon then follows a kind of inverted 'S' shape and comes out at a fork. You're going to want to take the left fork, because it goes down hill, but it comes out at a bad place. Don't go that way. Turn right and go up hill. It's gonna be hard in the snow, but that's the path. You're going to go northwest for maybe a mile, then you're going to come to the highest point, out in the open. You got a tough climb, maybe half a mile, and the snow will be deep. You got to keep a little south of west. I put it on the map, see, here. Three degrees south of west. Then, when you get to the top, you'll see the canyon below you." He squeezed in beside me, grinned and gave a small laugh. "You can go down on your ass..."

His mother scowled at him and he grimaced. "I mean, on, like... as though you had a sledge."

"I get the idea."

"Once you're in the canyon, you just follow it all the way down."

I slapped him on the shoulder. "Good man, Sean. That is going to be very helpful."

His face flushed with pleasure. "Jeez! I wish I could come with you. Mom, *please*?"

"No!

I patted his shoulder again. "You stay safe, Sean, and most important, keep your mom and your sister safe." To his mother, I said, "Walk me to my car."

We stepped out and she closed the door behind her. It was no later than four, but it was almost as dark as night. The clouds overhead were practically black and even in the relative protection of her small orchard, with her fruit trees and the rose bower providing some shelter, the wind seemed to drive needles of ice right through your skin.

I stopped her on the step, pulled my collar up, and asked her, "Have you got a weapon?"

Her face hardened.

"I'm not asking for it, Abi. You have two children to protect."

She shook her head. "He has never gone for a boy, and Primrose is older than..."

I interrupted her. "Abi, you need to start facing this

thing. It must be clear to you that we are dealing with two killers here."

Her eyes went wide. "What are you talking about?"

I stressed it. "At least two. You said yourself that the disappearance of the Ibanez family and the Gordons was suspect." I shrugged. "Who is it that the Martins are scared of? There is some kind of clean-up crew going around, and *they* are not fussy about age or gender."

She stared at me for a moment. She seemed astonished. "But why me? The Martins, perhaps, but why us...?"

"Maybe no reason at all, but maybe because I've been staying here, you have helped me, and they see me as a threat. Now please, answer the question, Abi. Have you got a weapon?"

She shook head. "No."

"Go inside out of the cold."

I went down the path to my car. I heard the door close behind me. I popped the trunk and pulled over the canvas kit bag I always keep there. It was sadly depleted. I had intended to drive to San Francisco, see Marni off, and drive home. I had not intended to cross a small mountain range on foot in the snow, or to make war on a gang of rapists and murderers. So it contained only the basics: there were my two Sig Sauer 9mm Tacops with their extended magazines, my take down, seventy pound orange osage bow with twelve aluminum arrows that formed a removable, rigid frame for the bag, and a Fairbairn & Sykes fighting knife with a brass, knurled grip. There was also some spare ammunition.

But the Heckler and Koch G36 assault rifle, the Smith & Wesson 500, the cakes of C4, the bugs, and all the rest of the kit—that wasn't even in my place in Wyoming. That was all

in my house in Weston, in Boston[1]. I sighed, pulled out the bag, slammed the trunk shut, and made my way back into the house.

I stamped the snow from my boots in the reception and went through to the kitchen. They were all sitting, silently staring at their cold cups of tea. I dumped the almost-empty bag on the table, pulled out the two Sigs and a box of ammunition. Sean's face lit up. Abi and Primrose looked like they'd just seen Freddy Kreuger peer in at the window.

"I am not going to argue with you guys. I want you and Primrose to have one of these each." Sean drew breath, but I gave him a look that silenced him. "I don't want to hear any bullshit." Abi drew breath. I gave her the same look I'd given Sean. "There are men in this village who are prepared to kill. We don't know why, we don't know who they are, and that makes them three times as dangerous."

Abi was shaking her head. "Lacklan, for God's sake, Sean is only thirteen..."

"And I would never expose a child to this kind of thing, Abi, unless I believed that the danger was real and present. And we all know that it is. If I could be here to protect you, this would not be necessary. But I am going to be gone for at least a day, and during that time you *must* be able to protect your family." I held up the Sig. "This is the only way."

I showed all three of them how the pistols worked. When I was done, I said, "Sean, I do not want you to touch these guns. You stay away from them, you understand? But,

---

1. See *Dawn of the Hunter* and *Double Edged Blade*

if the time comes and you need to protect your mother or your sister, I want you to know how to do it. You got me? This is not a game. This is real."

He looked at me with huge, solemn eyes and nodded, while his mother and sister looked sick.

I stressed to all three of them the dangers of the chambered round: if you eject the magazine and forget that you have a round in the chamber, that can cost lives. Too many people who should know better forget that. Then I took them out to the back yard to fire a few shots and get the feel of the weapons.

Back inside, I put the Fairbairn & Sykes in my boot, the rucksack they had given me with the food and flasks inside the kit bag, and slung the bag on my back. Primrose watched me do it and said, "You're not armed."

"I'm pretty sure they won't come after me. If they do, the weather is my first weapon, if that fails, I have a bow and my knife." I winked at Sean. "Believe me, I am a lot more dangerous than they are."

Abi stared at me a moment with the kind of strange, complicated expression that only women know how to make. It tells you they love the way you are and cannot wait to change you to the way they want you to be. She said, "I believe you probably are."

I zipped up my jacket and pulled on some thermal gloves Abi had given me, along with a thick, woolen scarf and a woolen hat, both of which I now used to cover my head and mouth. I made them stay inside, pulled the door closed behind me and set off along the track, past the dark, silent saloon, past the dark, silent houses with only the faintest glow creeping out from behind their drapes to touch with warm amber the deepening drifts on their front lawns.

The town of Independence was soon behind me and the track began to climb toward the pine forest that sprawled up both sides of the canyon and enclosed and protected the path. The sky was low and heavy and the snowfall was dense. A cruel wind gusted across the plain below, dragging huge white billows in its wake, reducing the poor visibility even further. There was no moonlight and no starlight, but even so, the endless blanket of snow seemed to emit a strange, blue luminescence all on its own.

But when I finally entered the long tunnel of trees that enclosed the path up the canyon, the darkness became almost impenetrable. The trade-off was that the snow was shallower, barely ankle deep, and the wind was nothing but a moan and a sigh, and an occasional wild scream in the canopy above.

What didn't change was the cold. I estimated it at somewhere around zero degrees Fahrenheit, minus fifteen or twenty Celsius. It was a numbing, penetrating cold, and I knew I had to endure it for the next nine or ten hours. And it could only get worse. All you can do in that kind of situation, in that kind of physical environment, is to create a rhythm with your walking and your breathing, and put yourself into a trance. Deep breathing to a rhythm has the double advantage of generating heat and distorting your perception of time.

So I breathed, five steps in, five steps out, five steps in, five steps out, and as I breathed and walked, in my mind, I went over, in minute detail, everything that had happened since I turned right at Mill City the day before.

I had been walking for maybe an hour, perhaps a little less, when I became aware that the path was beginning to veer slightly north of west, and as I became aware of that, I noticed also that the forest was beginning to thin slightly. This then was the first marker on Sean's map. I had covered barely two miles in slightly less than an hour. After this, the going would get tough. I pressed on for another five or ten minutes, until the sky began to show through the silhouettes of the trees above. Then, ahead, I saw the huge black bulk of the hills that Sean had talked about, blocking my path and forcing the canyon road north. The sound of the wind had changed. It was less muffled by the trees, but the howls and groans were deeper among the peaks of the mountains that now surrounded me.

As I turned slightly to follow the path, which bore now more north than west, out into the open among the wind and the snow, something made me look back. Perhaps it was instinct, perhaps habit and training. Whatever it was, it made me glance over my shoulder, and something caught my eye. I was not sure at first if it was the snow playing tricks or my imagination, but I stopped, hunkered down, and remained immobile, watching. Then I saw it again. It was unmistakable. It was the flash of a light. I closed my eyes and concentrated on the sounds I could hear around me. The wind dominated everything, so I focused on it and tried to detect what other sounds there were within it. Groans, whistles, cries, howls... the rustle of the canopy, the creak of branches... and there, just perceptible on the edge of hearing, the growl of diesel.

EIGHT

I RAN. I DIDN'T SPRINT BECAUSE I NEEDED TO preserve every bit of energy I could, but I knew I was making two miles an hour, and even up hill in the snow, if they were in trucks, they were making a damn sight more than that. So I set off at a steady jog, keeping close to the tree line where I could duck in if I needed to. I had a fleeting wish for my Heckler and Koch assault rifle, but pushed it from my mind and focused on what I did have; on what was real right there and then. I had a bow, twelve aluminum arrows, and a knife. They would have at the very least pistols and shotguns, and very probably hunting rifles. How many would there be? Impossible to say, but they had some idea of what I could do, so the chances were there would be at least four of them, maybe eight or more.

I was in trouble. I was in big trouble, and the only advantages I had were my head start and my training. Both were weighing light in the balance right then, and I knew that my best hope was to get ahead of them, and get lost on the slopes beyond the dogleg I was in right then. And that raised one, vital question—how far would they take the trucks?

My bet was that they would leave them at the tree line. They would not want to risk getting them trapped in the deeper snow. They'd take them as far as the end of the woods and leave them there. Try to track me on foot, kill me, and then drive back. That meant I had to put as much distance between me and the tree cover as I could.

Pretty soon I'd left the trees behind and the snow was falling heavily all around me. Visibility was worse than poor. I could barely see fifteen yards ahead of me, and though the wind was not as strong as it was down on the plain, it was bad enough to whip up the flakes and lash them painfully in my face. It was impossible to run for any distance in those conditions, so I did what the Brits call a rifleman's march: ten paces walking, ten paces running, ten paces walking, ten paces running...

After about ten minutes I stopped, crouched down, and looked back along my tracks. They were being covered fast by the snowfall and the wind. The weather was in my favor in that respect at least. Dimly, through the misty swirl of flakes, I could see lights—headlamps, four of them. They were making no effort to conceal themselves. They were either very confident or very stupid. Maybe they were both. Maybe they expected me to be curled up in a drift dying of hypothermia. I caught the sound of slamming doors on the gale. I thought I heard four, but I couldn't be sure. They sounded far off, but I knew that in that wind, they would have to be pretty close to be heard at all. I considered my options again and decided, for now, to stick with my plan and try to lose them. If they started gaining on me, which was a distinct possibility, as they were fresh and I was already very tired, then I might rethink my options. But for now I would press on.

I turned, ran ten paces, then walked ten paces, then ran another ten and kept going, following that relentless rhythm, barely seeing where I was going, channeled by the steep sides of the canyon, wondering how in hell I would know which way to go when I reached the open slopes: up would be about as close as I could get to a direction. I had Sean's compass, but with at least four men on my heels I would have no time to stop and consult it. After twenty minutes, my legs were starting to tremble and breathing was becoming painful. I could just make out, up ahead, about sixty or seventy yards away, where the canyon wall rose steeply, forcing the track to turn west again, and I knew I had reached the second bend in the inverted 'S'. It also told me that the snow was beginning to ease. And that was bad news, because it meant I might not be able to lose my pursuers on the slope.

I was sure I had pulled ahead of them. Unless they had been following the same regime of running and walking as me, there was no doubt that I had. But I'd paid a heavy price in my energy reserves. I would soon need to stop, rest, and have some hot soup and coffee. For that, I relied completely on being able to lose them beyond the dogleg, as I climbed the open slopes toward the peak. But if the snow stopped, or even eased too much, my tracks would be clearly visible and I would become an exhausted, exposed sitting duck, with a bow and arrows against at least four rifles and pistols. I'd be as screwed as a two-dollar whore during shore leave.

So I had to start thinking about modifying my plan. To modify my plan I needed intel, and to get intel I needed to get close.

I forced myself to keep up the pace a little longer. I could see that at the bend, the growth of trees and bushes was a little thicker. It was obviously a spot where water was trapped and accumulated during the rainy season, making it more fertile. That angle in the bend was the spot where I could come off the track without leaving obvious prints, get above my pursuers and observe them. However, coming off there also meant that if they did notice I had left the track, I would then be committed to taking them out, in a fight I was not sure I could win.

On the other hand, I was pretty sure that ship had sailed anyway.

I finally came to the bend in the track—there was no track to be seen; all there was was the bend in the canyon, the rock face ahead, and the empty, white space between the fringes of ferns and trees on either side. I put on a burst of speed, leapt over the fringe of ferns, and then walked backward in among the trees, throwing snow over my tracks. It wasn't perfect, but it was good enough, and the wind and the snow that was still falling would do the rest.

Then I started clambering, slipping, sliding, and crawling, clawing my way up through the trees toward a rocky outcrop I had seen sixty yards farther on, forty yards above the road. It would afford me a vantage point from which to observe, and possibly strike if I decided to.

As I clambered up, above the tree line I noticed that the snow was definitely easing. It was no longer a blizzard. It was barely even heavy snow. Which meant, among other things, that if I was not concealed behind rocks by the time they came around the bend, I would be in plain view against the white blanket. My breath was rasping painfully in my throat and my fingers were in a kind of numb, frozen agony from clawing at the icy rocks. I tried not to think of the fact that, if it came to it, I would have to use those numb, agonized, frozen fingers to set up and pull a seventy-pound bow.

I made it to the outcrop, crawled onto the rocks, dropped behind them, and landed in a painful heap behind a boulder. I gave myself fifteen seconds to wallow in self-pity, then took off the kit bag, tore it open, pulled out the take-down bow, and started clumsily assembling it with fingers that felt like anesthetized sausages—sausages that hurt despite the anesthetic.

I got it assembled and strung, extracted an arrow from the frame of the bag, and peered over the edge of the rocks. It was only about seven in the evening, but if it had not been for the snow, they would have been practically invisible. As it was, they stood out clearly against the perfect white background. There were four of them. I couldn't make out if Joe Vasco was among them, or my talkative pal Earl, but I could see that they were big, and they were all carrying rifles. They'd stopped walking and were just standing, looking around. I figured they were confused because despite the easing of the snow, my tracks had suddenly disappeared without a trace. One of them pointed at the forest opposite. Another pointed up into the hill where I'd come to hide. They couldn't decide. Eventually one of them walked on ahead. The others watched him a moment. He stopped and turned back to them, seemed to talk and point at the bend in the canyon that led to the open slopes. I knew what he was saying. He was saying what I would have said: "Wherever he's gone, wherever he is, he has to pass this way to get down to Lovelock. And this is where we'll kill him."

And that was when I made up my mind. I was never very good at being the prey. I was always more comfortable as the predator. Being the predator means you get behind, not in front.

I nocked the arrow, drew to my ear and sensed the shot. I gave it a second till I was sure, then loosed. The arrow whispered a moment, disappeared from sight, a heartbeat, two, and below, there was a moment of confusion. My mark leaned forward, with his hands on his knees. Then he sat down in the snow. His companions came up close to him, bending. There was a shout. The guy who'd walked ahead started running back. But by that time, I'd gone. I was crouching, running back the way I'd come, from rock to rock, tree to tree, placing myself behind them. All my thinking till that point had been based on the idea of trying to fight them off as they closed in on me and I fled toward Lovelock. But now everything had changed. Now they were going to be pursuing a prey they believed to be ahead of them, but who was in fact behind them, hunting them.

I came to the tree line, slipped in among the ferns and the pines, and made my way rapidly and silently, crawling on my belly, to the edge of the road. They were gone, only the corpse remained, sitting motionless on the white blanket of snow. It was what I had expected. I gave it a moment. I knew they were hiding in the trees, waiting for me to make a move. Now the deck was stacked in my favor. I was exhausted and needed the rest. I drew the blankets from the kit bag, wrapped myself in them, and settled against a tree trunk to drink half a flask of hot chicken soup and watch the area where I knew they must be hiding. While I was resting and drinking hot soup, they were lying in the snow, growing cold. I was confident they would move first.

They did. After fifteen minutes, they couldn't take it anymore and they came out onto the road. The wind was all but gone. Billows of condensation issued from their mouths, and snatches of their talk came to me on the frozen air.

"...Good damn it...!"

"...we been hidin' he's been getting away...!

"...we was sittin' ducks...!"

"...up there and look in them rocks...!"

One of them lumbered slowly up the side of the canyon toward the rocks where I'd been hiding, while his two pals covered him. After a few minutes his voice echoed across the dark. "*Nothin' up here...!*"

I smiled. Another voice, this one from below. "*Head in toward the slopes! See if you can find his tracks!*"

They were confident they would catch me there. And if I had continued to play the prey, they would have been right. But the game had changed, and now I was hunting them.

NINE

BEFORE I MADE MY SECOND KILL, I NEEDED THEM back together again. I didn't want them to scatter. If they did, I'd have to hunt in two separate directions. So I hung back and let them move down the track toward the point where it split and went through the pass and onto the open slopes. I figured that would be the point where the three of them would join up again. At that point there was no cover, and that would be the perfect place to claim my second kill.

I loped across the road and into the woods where they had been hiding just a little earlier. From there, I saw them round the bend toward the broad fork. Three great masses of rock rose toward the black sky, and two gaps yawned between them. I checked Sean's map. The one on the left sloped down, but as he had said to me, it led somewhere you didn't want to go. The other, on the right, lead along a broad, shallow canyon for half a mile and then opened up onto a steep escarpment, half a mile across at its widest point, two hundred yards at its base. Here they would be wading knee-deep in snow, climbing up hill, virtually immobile between one exhausting step and the next, and with no cover.

They were about fifty yards ahead of me. I watched their scout scramble down from where he'd been hunting for my tracks. They weren't put off by the fact he hadn't found anything. As I trailed them, I heard their voices. "If he wants to get to Lovelock, there is only one way he can go. If he's ahead of us, we'll get him. If he's hiding, we'll wait for him. One way or another, we got him."

As we walked, the snow continued to thin and I saw breaks begin to appear in the cloud cover: patches of blackness a little blacker than the clouds themselves, with frozen sparkles of starlight piercing them. Odin was not on the side of the prey tonight. Tonight Odin favored the hunter.

As they approached the end of the canyon, where it opened into the broad valley, I slipped in among the sparse trees and began to climb at a tangent to the three men, on an intercept course which would place me above them as they climbed. After five minutes, I found a tree and settled to wait.

I was invisible to them, in the shadows of the pines, but they were very clear to me, stark against the increasingly luminous snow. I saw them come into the valley beneath me, stand looking for tracks, then, grunting great billows of condensation, begin to climb. They passed within six or eight yards of me. They didn't look up or to the sides. They were focused too hard on the effort of climbing. I recognized the farthest of the three as Earl. I let them get twelve feet above me, then I stood, nocked an arrow, took careful aim, and shot the nearest guy through the heart. It was a silent kill. The broadhead punched through his ribs and sliced deep into his heart, causing a massive hemorrhage. He would have bled out in a couple of seconds. The other two didn't even notice. He sank to his knees, lay down, and slipped into the void.

I nocked a second arrow and aimed for the middle guy. He was a little ahead of Earl, but that was OK. I wanted Earl to see. I loosed and the barb thudded home through the back of his neck, severing his spinal cord and his windpipe and protruding six inches out of his esophagus. His body did a strange jerky dance and I saw Earl stop and stare at him for a moment. I figured from where he was he probably couldn't make out the arrow. By that time, I'd put down my bow and I was wading across the slope. He still hadn't seen me because I was behind him.

Then, the guy with the feathered neck leaned forward and slumped into the snow, and the shaft became clearly visible. Earl grabbed for the lever-action rifle he had slung across his back and as he did it, he saw his other pal lying face down a couple of yards behind him. I heard him swear violently, and that was when he saw me. But by then, I was just three paces away from him, pushing knee-deep through the snow. He tried to turn and take aim, but he was hampered by the drifts around his legs. He fired one shot that went wide. I lumbered two steps, circling further behind him as I went, forcing him off balance. He levered, tried to take aim again, and stumbled, unable to get his footing. My leg muscles were screaming, going into cramp, but I forced myself and surged two more steps toward him, struggling up the slope. He fell back and swung the rifle like a club. I tried to block it and he struck my elbow with the butt. The pain was excruciating. I fought to ignore it and pulled my knife from my boot as I fell on him.

He scrabbled up the slope, on his back, kicking at my face. I grabbed his ankle and stabbed at his leg, but he yanked it away and struck at me again with his rifle. I took the blow on my shoulder and scrambled to my feet, slipping and falling twice in the process. Meanwhile, he was fumbling the rifle around, levering another round into the chamber, trying desperately with frozen, gloved fingers to get a grip and take aim at me. I grabbed the barrel as he pulled the trigger and felt the bullet tear through my jacket. He was still on his back, lying on the slope. I kicked savagely at his hands where they were gripping the weapon, slipped on the icy slope, and fell again, yanking the rifle from his hands. I hurled it away and grabbed clumsily for his leg. He kicked at me and caught me a glancing blow on my face.

Next thing, he was on his knees and he'd pulled a big, ugly hunting knife from his belt. I was lying awkwardly on my side, with my knife hand pinned underneath me in the snow. He lunged, plunging the blade down at my chest. I caught his wrist in my left hand and rolled, pulling him on top of me. His face was twisted into a manic grimace as he grabbed the hilt with both hands and put all his weight on the knife. I held him with just my left hand. I knew I couldn't hold him long, but I also knew I didn't need to. Because I still had my Fairbairn & Sykes in my right hand, and now I rammed it savagely into his right shoulder. I could have gone for his armpit, but that would have killed him in a very short time, and I wanted this son of a bitch alive.

The long blade plunged two inches into the joint. I levered hard back and forth. He screamed and gibbered, spraying spittle from his lips, dropped his knife, and staggered to his feet, clawing at his shoulder as I yanked the blade free. I got on one knee and struck again in a straight thrust at his left thigh. He went down on his back and I went after him.

I knew his left arm was useless now, so I knelt on his right and held the long, razor-sharp blade to his throat.

"This goes one of two ways, Earl. I cut you badly and you bleed out here in the snow. Or I take you back to the trucks. What's it going to be?"

He was weeping like a child, sobbing and repeating over and over, "*It hurts! Oh God, it hurts!*" For a moment, I almost felt compassion for him. Then I remembered Peggy.

"Earl, focus. I can make it stop. I can stop the pain and I can get you to safety. Or I can make the pain worse and leave you out here to die in the cold. Get a grip, Earl."

"*Anything, anything, just please make it stop!*"

"Who raped Peggy?"

"I don't know, honest I don't."

"Was it Vasco?"

"*I don't know, I don't know, I don't know...* please help me..." he was moaning, slobbering.

"Who sent you after me?"

"Vasco. He told us to come and finish you. Please, *please...*"

"Who told him I was here?"

"Someone in the village...."

"*Who?*"

His face screwed up with grief and agony. "*I don't know! I swear to God I don't know! Have mercy, please! I can't take it! He just told us to come after you! And...*"

I waited. "And what? Abi? Did he tell you to go after her, too?"

He shook his head, still sobbing. *"Just you. You and Peggy-Sue. We had to kill Peggy-Sue before you! God forgive me...!"*

I didn't think, kneeling there in the snow, under the frozen stars in that black sky, that it was possible to get any colder. But a chill trickled through me that was colder than the ice and the snow, and froze my heart in my chest. I looked down at him, weeping, slobbering, begging for pity and mercy, and I couldn't find any of those things inside me. All I could find was an unwavering certainty that this being should not be allowed to live another moment. I placed the tip of the blade over his fifth intercostal, a terrible, monstrous roar came out of my throat and I hammered down on the hilt with my right fist; and drove that blade clean through his heart. Or whatever it was he had in his chest.

Peggy was dead.

I have long since forgotten how to weep. But I sat there in the snow that night with a terrible, unendurable desolation inside me; not for myself, but for that poor, fragile child who had been brutalized by these monsters and betrayed by her parents; and for this tragic, ugly world where these things are possible.

I don't know how long I sat there, but eventually an icy, silver moon rose over the mountaintops, raining a frosted light on the blue-white valley, and I got to my feet and started the long, frozen walk back toward Independence. There was no point in going on to Lovelock for an ambulance. The child was dead. And I would not go for the sheriff. I did not want a police investigation, an arrest, a prosecution, a trial. The courts were not equipped to dispense the kind of justice that Peggy-Sue was entitled to; the kind of justice that the black rage inside me demanded.

But I was.

I struggled back to collect my bow and my kit bag. Then I stumbled and slid down the slope, landing half-buried in a drift at the bottom. For a moment I lay there, looking up at the blackness, finely peppered with silver, wondering if I had the strength to get to my feet, thinking that perhaps a short sleep would help. I knew that sleep led irrevocably to death: a short sleep to eternal sleep.

Anger, hot and red, forced my arms and my legs to move. I pushed and struggled against the yielding, enfolding snow and got to my knees, then to my feet. I had begun to shiver badly. I was exhausted and hypothermia was setting in. I could not allow that. I had to get back. I had to avenge Peggy. I had to find and punish her killer. There was no logic or rationality to my thinking. It was a simple imperative.

I stumbled to the cover of some pines, sat on a fallen trunk and pulled the thermos from my kitbag. I swallowed some chicken soup, taking it slowly, one small sip at a time, and began to feel some strength coming back into my limbs and some clarity to my mind. Even so, when I thought of the walk back to the trucks, I wondered if I would have the strength.

I took some hot, sweet coffee, stood, and began to walk. It became a strange, surreal sensation: as though I were not really the man in the canyon, walking among the dark slopes and the trees, following that luminous, blue-white path, down into the dark bowels of Independence, where a child lay dead. It was as though I were up, in the crystal clear, freezing cosmos, beside the leering moon who rained frozen light down on that dark, luminous path. And through it all, there was the relentless rhythm of one foot before another, one foot after another, another step, just one more step.

I knew I was in a kind of delirium and wondered if delirium was one of nature's many ways of helping us to survive the unendurable. And, as I thought that, I saw ahead of me, death, mounted on a black horse, come to fetch me. I looked death in his eyes—those black, hollow caverns—squared my shoulders and told him I would not go until I had exacted my revenge. And death swung down from his horse, and as his black boot touched the blue-white snow, black wings enfolded me.

And then there was nothing.

TEN

I WAS COLD. I WAS VERY COLD AND uncomfortable. I wanted to turn over and cover myself, but I couldn't find the bedclothes. I tried to reach for them but my arms and hands were sluggish and found only cold, wet sludge. Then something was forcing itself into my mouth. I tried to fight it, but I was too weak. Whatever it was was sweet, like honey.

I opened my eyes and groaned. I saw the vastness of space spread out above me, and a billion brilliant, distant stars winking. Ice-cold air touched my face. There was somebody leaning over me, A spoon touched my lips. More honey. I took it hungrily and felt better. I blinked and tried to focus. Somewhere, a horse snorted and pawed the snow. My sight cleared.

"Sean...?"

He smiled at me.

"Can you sit up? We have to get you out of the snow.

Take some more honey. It's good for exhaustion, and hypothermia."

"What the hell are you doing here, Sean?"

"Not now, Mr. Walker. Take it."

I struggled to a sitting position. I was still trembling, and everything hurt. I took the honey. It was thick and waxy and sweet. It helped.

"Where...?"

"We're at the dogleg. I saw the man you shot, and the trucks further down. Can you get up? Can you get on a horse?"

"You brought *horses?*"

He grinned. "I borrowed a couple from the Wrights. They won't mind. Come on, Mr. Walker, we really need to get you back. Are there more men?"

I shook my head. He stood and helped me to my feet. The trembling was easing. I said, "I can ride."

He led me a few paces to where two horses were waiting, breathing great billows of condensation into the night. As I climbed into the saddle, he pulled the blankets from my kit bag and handed them up to me. Then he handed me one of the flasks.

"Coffee. I added more honey to it. Just keep sipping as we go. I'll lead the horse."

I nodded and took it. He hung the kit bag from the saddle. Then he swung up onto his own horse and we turned and headed back down the track. It was freezing cold and the horses knew they were going home, so the pace was brisk.

"It won't be long, Mr. Walker. It seems like a million

miles when you're on foot in the blizzard, but it ain't far on a horse, when it's clear."

"What are you doing here, Sean? Do you realize the risk you took?"

He nodded. "Mom is going to be real mad, but I don't see I had much choice."

"What do you mean?"

"My room is at the front of the house, which was how I saw you with my binoculars beating up those guys at the depot. Well, I was in my room, and next thing I hear trucks. Sometimes I see trucks going to the depot and leaving it, and sometimes trucks come to the saloon, but you don't often see them coming up into the canyon. So I looked out the window and those two trucks I just saw down the road drove up and stopped outside the doctor's house. Then I saw Earl and three other men go inside. They were there maybe ten minutes, then they come out and I saw them take off up into the canyon. I knew they were coming after you, and I knew you had nothing but a bow and arrows. I figured they'd have handguns and rifles." He shrugged. "After what you were trying to do for poor Peggy, I figured I had to help you somehow. I brought you one of your guns."

I nodded. "That was very brave of you, Sean. Your mother will be mad at you, but ignore her. What you did took guts. Thank you."

He grinned. "I borrowed a couple of horses from the Wrights, and when I saw the clouds clearing, I was glad I did. When the clouds break up, that means one thing. The temperature is going to drop, and I don't mind telling you, Mr. Walker. You would have froze to death out there tonight."

"I know."

Up ahead, I saw the body of the first guy I had shot. He was partially covered in snow, but clearly visible in the moonlight. I wondered how long he would sit there before he was found; he and his friends. As we passed him, Sean reached behind his back, pulled something, and handed it over to me. It was one of my Sigs.

"My mom put them in a drawer and locked it. Prim picked the lock and gave me one for you."

I took it, smiled, and shook my head. Some people are born to be victims. They can't help themselves. It was my lucky break that Sean and Primrose were not among them. He frowned at me. "What about the other three?"

I held his eye a moment, wondering if he was too young. I decided he was, but I also decided that life didn't give a damn how old he was, or how old Peggy was. Bad things happened, and either you fought back, or you went down. I shrugged. "They won't be raping any more girls."

He nodded. "Good."

Less than an hour later, we rode past the Martins' house, dark and silent, and into the small square. I swung down and told Sean, "You take care of the horses. I'm going to see if the doc is OK."

He nodded and rode away, down a side ally by the guesthouse. I tramped across the snow, still wrapped in my blankets, and hammered on the doc's front door. The moon was casting an eerie light over the luminous plain. Far off, a dog was barking and was answered by a coyote. Other than that, there was only silence.

I pulled my Swiss Army knife from my pocket, selected the small screwdriver, rammed it in the lock, and opened the door. He was on the floor, on his back. I switched on the light and knelt beside him. His face was swollen and badly bruised, but he was alive. I picked him up and carried him into his living room. There I laid him on the sofa and ran up the stairs to Peggy's room.

The bed was empty.

The room seemed to rock from side to side. I gripped the doorjamb to stop myself from falling. What had they done with her? Taken the body to dispose of it? That was what they were about, wasn't it? Trying to eliminate evidence.

I made it down the stairs and stepped back out into the snow. Somehow, in some kind of trance, I made it across the square and through the gate to the guesthouse. There I hammered on the door. It was wrenched open a moment later by Primrose. Abi was behind her, watching anxiously, and behind her was Sean, still in his coat. I pointed back, toward the doc's house.

"The doc, he needs help. And Peggy. Peggy's gone..."

And for the second time that night, I passed out.

———

THE FIRST THING I was aware of was clean, warm, fresh linen. It wasn't a sudden sensation, but I gradually became aware that I had been feeling it for some time. It was a luxurious feeling and made me smile. I rolled over and reached for Marni, found she wasn't there, and then the memories started seeping in. I groaned and opened my eyes.

There was sunlight lying warped across the foot of my bed. The fire was lit and I had an extra patchwork quilt laid over me. I levered myself onto one elbow and realized that I had been undressed and put to bed. My clothes were folded over the back of a chair, near the fire.

I swung my legs out from under the covers. Everything hurt. I noticed I had a big, ugly bruise on my ribs, a couple of inches below my left armpit. It had a large piece of gauze on it, held in place with sticking plasters. I remembered Earl's shot and guessed he must have got closer than I'd thought.

I walked stiffly to the en suite and stood for ten minutes under the hot water until I started to feel half-human again. I toweled myself dry and while I was dressing, the door opened and Abi stepped in. I had my jeans on but no shirt. She hesitated. I smiled. "I haven't grown anything you didn't see last night. Come in."

She flushed. "I heard the shower. How is your injury?"

"It's just a graze."

She stepped in and closed the door. "You lost blood. It looked like a bullet wound."

I put my shirt on and started to button it. "Earl came after me with some pals of his. He tried to shoot me. I guess he succeeded. How's the doc?"

"Bruised, concussed..."

I pulled on my socks and my boots and sat looking at her. "Do you know what happened to Peggy-Sue?"

She shook her head.

I said, "Earl told me Vasco ordered them to kill Peggy and then come after me. But when I got to her room last night, she was gone."

"They want to say a service for her at the church today."

I frowned. "A service?"

"They took her to the chapel..."

"She is dead, then."

"They want to hold a service for her."

I curled my lip. "It's a shame they weren't so concerned about her while she was still alive."

"Lacklan, don't... The reverend wondered if you would attend the service."

"Why?"

She looked down at her hands, as though she was holding something invisible in them. She looked embarrassed. "He wanted to thank you for what you'd done."

I stood. "Tell him he's welcome."

She sighed, still staring at her fingers. "He also wanted to talk to you."

"To warn me off? To tell me to leave it alone? To politely ask me to leave town?"

"I don't know."

"What about you, Abi? You also want me to leave town?"

Now she looked up me, held my eye, and spoke softly. "I don't know..."

She turned, yanked open the door, and left. I went out onto the landing and watched her hurry down the stairs. After a moment, I went back into my room. On the dressing table I found both my pistols. Neither had been cocked and the chambers were empty. I put one of them in my bedside drawer and slipped the other in my waistband. Then I put my jacket on and went downstairs.

I found the three of them in the kitchen. Sean and Primrose smiled at me, but Abi wouldn't meet my eye. I said, "What time is the service?"

She spoke to the table top. "In half an hour."

"I'm guessing the doc won't be going."

"He said he was going to stay in bed and recover."

"You looking after him?"

She nodded.

"You got a key?"

She looked up. "Yes. Why?"

"He gave me a pint of whiskey. I didn't drink it. I wanted to return it to him. I also wanted to see how he was. He's a good man, like your son."

Sean went puce and smiled at his sister. Abi's cheeks colored, but she didn't know whether to be pleased or mad.

"Sean is just a boy."

"With the heart of a man. May I borrow your key?"

She reached in her pocket and pulled it out.

I went over and took it. "I'll bring it to the church."

I turned to leave, but as I stepped through the kitchen door she said, "Lacklan…"

I looked back. "Yeah?"

"Not everyone in this town appreciates what you tried to do."

"I get that."

"I want you to know, in case you are in any doubt, that I do."

I gave her a lopsided smile. "Thanks."

ELEVEN

THE SKY WAS A BRILLIANT BLUE, LIKE IT HAD JUST
been washed and polished. The air was brittle, sharp, like
walking through ice. I pulled up my collar, pulled my jacket
tight, and loped across the square, doing a careful balancing
act and trying not to slip and fall. At his door, I slipped the
key in the lock and went in quietly. I figured if he was sleeping, I'd let him rest.

I climbed the stairs and stood on the landing for a
moment, looking at the closed door of the room where
Peggy-Sue had lain. I felt a twist of grief and anger at the
death of the child I had gathered up from the roadside,
broken and freezing, whom I had tried to save; who should
have lived.

I moved then to the doc's door, quietly turned the
handle, and pushed it open. Like Peggy's the night before,
the bed was empty. For half a second, my mind was paralyzed. Whatever angle I looked at it from, it didn't make any

sense. Then I heard the hammer click, too far away to strike at, and a voice, quiet, calm and steady, that said, "All right, mister, turn around nice and slow, so I can see your face before I blow your head off."

I sighed, raised my hands and turned.

"Doc, put the gun away. I came to see how you were, and to return your whiskey. I thought maybe you could use it."

He looked like a train wreck. Worse. It would have looked bad on a man half his age. On him, it was an outrage. My big regret was that I had already killed the men who'd done this to him. Most of the left side of his face was purple. His left eye was closed and his mouth was swollen. He was holding an old Colt .45 revolver in both hands, and he was wearing his pajamas and a robe. It wasn't so much pathetic as tragic. The gun wavered and he lowered it, releasing the hammer as he did so.

"Oh, it's you. Abi said you found me."

I nodded. "Back to bed, Doc."

"I'm hungry. I don't need bed, I need food."

"Stay in bed, I'll bring it up to you."

He ignored me, turned, and I followed him down the stairs to the kitchen. Once there, he sat at the table and said, "You can cook, but don't fuss over me."

I fried some bacon, mushrooms, and eggs and put it all on two slices of toast. I made some coffee, too, and laced it with the whiskey. Then I sat opposite him and we ate in silence for a while. When he was almost finished, he leaned back in his chair, drained his cup, and said, "You're going to get yourself killed."

I nodded. "Sooner or later, I guess that's true."

He studied my face through his one good eye. "But you don't figure that's going to happen any time soon."

I shrugged and chewed, watching him back. "It'll happen when it happens, Doc. I'm not easy to kill, but tomorrow a cow might fall on me out of a clear blue sky."

He snorted. "That likely, huh?"

"It happens. Joao Maria de Souza. Google it. Thing is, Doc, nobody gets out of here alive, and trying to is a waste of time. Meanwhile, I may as well do something useful."

He made a 'that's one way of looking at it' face and said, "You didn't get to Lovelock, though."

"Earl and his friends caught up with me."

He frowned. "What happened?"

"I killed them."

He blinked, one-eyed, and sighed. "Just like that. Can't say I'll miss them."

"What happened to Peggy?"

He watched me but didn't answer.

I said, "Before he died, Earl told me Vasco sent them to kill Peggy before they killed me."

He nodded, refilled our cups, and added some whiskey. "Yeah, they hammered at the door, when I opened it, they pushed it, demanding to see her. I told them to go to hell. He punched me a few times and they stormed upstairs."

"When I got here she wasn't in her bed, but her bed looked like it hadn't been slept in."

He took a drink, then sighed. "By the time they got here, we'd moved her to the church."

I narrowed my eyes at him. "In the blizzard?"

He raised his voice, not quite shouting, but mad. "When I heard your dumb-ass plan, I knew it would get back to them, and I didn't want those goddamn animals defiling her! So I went and called the preacher and between us, we moved her."

I stared at him a long while. "So they didn't kill her?"

"Not last night, no. But you tell me, Lacklan, if they didn't kill her, who did?"

"You're talking in riddles."

He shook his head. "Who beat her? Who tried to strangle her? Who dumped her by the side of the road?"

I nodded. "I hear you."

"You going to the service?"

I nodded.

"They're going to tell you to butt out and leave town, you know that, right."

"You want me to do that too?"

He shook his head. "No. And if you do, Abi and her kids will pay. You started, now you have to finish."

"I'm glad you think so."

He raised his cup. I raised mine back. He said, "I hope you get them before they get you."

I shrugged. "Everybody has a cow waiting for them somewhere."

––––––––

THE CHURCH WAS at the back of Main Street, where the Pioneer Guesthouse and the saloon were located, up a short track, on the southern slope of the canyon, with the pine woods spread out above and to the right of it. It was small and unassuming. The doors were closed, but I could hear the sound of singing. I crunched up the path and pushed through the heavy wooden door, stepped inside, and closed out the cold, bright sunshine behind me.

It was as plain on the inside as it was outside. The walls were whitewashed and there was a minimum of decoration of any kind. The congregation was a little less than three dozen people, including Abi, Primrose, and Sean. Most of them turned to look at me when I came in, and most of them bore expressions of resentment and hostility. I saw the Martins in the front row. Below the altar, at the end of the central aisle, there was the coffin.

The preacher ignored me and carried on with the service. He was a small, middle-aged man who was definitely more New Testament than Old. There was very little fire or brimstone going down, and he was more concerned with forgiveness and Peggy being received into the bosom of Christ than with her killer giving up an eye or a tooth for what he'd done.

Those who had turned to glare at me turned back to face the reverend and I slipped into the last row, which was vacant, and settled to wait for the service to end.

A couple of minutes later, the door opened again, letting in a blast of icy air, and with it came a tall, crooked man in his late sixties or early seventies with a shock of white hair brushed back from a long, craggy face. With him came a woman in her mid or late forties, once handsome but now drawn and prematurely aged, and a young man who bore a striking resemblance to both of them. He was probably in his late teens or early twenties, but he looked sickly and feeble. He was tall, like the man I figured was his grandfather, but he was stooped and pale, with hollow eyes and limp, blond hair that fell over his face. The woman, I guessed, was his mother, and he held onto her arm as they slipped into the back row, across the aisle from me.

When the service had finished, the reverend paused, as though thinking about what to do next. Then he spoke out suddenly, with a strength that had been missing during the worship.

"I will, in a moment, invite those of you who knew and loved Peggy-Sue to say a few words in remembrance of her, but before I do, I should like to say a few words myself. We are, first and foremost, a Christian community, and whatever the Old Testament may say about an eye for an eye and a tooth for a tooth, we follow the word of Christ, and Christ made it very clear to us that our way is the way of love and forgiveness. If there is to be punishment or vengeance exacted, let it be by the hand of God, not our hand.

"Now, if anybody here would like to say some words in memory of our beloved child..."

The tall man with the white hair who had arrived after me now stood. His voice was strong. "Reverend Cameron, I should like to say some words in Peggy-Sue's memory, if you will allow me."

"Brother Aloysius, I see you have brought your wife and your son. You are welcome."

So this was Aloysius Groves. I watched him walk with long, strangely jerky strides to a lectern that had been placed at the head of the casket. He had no prepared speech—at least it wasn't written on paper. He gazed at the congregation, like some ancient Celtic king, or a druid.

"It has been five years since we had anything like this in our small community. Ours has been a harmonious living together in peace and friendship. We are more than neighbors, more than a community. We are a family. The tragedy of Peggy's death strikes at all of us. Nobody who has not lost a child can begin to imagine the pain that Albert and Flora Martin are going through right now, but I know that each one of us here today, everyone who is a member of this family, has a deep, unquenchable pain in their hearts. When Peggy-Sue died, we all lost a member of our family."

He paused and looked down at his palms, first one and then the other, and he started talking like he was talking to his hands.

"Five years ago, after we lost Sally Ibanez, a year after we'd lost Rose and Alice Gordon, I promised you, here in this very church, that we would put a stop to it. And we did."

He fell silent. His gaze drifted. He was silent so long that people began to shift in their seats. Somebody coughed. He seemed to come out of his reverie, or a dream, and looked around at the faces, all looking to him for guidance, for a direction.

"I know that some of you are thinking that maybe we should call the sheriff, maybe we should call in law enforcement, maybe this is a case for the FBI. But before you take any rash steps or actions, I would say to you what I said to you all those years ago: I would ask you all to consider the consequences to our community of being portrayed nationwide as a ghoulish home of redneck rape and murder! Ridiculed from coast to coast as the small, backwater home of incest and rape, of inbreds and sodomites!" His face flushed. "That is not who we are. But I assure you, I have seen it, once the press and the media get a hold of this story, they will brand us forever, they will pry into each of our lives, they will lie and distort the truth just to sell their stories, to raise their ratings. Our small family will be branded and ridiculed from Los Angeles to New York."

He stood nodding, looking from face to face.

"And that will not be the end of it. The police will call in the FBI! And they will pry into every corner of our community, the will leave no life untouched, no closet unrifled, no secret unaired. And whether the culprit be one of us, in Independence, or whether he be from elsewhere—a stranger preying on our community—they will pin the guilt on one of us. They will make the evidence fit their prejudices, and one of our community will go down, guilty or not. You may be sure of it.

"I am going to ask you, as I did then, to give us a chance to look out for our own. Let the men of Independence protect their women and their children, as we did once before. And this time, you have my word, we will make it stick. Thank you."

Then, on his long, stiff legs, with his odd, jerky walk, he strode down the central aisle, gathered up his wife and his sickly, pallid son, and they stepped out of the church and into the snow. The door slammed closed behind them and a big silence settled on the temple. Nobody looked at me where I sat in the shadows, in the corner, but they all knew I was there, and they all knew I was the elephant in that room. Finally, the reverend said it.

"We have an honored guest among us today, a man who has fought bravely, albeit misguidedly, on Peggy's behalf. The man who found her dying in the snow, who brought her home, who delivered her into the doctor's care, and defied the blizzard to try to get her to a hospital. Today, we thank the Lord for sending him to Peggy in her hour of need, and we thank that man, and we honor him, for his efforts and for being among us today." He paused. "However, I also ask him, on behalf of this community, to desist from his efforts to find the culprit, to desist from his violent ways, to allow Independence to handle its own affairs, and continue on his way, with our blessing."

There was a lot of murmured approval and nodding. I slid to the end of the bench and stood.

"Reverend Cameron, people of Independence, I will be on my way..." I paused and smiled as I sensed the wave of relief ripple through the congregation, then added, "Just as soon as the weather permits, and I am through with what I have to do. You see, you made a mistake five years ago, and you made another one today. You think that Peggy-Sue's rape and murder is your business, and nobody else's. It's not. The rape and murder of a child is everybody's business. Peggy-Sue is not going to get swept under the carpet with Rose and Alice and Sally. I am here. And I am going to find who did this and I am going to make him pay. When I've done that, I'll leave."

I paused, looking around at all the people who now refused to look at me. Then, I added, "You don't need to worry about the law coming to Independence. I never made it to Lovelock. When your man, Earl, told me what he had been instructed to do to Peggy, I turned back. I decided I did not want the sheriff involved. You don't need to worry about the law. You need to worry about me. I am here to exact justice. You can pass that on to Vasco, when you brief him on this... service."

They didn't look happy. I didn't really care. I pulled

open the door and stepped out into the brilliant, freezing sunshine. I paused on the steps above the path and looked north. There were more clouds piling up. There was another storm building. This one would be worse. This time I'd be ready.

TWELVE

I was almost at Main Street when I heard her footsteps running behind me, crunching in the snow, and the breathless call of her voice: "Mr. Walker! Lacklan...!"

I stopped and turned. It was Primrose, with flushed cheeks and bright eyes, running to catch up with me. Beyond her I could see the church on the hill, gleaming white with its black, gabled roof. The doors were still closed. Nobody was leaving. They were still debating what to do about the stranger. She stopped running and drew level with me. She smiled.

"Are you going back to the guesthouse?"

I raised an eyebrow and smiled back. "Nowhere else to go."

She scowled and we fell into step. "That's true enough... Either way, you'll need a key."

"I was planning to shoot out the lock."

She gave a pretty laugh. "I'm sorry about the way they

treated you back there. They're basically good people, but..."
She shrugged.

I grunted. "Define good."

She glanced at me. "I guess so. The reverend isn't as chicken as he seems. He has stood up to Vasco and Al when he's had to. He believes what he preaches. He is a very committed Christian."

I nodded. "Groves' wife is a lot younger than he is. That surprised me. I thought it was his daughter."

"Karen, and his son Arnold. It caused a big stir when they got married. That was before I was born, 'course, but people still talk about it. She's about thirty or thirty-five years younger than him. They were married when she was just twenty and he was fifty or fifty-five. Almost straight away she got pregnant. There were those who said she was already pregnant and that's why they married. Either way, it was just gossip. Small towns love to gossip." She glanced at me. "I don't see it makes much difference what age they are, so long as they love each other, right?"

I nodded. "He's a pretty formidable man. But she doesn't seem very happy."

She raised her eyebrows high on her forehead and gave a small, pretty laugh. "They have a lot on their plates right now. He has four men missing, you threatening to call the sheriff and he *must* have a growing suspicion that his manager is involved in something pretty dark. He's talking about dealing with the problem, but taking on Vasco without getting the law involved ain't no easy matter."

"Why not?"

We'd arrived at the guesthouse. I held the gate for her and she made her way down the path. A shadow passed over the garden and I looked up at the sky. The first clouds were closing in. Primrose opened the door and we went inside. I followed her into the living room, where there was a fire burning. She took off her mittens and stood in front of it, warming her hands.

"Vasco has shares in the farm," she said. "And there are rumors..."

"What kind of rumors?"

"That Karen and Vasco are having an affair. Groves would do just about anything to avoid a scandal, he's real old school like that. So he turns a blind eye. On top of all that, his son is pretty sickly. He has some kind of disease. People say it's because of the age difference, but I don't believe that."

"An unhappy family."

She looked me in the face and seemed to study me. "What did you mean? What you said at the church, that you planned to make whoever it was pay, and they had to worry about you, not the law. What did you mean?"

I looked away from her, shook my head. "It's best you don't know."

"Why?"

"I need to get ready. I have to pack some things. I'll catch you later."

I climbed the stairs, went to my room, and closed the door behind me. The fire here also was lit. I emptied my kit bag on the bed and took stock of my weapons. I had the bow and nine aluminum arrows left. I had the two Sig Sauers, two extended clips, and a box of ammunition. And I had my knife.

I had all that and I had zero intelligence. All I knew was

that Vasco was four men down, five if you included the dislocated shoulder. What that left him, I had no idea. And of those that were left, how many were loyal to Groves and how many were involved with Vasco, I had no idea. On top of that, I knew nothing about the farm, its layout, or where Vasco lived. And if my gut was right—and it always was—I didn't have a lot of time for gathering intel.

I heard the door open behind me. I turned. It was Primrose. She was staring at the stuff on the bed. I said, "You don't knock?"

Her eyes went to my face. "I'm sorry."

"What is it?"

She came in and closed the door. "I need an answer, Lacklan."

I sighed. "You don't, Primrose." I sat on the bed and gestured at her. "You have a chance. Make a few smart choices, make an effort, you have a chance to be happy. I blew it. Without even realizing I was doing it, I devoted my life to killing. Some people are experts in law, medicine, building houses. Me? I'm an expert in killing."

I could see her breathing had quickened. "Are you going to kill Vasco?"

"Yes."

"And then?"

"Anyone else who was involved with him. Then I'll continue on my way."

"Take me with you, Lacklan."

"No."

"Why?"

I sighed. I stood and went to her. "Because I like you. Because you deserve better. Because I could never make you happy, or show you how to be happy. You don't want to know about me, or get involved with me, Primrose. I'm bad news."

She came closer and put her hands gently on my chest. Her eyes said she was confused. "I don't think you're bad news, Lacklan. I think you're good news. Don't leave me stranded here."

I felt my heart give a jolt and my belly was on fire. I shook my head. When I spoke, my voice was a rasp. "Don't, Primrose. Not now..."

She stepped closer, so that her body pressed against mine. I gripped her shoulders, not knowing whether to crush her to me or push her away. She whispered, "*Lacklan...*"

I growled, "I can't..."

Downstairs, the door opened. There was a whistle and a howl and I realized the wind was rising again. The glass in the window behind me rattled. Abi's voice called out, "Primrose! Where are you?"

Primrose closed her eyes and clenched her teeth. "*Shit! That woman!*"

She turned on her heel and wrenched open the door. "Yes, Mom! I'm here!"

The door slammed, cutting off Abi's reply, but it sounded like she was asking her what she was doing upstairs. I smiled without much amusement and told myself it had been a close call. I've never had much time for morality. It's too much like trying to fit square pegs in round holes. But Marni had flitted through my mind while I held Primrose, and that had troubled me. On the other hand, I told myself, if tonight was my night to die, that would have been a nice memory to take to Valhalla with me.

I returned to the bed and studied my weapons again. I had nothing like enough for a full assault, especially against an unknown target. That meant I had to divide my attack in two parts; an initial recon mission, and then an attack based on what I found. It was the only plan open to me, but it had a big drawback: it required time, and time was one thing I did not have.

So I would have to take all my weapons, do my reconnaissance, decide on an attack, and go for it. At least, I told myself, I knew my primary target—Joe Vasco.

I heard the door open behind me again and felt a stab of irritation. I turned and saw not Primrose, but her mother, standing in the doorway and looking at the weapons on the bed, like an echo of her daughter. She closed the door and stared into my face.

"What are you doing, Lacklan?"

I lied. "I'm packing to leave."

"You can't." She shook her head. "You can't do that."

I frowned. "Why not? I have to go. Apart from anything else, Abi, I can't put your family at risk, and as long as I am here, they are. You know that."

She came close to me and placed her hand on my arm. "The storm. You'll never make it. They're saying it's going to be heavier even than last night. You'll have to stay, at least for the night."

"Abi, I..."

"Lacklan, wait, what you said at the church..."

"That's why I have to go."

"No, wait." She took a step closer, looked up into my face. "What do you intend to do?"

It was like a weird replay of her daughter. I wondered if they realized how alike they were. I frowned, feeling I was repeating myself. "It's best you don't know, Abi."

"We have been lost, at the mercy of these men."

"Do you know something? Abi, if there is something that you can tell me, I need to know."

She shook her head. "No." Then she hesitated. "I mean... We were so scared, Lacklan. We were terrified. And Al told us, if we trusted him and his men, he would take care of everything. And we trusted them..." She moved to the chair and sat, staring at the weapons on the bed.

I waited, then said, "But..."

"It was unspoken." She looked up at me. "That's the word, the key word, 'unspoken'. Joe..."

"Vasco?"

She nodded. "And his men. It started with a free coffee now and then, then it was free breakfasts. Then they'd come in, in the evenings, and Joe would never pay for his drinks... It was unspoken, but it was understood that he and his men had privileges. The tradeoff was that we all knew that those privileges did not include our daughters."

"Your husband tried to do something about it?"

She nodded again. "He didn't like the way Joe was looking at Primrose. He didn't like the arrangement that had been made. He'd been a soldier, like you. He was a brave man. He went to confront Joe. We found him a day later by the side of the road. He'd been hit by a truck. That was the story."

"That's where Sean gets his spirit from."

She smiled at me, and there was gratitude in her eyes. "But spirit isn't enough, is it, Lacklan? You understand that."

"Yes, I understand that very well." I gave a small laugh she didn't understand, and echoed what I had said earlier to her daughter. "Some people become experts in law, or medicine, or architecture. They wouldn't win their cases or save their patients, or build their houses on spirit alone. Making war, fighting, killing people, is just the same. It requires skill, planning, and expert execution."

She studied my eyes for a long moment, speaking to me in a wordless language. Finally, she said, "I saw it in you from the moment you walked in, with Peggy in your arms. I knew it." She shook her head. "You don't need to leave. Whatever they said at the congregation, whatever Al said, I will stand beside you."

I gave her hand a squeeze. "OK, Abi. Thank you." I stood. "What can you tell me about the farm, about Aloysius and Karen Groves, and about her relationship with Vasco?"

She looked startled. "Very little. There are rumors about her and Joe, but I have no idea how much truth there is in them. Al is much older than Karen, and their son is very sickly and weak. They aren't a happy family. As to the farm, I know they employ a lot of Mexican labor that comes up from Arizona. Word is it's illegal, but he pays them a decent wage and nobody complains. Nobody ever sees them. They live and eat on the farm, so they are able to save and take the money home with them when they leave."

"Aside from the illegals, how many men has he? How many men can Vasco count on?"

"I guess about ten men, all told." She hesitated. "Is it true, what Sean says, that you killed Earl?"

"Earl and three others, Abi. They had instructions to kill Peggy, and then come after me."

She gave a strange, unexpected smile. "I guess he only has six men, then."

"I guess he has."

She stood and came close to me. She held my face in her hands and kissed me.

"Thank you, Lacklan. Thank the Good Lord that you are here. We need you... *I* need you."

THIRTEEN

FOR THE SECOND TIME IN LESS THAN TWENTY-FOUR hours, Sean came to my rescue. I heard his door burst open down the corridor and his voice hollering my name. Abi closed her eyes and sighed. I moved past her and stepped out of the room. Sean collided with me. He looked pale with fear.

"They're coming, Lacklan! I saw them with my binoculars! They're coming in their trucks!"

I took hold of his shoulders and stared hard into his face. "Stay cool, focus, tell me: how many trucks?"

"Two! Two trucks."

Two to four men. I turned to Abi, who looked as pale and scared as her son. I said, "Get out. Kitchen door, over the fence. Go to the church. Go! Now!" I turned and bellowed down the stairs, "*Primrose! Here! Now!*" But she had heard Sean and was already running up the stairs. I pointed toward the kitchen. "Vasco is coming. All three of you. Go. Now. Kitchen door, go to the church! *Now!*"

I turned back into my room, cocked one Sig, and stuck it in my waistband. I swept everything else back into my kit bag and went onto the landing. Abi and her kids had gone. I ran to the bedroom I knew was over the kitchen, opened the window, and looked down. There was nobody there, so I dropped the kit bag out and took the stairs three at a time down to the main entrance. Outside, I could hear cars pulling up. I put on my jacket, took a couple of deep breaths and saw, in my mind's eye, the big Kiwi Sergeant I'd had in the Regiment, staring at me and growling, "Never pick a fight you are not sure you can win!" I stepped out with a hot rage building in my gut. This was a fight I could not win, so I had to move it to where I could win it.

They had stopped, forming a kind of triangle, nose to tailgate, in front of the guesthouse. There were eight of them. Two in each cab, and two riding in back. They all had shotguns. The sky had grown dark, though not as dark as night. The wind had picked up again, but was not yet a gale. The snow was heavy and drifting. They jumped down and climbed out of the cabs. I knew I had a real problem, but my main worry right then was to give Abi and the kids time to get away. I raised my hands and walked slowly along the path toward them. Vasco was not there.

I didn't try to calibrate all of them. That was pointless. However good you are, you cannot take eight guys on your own, especially eight guys who probably wrestle bulls for fun. All you can do is reduce the odds and escape, then strike again. I selected two targets. The guy who seemed to be in charge, and the biggest guy I could see, who happened to be standing next to him, on his right—my left.

The guy in charge was at the front, just outside the gate,

pointing a pump action shotgun at me. He was wearing a sheepskin jacket and a white cowboy hat. On his right was Man Mountain McCoy; six foot six of solid granite with a jaw that would break Mike Tyson's fist, and a face completely undisturbed by thought.

I spoke to him, like he was the boss. "What do you want?"

He frowned, like he was trying to have a thought and didn't know how. The cowboy hat answered.

"You're coming with us, Walker. We're going for a ride. Time for you to be moving on."

I ignored him and kept talking to the gorilla. "I don't want any trouble. You didn't need to bring an army. I was just packing to leave."

Now he looked distressed, like he had brain-ache. He glanced at his boss, who answered and sounded pissed. "Hey! I'm talking to you! Are you armed?"

I glanced at him briefly, like he wasn't important, then answered the gorilla as I moved through the gate and into the road outside. "I have a nine millimeter. It's in my waistband." I still had my hands up. "I'm going to pull it out, release the clip, and put it on the ground. Are we cool?"

I waited. The cowboy hat who was supposed to be in charge was seven feet away from me, slightly to my right. The man mountain was a similar distance, slightly to my left. Just behind him was the red Toyota pickup he'd arrived in. Scattered behind the cowboy and around a Ford were the six remaining men. It was going to be tough.

The cowboy spoke in a tight voice. "You gonna talk to me, boy, or I'm gonna whip you within an inch of your goddamn life! Let me see the gun, and drop it!"

I reached behind my back very slowly. The key thing was slow down reaction time as much as possible. I had the cowboy and Man Mountain McCoy thinking about why I was talking to the gorilla instead of the boss. Now I had to make the six boys relax. I held up the Sig with my finger on the trigger guard so they could see it. I released the clip into my left hand and held both up for them to see. I gave them a second to relax. They were now sure that they were in control. I spoke to the man mountain.

"I am going to put it down."

He was very confused as I bent slightly forward to drop the weapon in the snow. The cowboy was real mad and real determined to make me respect him. He was stepping forward when I shot him right between the eyes.

The 9 mm hollow point made a neat hole in his forehead but sprayed about twenty-seven cubic inches of blood, brains, and bone all over the six guys standing behind him. Everybody was going to be very confused for about three or four seconds, and I had a lot of work to do in that time. I had the magazine reinserted and the weapon cocked before the cowboy hit the snow. Man Mountain McCoy was gaping at his boss, still trying to have his first thought, when I shot him through the temple. Then I was running, with two seconds in which to put the trucks between me and the six guys with shotguns.

My plan was simple, and had the advantage of being what they would least expect me to do. I needed to lead them away from Abi and the kids, which meant away from the guesthouse, and away from the church. That in turn meant leading them toward the woods, where I could lose them and circle back behind the saloon and the terrace of houses, toward the plain. The last thing they would expect was for me to go to the farm. And that was exactly what I planned to do. I was going to strike at Vasco while all his men were searching for me up in the canyon.

That was my plan.

I ran four paces, turned, and ran another four paces backward, firing four shots randomly at the trucks. I smashed a windshield and popped a spotlight, then sprinted as best I could through the snow toward the cover of the trees at the foot of the north canyon wall. I heard two shotguns go off, but at that distance and in the snow they had no accuracy.

In among the trees I stopped, turned, dropped to one knee and raised my weapon. I'd expected to see six men chasing after me. Instead I saw empty snow, and in the distance the two trucks parked outside the Pioneer Guesthouse. Four men had taken cover behind the trucks, one was on a radio in the Ford, and another was aiming his weapon at the garden path, where Sean was standing in front of his mother, holding a kitchen knife, and Abi was weeping and begging him to drop it.

I went cold inside. Right there was the full impact of Sergeant Bradley's wisdom. Sean had picked a fight he could never possibly win, and in his wild courage he had brought us all down.

My mind raced, weighing my options. If I handed myself over, all I would achieve would be to guarantee all our deaths. Also, Primrose was not there. She had been smart. She had gone to the church. So my plan was clear. Go to the back yard, collect my kit bag, ensure Primrose was safe, then cross the plain to the farm and open the gates of Hell.

That was a fight I could win.

I ran through the trees, up along the canyon until I was sure I'd be out of sight. Then I crossed the path into the southern slopes, at the height of the church, and crossed the woods till I came to the road that led down to the back of the guesthouse. There, I lay hidden among the trees, watching and listening, dissecting the sounds and the shadows. There was the sigh of the mounting wind in the pines, the distant, growing moan as it swept across the plain to the east and into the hills. There was the creaking of the boughs and the rustle of the branches, and there was another rustle that did not belong. I remained motionless, waiting, and after a moment a shadow broke from among the other shadows of the forest and slipped across the snow toward the church. I rasped, "*Primrose! Here!*" She stopped and turned. "*It's me, Lacklan!*"

She ran unsteadily toward me. I pulled her in among the trees. She grabbed hold of me. "Mom and Sean! I lost them!"

"I know. Sean tried to take them on. Your mother went after him. Now I need you to listen really carefully. We're going back to the guesthouse."

"*What?*"

"They're going to do one of two things: they'll either interrogate your mother and Sean at the guesthouse, or they'll take them back to the farm. If they interrogate them, I'm going to need your help. If they leave and go back to the farm, the guesthouse is the safest place you can be, because it's the last place they'll look for you."

She looked scared. She looked sick. "My help...?"

"Let's hope it won't come to that. Follow me."

I led her to the edge of the tree line, past the Wrights'

house and on to the short path that led from the church road to Main Street. I hunkered down at the corner and peered around. Through the heavily falling flakes, I could see the lights from the Toyota on the snow and two guys leaning on the hood watching the woods where I had disappeared. They couldn't see me, but I covered them anyway and signaled Primrose to run quietly to the back yard of the guesthouse. She managed that without making a sound and I signaled her to wait.

I'd seen one of those guys talking on a radio earlier, and I wanted to know what they had talked about and, above all, who they'd been talking to. I moved across the path to the guesthouse wall and slid silently along till I came to the corner. The answer to my questions came almost immediately. There was a man talking.

"We checked out the whole house, Joe, there ain't nobody here. We checked the back yard and there were footprints leadin' to the fence. I reckon Primrose upped and ran, vaulted the fence."

Vasco's voice came back. "They ain't got nowhere to go. They gotta come back here. Pete, you put the truck over there, down by the side of the saloon. Leave everything just as it is, door open and everything. You and Davie go and wait inside. Primrose is gonna come back. It's gonna look like we left, see? When she does, you take her and you keep her here. I got something special in mind for her. If that son of a bitch Walker comes back, you shoot him, y'hear? You don't mess around or try an' bring him in. You just shoot him dead. And make *sure* he's dead."

"OK, Boss. We got it."

"All right! Let's get back to the farm before this storm

gets any worse. I think this pretty lady has something she wants to tell me. Ain't that right, Abi?"

Pete had climbed in the Toyota and was driving it across the road. He pulled in down the side of the saloon and disappeared from view. There was a lot of movement. I heard somebody, presumably Davie, go inside the guesthouse. Then, six truck doors slammed. I figured the Ford and a four-door, maybe the Jeep I'd borrowed the day before. That was eight men: Pete and Davie, and six who'd got into the vehicles. Then there were boots clattering into the back of a pickup. Two, maybe three men. So I was facing ten or twelve men; more than I had expected. I ran back along the path to where Primrose was waiting.

"Two men inside. They've taken Sean and your mother to the farm."

She pointed to a damson tree with branches overhanging the road. I pulled myself up into the lower branches, slipped across the fence, and dropped into the back yard, twenty feet from the kitchen. The kitchen light was off, but there was light seeping through from the living room. Primrose slipped down beside me. I signaled her to be quiet and stay by the tree. The snow was falling heavier and the poor visibility, plus the partial frosting on the glass, were going to play in my favor. I crossed the garden, crouched down seven feet from the door, and got a good, clear look into the kitchen, just as Pete closed the door into the living room. I smiled. It was a cold evening. He wanted to keep the warmth in.

I was going to let the cold in. I was going to ice them.

FOURTEEN

MAN'S BIGGEST ENEMY WHEN HE IS FIGHTING FOR his life is his brain's instinct to predict what is going to happen next. It's one of the reasons Zen advocates the empty mind. The empty mind is not a fancy spiritual state of consciousness. It's a very difficult state to achieve and takes years of training, and consists simply in not thinking, not predicting what is going to happen next, so that you can react instantly, without having to work it out or make sense of it.

Pete and Davie obviously hadn't been attending the local Independence Zen workshops. When I stepped into the kitchen and moved to the living room door, I could hear them inside, sitting in front of the fire, predicting what Primrose and I would undoubtedly do.

"There ain't no way they's coming back here, Davie. He's smart. He holed up in them woods waitin' for us to go after him. She went out back, you saw the footprints. She went over the fence and circled 'round through the woods to meet up with him. What he's gonna do is hole up in a barn, wait out the storm, steal a truck, and git the hell out here with the girl. 's what I'd do."

Davie wheezed a laugh. "Can't say I disagree with you, Pete. I'll tell ya! I'd sure like to get that Primrose alone. Boy! You see that ass? I can't blame him for takin' off with her."

Pete laughed. "We'll, least we got an easy evenin' ahead. You reckon she's got some beer in the kitchen…?"

I figured I'd heard enough intellectually-challenged conversation for one night and I opened the door and stepped in. They had predicted I was holed up in a barn making hay with Primrose. So it made no sense at all that I should walk in through the kitchen door. Unarmed, it made even less sense. Their brains needed time to process and readjust to the new data. It was only a couple of seconds, but it only takes a quarter of a second to kill somebody.

Pete was in an armchair, sideways to me. Davie was in front of me in the other chair. They were both gaping. I had taken two strides before they reacted. Pete fumbled for his shotgun while he tried to stand, which meant his guard was down and the side of his head was exposed. My right fist caught him full in the ear and sent him crashing over the side of the chair. By the time I got around, Davie was on his feet with the barrel of his weapon aimed straight at my belly. He was six feet away, which put the barrel just within reach. He pulled the trigger as I leaned to the left and stepped forward. The pellets ripped at my jacket. I levered the shotgun up and grabbed it with both hands. He wrestled me for it and I smashed my boot into the side of his right knee. His face went white and his eyes bulged. I used his hands as a pivot and rammed the butt of the shotgun into his jaw. His eyes rolled and, as he slumped, I took hold of the back of his head and his jaw.

You don't twist to the side like they do in the movies. All that does is cure a headache. You yank the back of the head hard to the side, and push up hard on the jaw. That breaks the neck. I let him go and he folded to the floor.

Pete was tough. When I turned around, he was on his feet. His eyes weren't focusing all that well, but he was ready to make a fight of it. He threw a right jab. I stepped left and leaned away from it, and in the same movement put my left forearm against his elbow. Then with savage speed and force I brought my right arm up against his wrist. I felt his elbow crunch. His bicep ripped and he screamed. I didn't stop. I gripped his wrist and pushed hard on the broken joint. He sprawled face down on the floor, screaming and gibbering, trying to beg me to stop. I did. I let go of his arm. It flopped to the floor, horribly twisted. I shifted my left foot and slammed the blade of my right into the back of his neck. I felt the vertebrae crunch and, apart from a few twitches in his feet, he went quiet. His fighting days were over.

I turned to call Primrose. She was standing in the doorway watching me. She looked like she'd just swallowed a pint of last week's clams.

I said, "I'm sorry you had to see that. You should have waited till I called you."

She shook her head. "That's not how we do things. I thought you might need help."

I couldn't restrain the smile. "Thanks."

I searched in Pete's pocket and found the keys to the Toyota.

Outside, the sky had gone black. I didn't know what

time it was, but it was dark as night. The wind was blowing hard from the north and lashing the snow like rain against my face. I struggled across the small square and down the side of the saloon. The Toyota was there. The windshield I had shattered with a shot had been kicked out and removed, and the seat and the dash were spattered with snow. I climbed in and reversed it, with difficulty, back to the guest-house. Then I went in, dragged Pete and Davie, or what was left of them, out to the street and, with Primrose's help, heaved them into the back of the 4X4. After that, I collected my kit bag from the back yard where I'd thrown it and slung it on the passenger seat.

I knew the road from the depot to the farm had been cleared of snow the day before, I just hoped the Toyota would get me as far as the depot. Primrose took hold of my collar and turned me to face her.

"What are you going to do?"

"I'll go to the farm and get your mother and Sean back."

She searched my face for a moment. "And then?"

"Then I'll make Vasco pay for everything he's done."

"Let me come with you, Lacklan. Let me help."

I shook my head. "No."

"If you die, I want to go down with you. If you live, when you leave, I want to go with you."

I grabbed hold of her shoulders. There was a hot, wild excitement inside me which I fought to control. I growled, "No! Stay here, Primrose, stay safe. I will come back and I'll bring your mother and Sean with me..." I hesitated, then shook my head. "I don't want you hurt... Go inside and wait for me."

I clambered into the cab, slammed the door and, with

the lights off, began the slow descent toward the depot. For a mile and a half, the snow was deep, and a layer of ice had formed under it, covering the road and causing the truck to slide and swerve as I moved forward, forcing me to crawl at a snail's pace, with the freezing wind lashing at my face through the yawning hole where the windshield should have been. It took me almost ten minutes to get to the turn off to the depot. And there, something made me stop and stare. Suddenly, the place looked incongruous, absurd, with its high wall, its gate, and a snow plow clearing the path during a blizzard. A path for what?

I remembered the ten-wheeler truck I'd seen leaving, headed south. I tried to see in my mind what lay south. South was just desert: hundreds of miles of desert, and route 400, which turned west near the end of the Humboldt Range to connect with the I-80, just north of Lovelock. Whether you were going southwest to California or northeast, it made more sense to turn left and north at that junction. It made no sense at all to turn south.

I didn't know right then why it was important, but I knew, with absolute certainty, that it was. I spun the wheel and turned off the road and down the track, bumping, sliding, and skidding toward the structure. I pulled up outside the gate and swung down from the cab, wincing in the icy wind, shielding my eyes with my hands, and made my way around the hood. The gale whistled in the pylons and groaned over the plain, raising great clouds of snow and rattling the wooden fence. The gate was padlocked. I pulled my Sig from my waistband and put a round into it. It came loose and I put my shoulder to the boards, forcing it open.

I found myself in a broad yard stacked with heavy-duty

plastic drums, about four feet tall and three feet across. At a rough estimate, I guessed there must have been at least a couple hundred of them, maybe twice that number. In the poor visibility, with the darkness and the blizzard, it was hard to tell. I waded through the snow, struggling to keep my footing against the wind, and came to the closest of the drums. The lid was sealed on with steel bands. Whatever was in them, it sure as hell wasn't carrots. I took my Sig again and shot off the two bands, then unclipped the lid and pried it off. I shielded my eyes and stared. It was full of dirt. I reached in with my gloved hand and grabbed some to look at it more closely. It was coarse dirt.

I stood back and stared at the rest of them, stacked three high, five deep against the fence. Why? Why would you store tens, maybe hundreds of tons of dirt like that? I looked at the shed. It was huge, and suddenly I was wondering, if outside there were hundreds of drums of dirt, what the hell was on the inside? And as I wondered that, I saw there was a window, high up on the near side, and in it I caught a glimpse, a dim reflection, of light.

I explored further and found that there was a huge, steel roller blind at the north end, and a wooden door on the far side, away from the gate. I struggled over to it. It was locked, and at the top and bottom of the door, there were also deadbolts.

On the outside.

I slid back the bolts, took my Swiss Army knife from my pocket, rammed it in the lock, and, with my Sig in my right hand, I eased the door open.

More than a barn, it was a huge hangar, easily fifty feet across and at least seventy feet long. The ceiling was high, maybe twenty feet, supported by an A-frame of rafters. Here, inside the hangar, there were also drums stacked against the walls, three and four high, five and six deep. But what struck me most, as I took it in, was the peculiar structure against the wall in the far right-hand corner. Made of drums, it formed a kind of pen, or enclosure, with blankets laid across the top as a roof. And through an opening, about four feet across and five feet high, I could make out the unmistakable wavering light of fire. I wasn't exactly surprised. A deadbolt on the outside of the door can only mean one thing: you want to keep somebody on the inside.

I closed the door and walked slowly toward the enclosure, keeping my gun trained on the opening. There was total silence. When I was ten feet away, I said, "Whoever you are in there, come out with your hands in the air."

After a moment, there was a slight movement, a rustling, and then a pair of feet in Nike trainers appeared, followed by a pair of filthy jeans, and then the torso and the head of a man, probably in his late thirties, ducked out. He had black hair and olive skin, and two got you twenty he was one of Aloysius Groves' illegal Mexican employees; and this was his fair and equitable food and lodging. I beckoned him out and pointed at the portal through which he had emerged.

"Are there more of you in there?"

He shrugged and shook his head, looking back at the opening. Another face appeared, this time a woman, probably also in her mid-thirties. She came out too and I took a step closer, peering in. I caught a glimpse of bodies, legs, people sitting, cramped together in firelight, improvising warmth against the storm.

I slipped my gun back in my waistband and said,

"*Amigo.*" I put my hand on my chest and repeated. "*Amigo.*" I pointed over at the enclosure. "*Cuantos? Cuantos hombres y mujeres?*" How many men and women? They looked at each other, wary, but afraid and beaten down. The fear was written large in their eyes. The man spoke.

"*Cien, cincuenta hombres, cincuenta mujeres. Somos familias. El lo quiso así.*"

My Spanish is poor, but I knew enough to get it: there were a hundred of them, fifty men and fifty women. Families. And from what I could make out, '*el lo quiso así*' meant, 'He wanted it that way.'

Slowly, one by one, others began to emerge, most of them in their mid to late thirties.

I frowned, shaking my head, telling them with my face that I didn't understand. "*Quien?*" I asked. "*Quien lo quiso así?*" Who wanted it that way?

"*El jefe. El señor capataz, el señor Vasco...*"

Vasco. Vasco wanted it that way.

Why?

FIFTEEN

THEY TRIED TO TELL ME. THEY TRIED TO EXPLAIN, and they bombarded me with questions, too, streaming from the small opening in the enclosure in their dozens, gathering around me, grabbing hold of me and talking all at the same time: was I a cop? Was I immigration? Was I FBI? Who was I? Why was I there? They wanted to go home.

I tried to tell them I didn't speak Spanish, I was not a cop or a Fed, but they weren't listening. They were talking, terrified, clamoring, begging, pulling at my sleeves, clawing at my arms. I backed away toward the door, signaling with my hands that they should stay, and be quiet. Gradually, they stopped, fell silent, and stood, a small, frightened, bewildered crowd in the middle of a vast, frozen hangar, with the flickering light of the flames behind them.

"*Esperen aquí,*" I said. "*Con el fuego. Volveré.*" Stay here, with the fire. I will be back.

I stepped into the freezing gale and, pulling up my collar and hugging my jacket close around me, I struggled back to the truck. My mind was in a whirl, but I had no time to think it through. I fired up the engine and drove slowly back to the road, not daring to go above six or seven miles an hour. Every time the needle edged toward ten, the wheels began to spin and the truck skidded and slewed on the ice beneath the snow.

Finally, I made it to the blacktop, Route 400. Already it was beginning to disappear under a thick, white blanket. The entrance to the farm on the other side was invisible among the billowing clouds of white flakes, but I had a fair idea of where it was. I crawled onto the road, pointed the nose of the truck at where I thought it should be, and gently pressed the gas. The truck trundled forward and gradually the white wall, and the big white arch, emerged from the blackness at the end of a short driveway, among the mist of wind-blown snow. When I was sure I was lined up with the center, I floored the pedal and rammed nearly four thousand pounds of truck right through the big, iron gate.

It gave and I slithered and slewed through to the sound of screeching, tortured metal. Any other day and the noise would have been heard for miles, but with that gale blowing, the crashing, grinding, and scraping of iron and steel was lost, blown away on the wind.

I continued for fifty or sixty yards up the driveway toward the house, but eventually the truck skidded on the frozen track and buried itself nose-first in a snowdrift. It was good enough. I grabbed my kit bag and jumped down from the cab. Squinting and wiping the freezing flakes from my eyes, I made out the glimmer of light from the farmhouse windows. I shouldered my bag and started to trudge through the drifts toward the lights. Nobody tried to stop me. There were no shouts, no dogs, no spotlights, no gunfire.

The house turned out to be a big, mock Georgian manor. At the front there was a gabled portico supported by Greco-Roman columns. But at the back, where there should have been a landscaped, formal garden, instead, maybe fifty yards away, there was a complex that looked like stables, a barn, and some kind of living quarters for the hands. I figured the fields and the crops were further back, made invisible by the storm.

I didn't pause or hesitate.

Vasco was confident he had me. He had a dozen men, and his opponents were a teenage girl and a single man, struggling to survive in a blizzard out in the wilderness. But the SAS is founded on the principle that a single man can sometimes do more damage than an entire army, if he knows what he is doing. To say I knew what I was doing might be to overstate the case. I was making it up as I went along. But I knew that when the time came, I would know what to do. That single man struggling to survive in a blizzard was now wading through the snow up to his kitchen door, with murderous intent.

He hadn't posted perimeter guards because of the blizzard, and the ones he had posted inside the house were, like him, confident that their enemy was either freezing to death or being shot to death back at the guesthouse. I stood back from the light and peered through the kitchen window. It was hard to make out details, my eyes were watering from the freezing wind, and the glass was frosted with ice, but I could see a guy sitting at a large, pine table, watching something on a small TV. On the table beside him was an automatic. One here, another presumably at the front door. How many more?

I turned and looked over my shoulder. There was the long building that looked like the living quarters for the hands. There was light filtering out of the windows. Some of his men, at least, were in there. There was only one thing to do. I couldn't stay put in those temperatures much longer. I had to go inside. I buried my kit bag under a drift, walked up to the door, and banged. The guard's logical assumption would be that it was one of the hands. Usually your mortal enemies don't come up and knock on your kitchen door in the middle of a blizzard.

I saw him turn and look. He got up, picked up his piece and walked over to the door, looking over his shoulder at the TV and laughing as he went. I pulled my Sig and cocked it, and aimed at where his head was going to be. I wanted to shoot him while I was outside where the gale would muffle the sound.

The door opened and he stood staring with his mouth open. I said, "Make a sound and I'll blow the back of your head off. Do as I say and you'll wake up alive tomorrow."

He closed his mouth.

I said, "Step outside and throw your weapon in the snow."

He did as I said and held up his hands.

I asked him, "How many inside the house?"

He wasn't about to be a hero. "Mr. Groves and his wife and the boy, me and Phil in the entrance hall. All the other boys are in the lodgings over yonder." He indicated the long building I'd pegged as the living quarters. "Look, mister, we never meant no harm. It's just..."

"Can it. What about Abi and the boy?"

"They're upstairs, safe and sound..."

I shot him between the eyes, picked up his piece—a 9mm Taurus, Beretta look-alike—stepped inside, and closed the door. A burst of canned laughter greeted me, like what I'd done was funny. I stood in the middle of the terra cotta-tiled floor and listened. The kitchen was big, spacious. Outside, I could hear the moan of the wind, with an occasional high whistle. There was the babble from the TV, the hum of the large, silver fridge, and nothing else.

I moved toward the door that gave on to the rest of the house. I had no idea of the layout or if the exit from the kitchen would take me past the hall and Phil. I eased it open and peered out. Still no sound. I was looking down a passageway toward a beveled column, a large fern, and a white, marble floor that seemed to open to the right. Opposite me was a wall that, after a moment, I realized was the side of a staircase that rose to the upper floor. That meant the column and the fern were in the hall.

I slipped my Sig in my waistband and drew my knife from my boot. Then I moved very slowly along the passage. Step by step, the hall came into view. It was spacious and absurdly ornate, with a statue of Eros in the centre of a circular floor. Imitation Louis XV furniture with gilded legs stood against the walls, and ferns were positioned beside multiple, unnecessary Greek pillars. It was like the lobby of a gaudy, nineteenth-century hotel.

Seated with his back to me in one of the Louis XV chairs was a man in his late twenties. He had no TV to watch, so I guess, in desperation, he had picked up a book. He seemed to be absorbed in it. I paused and listened. There were still no sounds. I took two long, silent steps that brought me beside the column just behind the fern. He was six feet away, with his head slightly inclined, looking down at the book in his lap. He was angled slightly to the left, facing the door. The fern would be in my way, making it awkward, but it was doable.

I slid my left foot forward, brought my right level. He was now three feet away, and I acted swiftly and brutally. I took another step with my left foot, clamped my left hand over his mouth and nose and simultaneously rammed two inches of the blade into the vertebrae in his neck, an inch below where they meet the skull. Bleeding was minimal, but it severed all communication between his brain and the rest of his body, including his vital organs. His heart stopped, his diaphragm stopped, what air he had in his lungs hissed out, he could not scream.

I left him looking at his book with dead eyes and ran silently up the stairs to the galleried landing that overlooked the hall. It extended in two passages from left to right and led to bedrooms on either side. At the end of each passage there was a sharp, right angle bend toward the back of the building, where the two wings formed a kind of horseshoe. I moved to the right and out of sight, and again stopped to listen. This time, I heard the faint murmur of voices.

I moved slowly, pausing after each step, homing in on the sound. It grew steadily louder until I came to a door at the end of the corridor, by the corner. I couldn't make out the words they were speaking, but it was a man and a woman. The woman's voice was soothing, gentle. The man's voice was whining, complaining. It wasn't Abi and Sean, so it must be Karen and the boy, Arnold. I had no use for them, so I moved on, around the bend. At the far end there was a window, black glass smeared with snow, in the walls, and two more doors: one in the far wall; the other, by its position, must give on to the same room where I could hear the murmured conversation.

The far room was empty, and I was about to return and explore the other wing when a noise made me stop. It was a voice, clear and distinct, coming from the room where Karen and Arnold were. I froze. He must be right by the door.

"Mommy, please talk to Daddy. I really miss her and I want her to come and visit me..."

Then the unmistakable sound of a toilet lid being put down and water flushing. A door closed and the talk was muffled. Clearly it was an en suite with a door to the passage. The words he'd spoken intrigued me and a gut feeling told me that what I had listened to was important. I tried the handle. The door was locked, but thirty seconds with my Swiss Army knife changed that and I slipped in and closed the door softly behind me. There was another door opposite that led into the bedroom itself. It had an old-fashioned keyhole and I knelt down and peered through. I couldn't see much, but there was a large bed on the right, and to the left I could make out some armchairs in front of an open fireplace. I figured they were fifteen or twenty feet away and were turned with their backs to me, facing the fire at an angle. I could risk easing the door open a few inches. I turned the handle and pulled. Karen was speaking.

"Sweetheart, there are things you can't always understand and it's best to leave those things up to Mommy and Daddy. And sometimes, the people you want to be with and play with..."

"I don't play anymore, Mommy, you know that! I'm twenty years old now!"

He laughed and she answered with a smiling voice. "To me you'll always be my special baby boy. And even if you *are* a big man now, you still you have to realize that you are not just any man, you're *Arnold Groves!* And that makes you special. That means you can't just have any old person coming to visit you."

They were quiet for a moment. Then, he said, "But, I used to have friends come and play..."

"Well, that was when you were a child, Arnold, honey, and it's different when you're a child."

His voice turned resentful. "Everything changed when Joe came to live with us. He ruined everything. I don't like Joe!"

"Now I don't want you talking like that about Uncle Joe. He's our special friend and he helps Daddy a lot. Why, I don't know what we'd do without Uncle Joe!"

"He takes all my friends away..." There was silence, then he added, with a bitter twist in his voice, "He takes you away!"

"Now, Arnold! That is *not* true! I don't want you talking like that! Nobody will ever take me away from you! *Ever!* You hear me, mister?"

"I guess..." He didn't sound very convinced.

"Now, I think it's time for you to have a little lie down and a rest. What do you think?"

I glanced at my watch. It was barely eight thirty. I heard Arnold's voice, still sulking. "OK. Will you stay till I'm asleep, and sing to me?"

"Of course I will, my darling. You're still Mommy's baby boy. Come on, sweetheart, I'll help you to the bed."

I saw her stand and bend over him. He stood too, apparently with difficulty, and then they moved across the room, toward the bed and out of view. After a moment, I heard her start to sing. He said, in a sleepy voice, "I do wish Prim could come and visit me, Mommy. She's so pretty and sweet..."

But she ignored him and kept on singing. I pulled the door closed and slipped into the corridor again. There, I leaned against the wall and slowly slid down to sit on the floor. My mind was racing: the men and women in the depot, Arnold and Karen, and Joe and the snow plow... It all began to make some kind of horrible sense.

SIXTEEN

I HEARD THE DOOR OPEN AROUND THE CORNER AND rose silently to my feet. I heard her steps move briskly along the landing and then thud softly down the stairs. I had to decide quickly whether to follow her or find Abi and Sean. I decided I knew to within five rooms where they were, and all of a sudden I was very curious to hear more of what Karen had to say. I followed her.

I moved to the top of the stairs and watched her reach the hall and walk past Phil without looking at him. She crossed the tiled floor, her heels tapping loudly, knocked on a tall, walnut door, waited a moment, and went in. I took the steps three at a time, wondering how I was going to manage to eavesdrop on their conversation. I moved silently to the door and listened. All I could make out was a muffled exchange that sounded vaguely irritable. Then suddenly Aloysius' voice was getting louder and I realized he was approaching.

On my right there was a column with the bust of somebody who looked Greek and wise, like his name should have been Platocrates. Beyond it was one of those mock Louis XV sofas. Two long strides took me past them both and I crouched down as the door opened. Aloysius came out on his long, stiff legs with his odd, jerky walk. He was talking and he didn't sound happy.

"Why you can't tend to the boy is beyond me. Don't I do enough for him as it is?"

She followed him across the hall and up the stairs. Phil kept on reading. She was saying, "Really, Al, all he wants is for you to tell him he'll be able to play with Prim soon..."

"He's twenty years old, for God's sake, Karen! And the girl must be that age herself! They don't *play* anymore!"

"You know what I mean, Al. Don't be grouchy. I have a headache. Just promise him..."

"I can't promise him! It's out of the question...!"

They moved onto the landing and their voices trailed away toward the bedroom. I slipped across the floor and silently crossed Phil's right leg over his left and turned a couple of pages. I was flying by the seat of my pants and I knew it, but that didn't mean I couldn't be thorough. I went back to the walnut door, opened it, and went in. It was a library-cum-study. A fire was burning in a marble, mock-Georgian fireplace. A couple of old leather armchairs and a sofa that looked authentic stood around it. Beyond, there was a heavy oak desk, and beyond that heavy, burgundy drapes were drawn across what I assumed were glass doors out onto a garden.

I had a quick look at his desk, but there was nothing worth seeing and the drawers were locked. I was aware I was running out of time. Sooner or later, somebody was going to realize Phil was dead and raise the alarm. My priority was to get Abi and Sean out of there and after that, do what damage I could to Vasco and his men. But something was telling me I needed to listen to Karen and Al. They had something to tell me. Something important. So, the guards were dead, why not just put a gun to their heads and make them talk?

Because they wouldn't. It was just instinct, but I knew that whatever their story was, they would rather die than let me in on it.

I heard their voices again coming down the stairs. I stepped quickly behind the drapes and nestled in where they met the bookcase. She was talking as they opened the door. Her voice was tight with anxiety.

"Maybe he should see a doctor, Al. He just seems to be getting so weak..."

"No! I am adamant on this, Karen. It is out of the question. We take care of our own. We always have. Close the damn door, woman!" I heard the door close and he continued. "We see to his needs, we feed him and care for him, but if the Good Lord sees fit to take him while he is young, then so be it!"

"Oh, Al! Don't say that!"

His voice rasped at her, "He's weak! He's feeble! There are days he can barely stand on his own feet! What quality of life is that for the boy? He barely eats or drinks, he can't have a normal relationship... That's not a *life!*"

"But Al, that's not true! That's a wicked thing to say! There are days when he can walk if I help him. You saw him when we went to poor Peggy's service. He was quite lively! And those days make it worthwhile. What does he want women for? He has me! He gets so much joy from a little bit of affection..."

He growled, "It's not natural! You're *blind*..."

"Not natural? What are you talking about? He loves his mother! Of course that's natural! He doesn't like filthy harlots! Or these tramps from the village! *And neither do I!* In his heart he is still a child. Is it natural to let your own son *die!*"

"Be *silent*, woman!" There was a loud knock at the door. He roared, "*Come in!*"

I heard it open and there was a heavy tread of boots before it closed again. I had my Sig in my hand, but the new voice, Vasco's, didn't say anything about Phil or the unattended kitchen. Instead, he said, "We ain't heard nothing from Pete yet. Weather's getting pretty wild and I can't see them staying out in this. They won't live long if they do."

"What's your point?"

"Either they're dead or he's killed Pete and Davie."

"Those are not the only two options, Joe. He may have sought refuge in a barn, or he may have stolen a vehicle and tried to make a getaway."

Vasco snorted. "If he's done that, he's sure as hell dead. I guess he may be holed up in a barn, but the nearest barns are at least a mile from Independence. I can' see it myself."

It was Karen who answered him. "Either way, there is nothing we can do till the blizzard passes. It should have eased by the morning. Then you take the plow and clear the road not just to the depot, but to the Pioneer. Take men. If you see this Walker character, shoot him on sight. Shoot Prim too."

"Uh-uh, Prim is for me."

"I want her dead!"

"Don't sweat it. I'll deal with it."

Al cut in, "The way you're dealing with Abi and the boy? Why are they still alive? They are a liability. This whole situation is getting out of hand, Joe. Instead of containing it, you're turning it into a catastrophe."

There was something dangerous in Joe's voice when he answered. It was low and quiet. "Take it easy, Aloysius, I know what I'm doing. Word in the village is that Abi and this guy were getting sweet on each other..."

"In two days?"

"It happens. Either way, we've got nothing to lose. If it's true, we may have an edge over him while we hold her."

"If he hasn't shown up by tomorrow morning, I want her dead. You take the plow to the Pioneer. If he and Prim are not there, you start a search, house by house, room by room, barn by barn. You find them!"

"OK..."

"Meanwhile, we clear the road to Rochdale." He was silent a moment, then, as though distracted, "It may do Arn some good to go to Rochdale, too. Maybe that's what he needs..." He paused again, then snapped, "I need those damned Mexicans working! They are costing me fucking money just sitting there on their skinny fucking asses! Clear the road, then you take Abi and the boy to Rochdale and you *fucking bury them there!* Walker or no Walker! You understand?"

"Keep your hair on, old man. Don't shout at me. It upsets my digestion."

"Don't be impertinent!"

There was a strained silence for all of five seconds,

counted slow, then Vasco's voice, low, "I'll see to it, old man, but tomorrow, we're going to sit down and talk about a new arrangement. I figure, the risks and responsibilities I take, I deserve a bigger cut of the cake. What do you say, Karen? You think I deserve a bite of that cherry...?"

There was a nasty leer in his voice. She snapped, "Stop it, Joe!" But there wasn't much conviction in her voice. "Let's stop this before it gets out of hand. You have your orders..."

There was a snort. "Yeah, I have my orders..."

I heard his boots cross the floor and the door open. I heard Karen's voice, subdued, "You want to take Arn to Rochdale...?"

Al's voice came back, heavy and dull. "It may be what he needs."

I was waiting for the door to close but it didn't.

"I don't like it. He's so weak at the moment. It's so cold..."

"It'll do him good. He always feels better after a visit."

She said again, "I don't like..."

Suddenly he roared, "*Is everybody going to argue with every damned decision I take today?*"

"No, Al, no, I'm sorry..."

In the background I could hear Vasco calling, "Hey! Phil! You gonna turn that page or you gonna stare at it all night?" I heard his heels on the tiled floor, and his voice farther away, "Hey! Phil! What's the matter with you...?"

I had to decide, attack or run?

Vasco's voice bellowed, "*Holy mother of...! Jesus Christ! He's fucking dead!*"

I could come out from behind the drapes, kill Vasco. Karen and Al would be easy to deal with. Or I could step out through the French doors I was leaning against, and follow them tomorrow to Rochdale. But while I was debating it, I heard Vasco shouting, "*He's in the house! He's in the fucking house!*" And then there was the crackle of a radio and Vasco's voice again, "*He's in the house! Get your asses here now! Now! Now! Cover the back doors and the front! Now!*"

Then Al was shouting, "*Abi! Abi! Upstairs! Quick!*"

They ran from the room and I heard their feet clattering up the stairs. Through the glass panes on the French doors I could see the lights streaming from the open door of the lodgings, and the dancing black silhouettes of the men pouring out of it.

I had one option. Pursue them upstairs, kill Joe Vasco, use Al as a hostage. I stepped out from behind the drapes and ran silently across the study and then the hall, up the stairs and onto the landing. Down to the left I saw an open door. Karen was standing in it with light bathing her face. She was looking over Al's shoulder. Al was scowling. From within, I could hear Joe's voice. "*Where is he?*"

And Abi's weeping. "*I don't know!*"

I sprinted toward them, raising my gun. Karen turned and stared at me. Her eyes went wide and she screamed hysterically, "*He's here!*"

Then Al was being dragged into the bedroom by the scruff of his neck. I heard Abi's voice screaming and as I opened my mouth to shout, "*Give it up or Karen dies!*" Joe Vasco burst out of the room, dragging Abi with a .44 semiautomatic pointed at her head.

He was sneering. "Go ahead, shoot her. It makes no damn odds to me. But if you don't drop your weapon by the count of three, the lady gets it, and then the boy."

I looked into the room. Al had Sean by the hair, and he was holding an automatic at his head.

Checkmate. I might shoot Vasco, or I might shoot Al, but I couldn't get them both and guarantee Abi and Sean's survival. I'd been outmaneuvered. And now I was probably going to be shot. I held up my hands, showed him the gun and laid it on the floor. Vasco glanced at Karen, who was shaking badly. He jerked his head at me and said, "Frisk him."

She approached me with fear in her eyes. She found the Taurus in my jacket and the Fairbairn & Sykes in my boot. She handed them to Vasco. He inspected them and scowled at me. "This is Julio's gun."

"He doesn't need it now."

There was rage in his face. "I ought to gut you right now..."

I looked deep into his eyes. "Yeah, you ought to. Use my knife."

He took a step but Al snapped at him, "No! It's too risky. Lock him up, with the woman and the boy. We'll dispose of them tomorrow at Rochdale." Downstairs, there were feet running. The boys had arrived. Al came out of the room and shouted, "Up here!" Then to Vasco, he said, "We'll keep four guards on him at all times. If he steps outside that door, shoot him dead, along with the woman and the boy." He stared into my eyes. "You got that?"

I nodded at him. I'd got it. I also knew he'd made the biggest mistake of his life. He should have killed me while he had the chance. Now I was going to kill him.

SEVENTEEN

THE ROOM WAS A SMALLER VERSION OF ARNOLD'S room, only the bed was a large four-poster. Like Arnold's room, it had chairs arranged around a fireplace, though there was no fire burning in it. Drapes were drawn across a broad window that overlooked the back of the house. Abi was sitting on the bed, with the fingers of her right hand held over her mouth. She was struggling to control her sobs. Sean was sitting next to her with his arm around her, comforting her, though I could see from his expression that he was fighting hard not to cry himself.

I eased back the drapes and examined the window. It was triple-glazed and locked, and from what I could see, even if I could get it open, it was a twenty or thirty foot drop into the unknown. I turned and looked at the door. Outside, I could hear four guys drawing up chairs and a table further along on the landing, at the top of the stairs, so they could play cards and block our escape at the same time. Again, even if I could get the damn door open, I'd give them plenty of warning and I'd be unarmed against four men with guns and grudges. So far I had accounted for six of their guys—that they were aware of—and that made up a lot of grudges.

I turned and looked at Abi. Her sobs were subsiding. I said, "Why don't you go and sit in the chair, I'll make us a fire."

She looked at me with puffy, red eyes. "There are no logs..."

I smiled. "I know where to get some."

She frowned and looked around, but stood and went with Sean over to the chairs. I grabbed hold of the mattress and heaved it and the bedding off the bed, exposing the wooden structure. The posts were held to the main frame by large, iron bolts. Once I had loosened one of them, a few good kicks broke the post free, and the slats that formed the base on which the mattress rested snapped easily when I stamped on them. They made excellent kindling. Abi and Sean were looking at me like I was insane. I ignored them and kicked off a second post, then laid both across a stack of kindling and set fire to it with my Zippo.

Once it was burning, I sat cross-legged on the floor and gazed at the flames for a moment.

"Abi, Sean." I turned to face them. "I want you both to listen real carefully to me. I have been in situations a lot worse than this one, and I have come out alive." I smiled. "Sometimes bruised, a couple of times injured, but always alive. Now I am giving you my solemn promise, we are going to survive this. I am not going to let anything happen to you two, or to Primrose."

Abi said, "Where is she?"

"She's safe."

"Lacklan, he must have a dozen men…"

"Less than that now."

She paused, staring at me like she didn't know whether to love me or fear me. Her voice was incredulous, but there was hope in it, too. "How can you stop them?"

"Leave that to me." I turned to Sean. "Now, Sean, I have very precise orders for you, OK? I know you're brave and tough and resourceful, but I need you to be disciplined, too."

He frowned, like he didn't like that idea so much. "Disciplined?"

I nodded. "It's the toughest thing to learn, but it's what makes the difference between a brave soldier and a great warrior. It doesn't just mean following orders, any sheep can do that." He smiled, he liked that more. "It means keeping a cool head and doing what you know you need to do, to win."

I waited a moment for that to sink in. He liked the sound of winning, so he nodded. "OK."

"And *that*," I said, "means that sometimes you have to walk away from a fight, no matter how much you want to beat the guy up."

His cheeks flushed red. "Yeah, I'm sorry."

I ignored him. "Never, *never* go into a fight you know you can't win, because when you do, you drag your comrades in with you. So I want you to promise me that tomorrow you will stay with your mother, look after her and keep her safe. You understand me?"

He nodded. "I promise."

"And if each one of us plays his part, and if I *know* that I can trust you to play yours, tomorrow we go home, safe and sound. Deal?"

He smiled. "Deal."

We shook on it. Abi was studying my face, trying to read me. She said, "Can you really promise that?"

I nodded. "I can promise that if we believe it, we can make it happen. It's not up to them. It's up to us."

She made a face that said she wanted to believe me but was afraid to hope. There was nothing more I could tell her, so I said, "Abi, on my way here I broke into the depot. Do you know what's in there?"

She shook her head. "It's a kind of unspoken understanding, we stay away from the depot, and we don't talk about it."

Sean had sat up straight and was grinning. "I know!"

Abi snapped at him, "Sean! I hope you haven't been near that place!"

"No, Mom! I've been watching it from my room, with my binoculars. I know what goes on there!"

"What did you find?" It was Abi, looking like she really didn't want to know.

I sucked my teeth. "I found big, reinforced rubber drums of dirt. Hundreds of them."

She frowned like I was talking a language she didn't understand. But Sean interrupted. "I bet you found people too, didn't you? He has people living there!"

I nodded. "One hundred Mexicans, fifty women and fifty men. And hundreds of drums of dirt. Tell me what you've seen."

"Every day, early in the morning, a truck arrives, one of those ten-wheeler jobs, and all these people climb in the back. Then the truck takes off and goes south. And every evening two trucks come back. One of them unloads the people and the other unloads something else, I can never see what it is because it goes inside the fence. But I guess it must be those drums of dirt."

Abi was shaking her head. "Why dirt?"

Sean put his hand on her arm. "Wait, Mom, there's something else. Once a week or every ten days, a truck comes from the north. It's bigger, it loads up and then heads back north again."

I studied Abi's face. I was pretty sure I knew the answer, but I asked her anyway. "Have you any idea what it means?"

She shook her head. "Why would anyone ship dirt? It doesn't make any sense." She frowned at me. "Have you any idea?"

"I'm not sure. What or where is Rochdale?"

"I don't know of any Rochdales around here." She hesitated a moment. "It sounds more like a name from the east..."

I smiled. "I know two, New York and Massachusetts, but I'm pretty sure he isn't taking us east tomorrow. There has to be a Rochdale around here, close enough to drive a snow plow to, and two gets you twenty it's south on Route 400."

Sean was nodding vigorously. "Six or seven miles south of the crossroads where you found Peggy, the road turns west and crosses through the mountains. It comes out on the I-80, just north of Lovelock. I bet you anything you like, Rochdale is somewhere along that pass through the mountains."

I nodded back at him, a little more slowly. He had echoed my thoughts. There was, as my British comrades in the Regiment would have put it, sweet fuck all south of Independence until you got to the Mexican border, more than five hundred miles away; just desert, and then more desert. And the only road around here, Route 400, took you straight to the I-80, as Sean had said. But the quickest way to I-80 was north, back up toward Mill City. The only reason you'd go south on Route 400 would be if you had some reason to go through that pass. So the question was no longer 'where is Rochdale?' but, '*what* is Rochdale?'. And I had a nasty feeling that I knew the answer.

I stood. "Let's try and get some sleep. Tomorrow is going to be a tough day. You guys get those chairs out of the way and I'll pull the mattress over."

I dragged the heavy mattress and the bedding in front of the fire. We took off our shoes but left the rest of our clothing on, and climbed under the covers. Sean was dispatched to turn off the light, and by the flickering glow of the flames Abi put her arms around me and her head on my shoulder, and Sean curled up next to her. Outside, the wind howled and wailed, and the snow fell thick and freezing, and I lay staring at the wavering orange light on the ceiling, wondering what the hell I was going to do in the morning, how the hell I was going to keep the promises I'd made.

————

I SLEPT eight hours and was awake before six. I spent an hour training and then had a shower. When I came out of the bathroom, Abi and Sean were awake and looking depressed and frightened. I wondered absently when they had last eaten. If they were planning to kill us later that morning, they would not waste food on us.

The door opened and Vasco was there with his four goons behind him. They were all holding guns. I suppressed the impulse to kill him where he stood. It would not have been difficult. But the risk of getting Abi and Sean hurt was too great. Instead I watched, and enjoyed the expression on his face as he stared at the broken bed. He narrowed his eyes, like he was trying to squeeze understanding out of his brain. "What is *wrong* with you?" He gestured at the broken mess with his hand. "That bed is two hundred years old! It's worth a fortune...!"

"Was," I said. "It was two hundred years old, and it was worth a fortune. And we were cold. And it was my idea. I did it. You want to punish somebody, punish me."

He was nodding. "You'll get your damn punishment, Walker." He jerked his head at Abi and Sean. "They get breakfast. You get to come for a ride."

I raised an eyebrow at him. "They get breakfast why?"

"Mind your own damn business!" Over his shoulder he said, "Take 'em down to the kitchen. If they try to run, shoot them."

I put my hand on Sean's shoulder. "Remember what I told you. Stay cool. OK?"

He nodded and one of the goons led them away and down the stairs. I smiled at Vasco. "So you didn't find Primrose, huh?"

He frowned.

I shrugged. "Why else would you keep them here? Last night he wanted to bury them in Rochdale. This morning you're giving them breakfast. So what happened? You took the plow over, found Pete and Davie dead in the Toyota and no sign of Prim. So you put the word around the neighbors: you have Abi and Sean and if she wants to see them alive, go to the farmhouse, Al and Karen just want to make things right, no harm will come to anybody."

He studied my face a moment. He wanted to hit me but he dared not get that close. He stepped back and gestured at the door. "Downstairs, genius. We're going for a ride."

I stepped out and made my way down the stairs with the four gorillas behind me. Over my shoulder I said, "Where are we going, to Rochdale?"

They all laughed, but that was the only answer I got. Vasco went ahead and opened the door. "There ain't one of us couldn't shoot a fly off a hog's back, Walker. Don't try and run."

I stopped dead and stared at him. I made no expression, but my eyes told him everything he needed to know. "I won't run, Vasco. Before the day is out, I'm going to kill you. But before I do that, I want to see what you have going down at Rochdale."

He curled his lip. "Put him in the back of the truck. If he moves, blow his kneecaps off."

They shoved me outside. The sky was still heavy. The snow drifts were five and six feet deep, but the snow had eased and there was a path cleared to the road. They tied my wrists and shoved me in the back of a Dodge RAM. Then we moved down the drive. At the intersection we turned south, and headed down, under heavy, leaden skies, toward Rochdale.

EIGHTEEN

THE SKY LOOKED LIKE ODIN JUST TOLD THOR HE punched like a girl. It was an angry sky, with low-bellying clouds heavy with menace and frozen water, though only the odd, desultory flake drifted down, hinting at the Norse fury which was to come. The road, straight for almost seven miles, plunged away from us through a white wasteland, looking exposed and vulnerable under the awful sky.

Eventually the road turned right and became a broad, dirt track, and we followed that for about two miles west, moving toward the Humboldt Mountains. Then the road began to climb, and the brush and gnarled bushes that poked up through the mantle of snow became trees, naked and skeletal, half-buried in frozen white. We climbed for another two miles, then slowed and eased off the road onto a wide, pitted, rutted track.

Now we ground slowly, winding and bumping up ever steeper hills until eventually we came to a broad esplanade and I saw that Rochdale was exactly what I had thought it was: the only thing it could be in Nevada.

There was very little snow here. Most of it had been removed. It was dirt, like a big scar on the face of the Earth, where the mountain had been flattened with dynamite. On the right, as we drove in, I saw two trucks. Beyond them there were two ten-wheelers, which told me that the Mexican couples were here already.

Beyond the trucks, there were three buildings set in a horseshoe around a kind of courtyard, with the open end toward us as we approached from the south. The two buildings to right and left were long, maybe thirty or forty feet, and comparatively low—not more than ten or eleven feet high. They were made of wood and had no windows. The building at the end was different. It was made of concrete, two stories high, and had two SUVs parked out front. I figured that was where the offices were.

But the two things that struck me as most interesting about the place were, first, the vast stretches of cleared earth, excavations and huge terraces that stretched for nearly a mile to the west and to the north, with groups of people working among trucks that were being steadily loaded with dirt; and second, the armed men who stood guard everywhere. In the courtyard I counted three, plus two outside the office building. And in the quarry I spotted at least seven. Rochdale was, as I had suspected, a mine, and the Mexicans were slaves used to work it.

We pulled up in front of the office building and I was dragged out the back of the truck. The air was freezing here and our breath billowed in thick clouds from our mouths.

Vasco turned to the two armed guards and shouted, "Ern! Jerry! Come here!"

As Ern and Jerry approached, I took a better look around me. The two long, low buildings intrigued me. One might be for storage and equipment, but what was the other for? It wasn't a big, mechanized operation, and by the looks of it, they were shipping the raw product out for refining every day and storing it at the depot. So what was in the second building?

The realization dawned suddenly. It was like the icy air had got inside me and clutched my heart with frozen fingers. Everything I'd seen and everything I'd heard fell into place, and I knew what it was for. I knew what they kept in there. But I had no time to process the realization, because Vasco was saying to Ern and Jerry, "Take him away. Bury him in the north quarry. I never want to see this son of a bitch again. *Comprende?*"

I took a moment to calibrate the two guys. Jerry was six two, powerfully built and had a crew cut and pale blue eyes. His face looked like his wife had been doing frying pan practice on it, and his expression had all the bright intelligence of a bad hangover. Ern was much like a Latino version of his pal. He was shorter and broader in the shoulders, and had a neck like a redwood tree. His eyes expressed the Zen ideal of a total absence of thought, but for all the wrong reasons. He jerked his head toward the side of the building and said, "Walk."

I walked. They shoved with their rifle butts. I walked faster.

We rounded the building and I saw a track climbing up

toward a steep, open cast quarry where the snow had been allowed to gather in drifts, presumably because the vein had been exhausted. I figured what they were going to do was to take me to the top, shoot me, throw me into the pit, and then bury me using one of the excavators. It made sense.

It was a ten-minute walk to the top of the quarry. The snow up there was not so deep, because it was exposed and the wind had carried most of it away. By the time we got there, Jerry and Ern both looked bored. Maybe they'd done this so often it wasn't fun anymore. Ern pointed over at the edge of the mine and said, "Go and stand over there." He had a surprisingly high-pitched voice.

I smiled at him but didn't move. I asked, "Have you got a knife, Ern?"

He frowned and glanced at Jerry, then looked impatient. "Just go stand over by the edge. Dumb-ass question…"

I shrugged. "Just grant a dying man a wish! I'm not asking you to explain the golden mean. I'm just asking you if you have a knife!"

"No! I ain't got a knife! OK? Now go stand over by the goddamn ledge!"

I smiled at Jerry and spoke in an exaggeratedly elaborate voice. "How about you, Jerry? You look like a guy who likes hunting and all sort of outdoor recreational activities. Have you got a knife?"

He stared at me a moment. "I don't know what in the hell you are talking about, mister. You playing for time or what?"

I sighed and smiled sadly. "So what if I am, Jerry? Is that such a bad thing? Ask yourself, if you were going to be shot and thrown over a cliff into an open cast mine, would you play for time? Is it too much to ask that you answer a simple question? Have you got a knife on your person?"

He had that look people get when accountants try to explain to them exactly what they do. He creased his eyes and started to shake his head. He pointed at the ledge.

"Yeah! Yeah! Yeah! I have a knife. Now go! Stand over there."

I sighed noisily and made a face of huge relief. "That is great news!"

"What are you *talking* about? Just go over..."

I interrupted him, but stopped smiling and spoke in a dead voice. "I don't want to have to go searching in this cold. I'll need a knife to cut the ropes on my wrist after I kill you."

And there it was. The two seconds of surprise that I needed.

You either hate tae kwon do or you love it. Personally, I love it. It has definite weaknesses, like the lack of hand techniques, but if your hands are tied behind your back, who cares? It's exactly the fighting style you need. I turned the toe of my left foot in, and spun. Suddenly his rifle was aiming at empty air and the heel of my boot was smashing into his sternum, shattering the cartilage and fracturing his ribs. The pain of that kind of blow is paralyzing. It can cause cardiac arrest. Every breath is like having a thousand shards of glass dragged into your lungs.

The kick took less than a second. Ern was gaping and, all credit to him, he reacted and brought the barrel of his rifle around, but it was too late. As my right foot came down I stepped toward him and kicked savagely up into his elbow with my left foot, deflecting his weapon and badly damaging his joint. He staggered back and I smashed my right instep into his testicles. His eyes bulged and his face turned purple as he went down.

I kicked his rifle out of reach, just in case, and went back to Jerry. He was making a bad noise in his chest as he tried to breathe, and by the look of him, he was suffocating. I used my foot to move the hem of his jacket back, and saw his knife in a sheath hanging from his belt. I knelt down, leaned back against him and, with difficulty, managed to ease out the blade with my fingertips. Then I maneuvered it around so I could cut my bonds. The knife was sharp and within thirty seconds my hands were free.

I am not big on philosophical beliefs, but one thing I am clear about is that suffering is worse than dying. So as soon as I had my bonds cut, I turned his head to expose the left side of his neck and sliced deep through his jugular and his carotid. Death came quickly in a couple of heartbeats. I did the same for Ern, collected their rifles, and went to lie on my belly at the edge of the cliff to look down at the mine.

In the distance, I could see the small groups of people digging at the quarry face, loading the rubble into the trucks. It was hard to make out any details, or how many there were, but all in all I figured there must be two or three hundred people there. I remembered the Mexican guy at the depot: "*Cien, cincuenta hombres, cincuenta mujeres. Somos familias. El lo quiso así.*"

One hundred, fifty men, fifty women. They were families. Vasco wanted it that way. But there were more than a hundred people working out there. There was more than double that number. And that confirmed for me what I had realized earlier: that the long building I had been wondering about was a dormitory, a dormitory for the rest of the family: for the kids.

I didn't try to repress the rage I felt. I encouraged it. I fed and fuelled it. But I set it on one side for later. For now I had to remain as cold as the snow I was lying on. My mind had to be clinical and clear.

I had at least answered one of my questions: how Al and Vasco seemed to be able to replenish their men so easily. Now I saw how. They kept a handful at the farm and more at the mine. This, what I could see now, I figured was the full compliment of what was left. Three in the courtyard, plus seven more dotted around the mine. That was ten, plus Vasco—and a couple he had kept back at the farm. I'd deal with them later.

I lay and watched for half an hour, trying to ignore the cold and formulate some kind of plan in my mind. After about twenty or twenty-five minutes, a dark blue SUV pulled into the courtyard. It looked like an Audi Q7. It stopped outside the office building and I saw Al climb out. He stood looking around for a second or two, like he was thinking you just couldn't get decent service anymore. Then Vasco came out and they talked for a moment. I guessed Al was asking him where the two guards were, and Vasco was telling him they'd taken me up to the quarry, to get rid of me. They called over one of the armed men who was standing by the building I'd pegged as the dormitory, and he approached them at a run. They talked and then he and Vasco went around to the passenger side of the SUV and opened the door.

I watched as they helped Arnold down. He could barely

stand, but between them they walked him across the yard to the dormitory and went inside. I lay chewing my lip for ten minutes, then crawled backward out of sight, stood, took Jerry's jacket and his baseball cap and started a slow, careful descent back toward the mine.

NINETEEN

I KEPT MY HEAD DOWN AND MY COLLAR UP, AND walked around the corner and over to the main door of the office building. If anybody saw me, they assumed I was Jerry. I pushed the door open, stepped inside, and closed it behind me. I didn't know how many people I was going to find, or who they might be. I was kind of hoping Vasco would be there, but he wasn't. Nobody was. There was an empty front office with a tin desk, a filing cabinet, and a telephone. There was a staircase leading upstairs and to the right there was a door that led to a back office that was just as empty. It didn't surprise me much. It was pretty clear this was an illegal operation and any bookkeeping and admin paperwork was going to be kept to a minimum. What there was would be done by Al and Vasco at the end of the day.

The back office was bigger and afforded a view of the courtyard. It had an old wooden desk with a map on the wall behind it. There was a fire extinguisher and a large fire axe in the corner by an old steel safe. No doubt the gang's wages were kept in there. I wondered briefly what the pay was these days for an assistant slave driver. I had the feeling that at one time, long ago, this had been a legitimate operation. Obviously it had closed down, somehow come into Al's hands and, presumably, he had found a new vein of whatever it was they were mining.

I had a fair idea of what that was, too.

For a moment, I was startled by the sound of a siren. It sounded like a World War II air raid warning from the blitz. Then it dawned on me: it was lunch time. That made me stop and think. They'd be bringing them back to the dorms for lunch. I rested my ass on the desk and looked out the window at the courtyard. They were obviously keeping the parents and the children separate. That was how they controlled them. The kids lived in terror of what might happen to their parents, and the parents were perpetually in dread of what could happen to their children. All lived in hope that they would eventually be reunited and allowed to go home. Meanwhile, in that hope, they kept quiet and did as they were told.

So the children would go to their dorm to eat, and presumably the parents would be taken to the long building opposite. There they would make their food, rest for however long they were allowed, and then go back to work.

I wondered where the guards and Vasco would go. I wondered where Arnold was. The Audi Q7 was still parked out front. The answers were not long in coming.

First, two trucks rolled into the courtyard and, supervised by the armed guards and the drivers, men and women started to climb down from the tailgates and file into the long building on the left. The sight was pathetic.

Seen clearly, in the light of day, these were a hundred broken, hungry human beings who had made a bid for a better life and had walked straight into a nightmare that was beyond unimaginable: they were slaves, and every day they woke up to the unending terror of what might happen to their children. Children they only ever saw at a distance, abused and exploited, and unable to go to them and help them.

When the last of those wretched people was inside, the doors were closed and locked with deadbolts, just like the one at the depot.

The trucks withdrew and a couple minutes later, two more trucks rolled in. The drivers swung down from the cabs and three armed men jumped from the back. All told, they made up the seven men I had spotted earlier, keeping watch over the mining operation.

After that, the kids started to pour from the back of the vehicles. If the parents had been pathetic, the kids were almost impossible to watch. But I forced myself, because I wanted to feed the rage. It was hard to keep count, but I figured my estimate of a hundred and fifty was about right. They all seemed to be aged between twelve and sixteen—too young to be independent, but old enough for hard labor. They were skinny, undernourished, drawn, and pasty. Their eyes looked hollow, their hair was matted and uncombed. They didn't cry or wail. They didn't even look toward the other building, where they must know their parents were. They had learned well all the things not to do. They moved with fear in their hearts, bowed, broken before they'd even lived, toward their dorm. After they'd filed in, two armed men went in with the parents and the rest followed the kids.

Obviously they figured that as long as they controlled the kids, they owned the parents.

I stayed a while, staring. The courtyard was silent and empty. I thought about what I was going to do. After two minutes, when I had just about made up my mind, the door to the kids' dorm opened again and Vasco emerged, holding a girl by the arm. She was thirteen or fourteen, and pretty—or had been, before they'd beaten and starved her, exploited and abused her and crushed her spirit and her joy. He marched her toward the office building. She glanced anxiously across at where her parents were. She knew something was wrong. It was hard to imagine the terror she must be living through in that moment. I picked up one of the rifles and waited for them to arrive.

Then the dorm door opened again and Al came out with one of his guards supporting Arnold. They proceeded slowly after Vasco.

Vasco did not come to the offices. Instead he went to the Audi, opened the back door, and pushed the girl in. Then he stood waiting for Aloysius and his son. When they arrived, Arnold climbed in the back with the girl. Vasco slammed the door and exchanged a few words with Al. Then he and the guard went back toward the dorm, and Al climbed in behind the wheel. The Audi turned and drove away.

I stood for another minute, thinking, trying to make sense of what I had seen. In the end, I decided I couldn't. There was too much information missing. And besides, I had plenty to do right here, right now. I picked up the two rifles and slung them over my shoulder, took the axe from the corner, and made my way out of the office building and across the freezing yard toward the long outhouse where the parents were being held. I knew the odds were stacked hopelessly against me. I knew I didn't stand an ice cube's chance in a supernova of surviving. But there was a kind of madness in me. A rage against the kind of people who could do this to families, and above all to children. A rage against the evil that dwells in people's hearts. A rage that had become so wild I could no longer contain it.

And besides, I had always known that one day I would face a battle I could not win; I would have no choice but to fight that fight, and I had long ago decided that when that time came, I would not turn from the battle. I would unleash the demon within and go down wreaking unholy havoc. Maybe, I told myself as I approached the door, maybe this was that day, and that fight.

I reached the entrance, slid back the deadbolts, put one rifle to my shoulder, and kicked open the door. I stepped in, took a second to locate the two guards. They were sitting at a table on their own, gawping at me. I put one round in one forehead, adjusted my position and put another round in the second forehead. Three seconds.

The one hundred parents were staring at me. Somebody whispered, "*Es el mismo...*" It's the same one...

I put my finger to my lips, then made a gesture with both hands to wait, and said, "*Sus hijos vienen, esperen aquí.*" Your kids are coming, wait here.

After that, I crossed the room to where the two corpses were lying face-down in their food. I went through their pockets till I found the keys to one of the ten-wheelers. Then I went outside into the freezing courtyard, leaving the door open. I made my way to one of the trucks I'd seen the parents arrive in. It was either this one or the one parked next to it. I guess I got lucky. I stuck the key in the ignition, turned it, and the engine roared into life. I put the transmission in reverse and floored the pedal, guiding it across the yard, straight toward the big wooden wall.

The noise was horrific, bone-jarring and ear-splitting. The wall shattered, wood screeched and splintered, the roof groaned and sagged, snow cascaded over the windshield, and planks, pillars, and rafters fell all around me like rain. I shifted to first and pulled away, leaving a huge, gaping hole in the side of the building.

I climbed down, taking the rifles and the axe with me. Inside, I could hear men shouting and a hundred and fifty kids screaming. My heart was pounding and my belly was on fire. I walked away from the hole and back toward the door they had gone in through. I wrenched it open and looked around. The kids were in the middle of the floor, standing, huddled together, screaming and crying. The nine men were closer, gathered around a long, wooden table perpendicular to the walls, maybe twenty or thirty feet away. Everybody was staring at the big, gaping wound in the side of the building. I aimed randomly into the group of men at the table and pulled the trigger. The shot was like thunder in the enclosed space. I saw a guy go down, but I didn't care about that. The shot was to scare the kids out through the hole in the wall. I didn't want them to witness what I was about to do. They'd had enough ugliness in their lives as it was.

They started screaming again and I fired two more times into the group. I don't know if I hit anyone, because by then I was roaring like a demented monster. The kids were running, streaming through the gap. I knew that their parents were out there waiting for them. That was all I cared about.

Somehow, in that moment, I saw everything in slow motion. It happens sometimes. I hurled the rifle away from me, grabbed the fire axe and ran, screaming like I was possessed, toward the head of the table. The men seemed frozen, some gaping in shock, others reaching for their weapons. I saw two men on the floor, lying in large, oozing puddles. There were five more on my right, three standing, two sitting, one of those leaning behind him for his rifle. On my left there were two, both standing, the closest pulling a revolver from his holster. On the table there were plates of beef and beans, glasses of beer and bottles. Everything was stark and clear and frozen.

The first swing of the axe tore through his forearms, ripping the revolver from his hand and sending it skidding across the concrete floor. He screamed and staggered back into his pal, staring at his bloody stumps. The second swing was the return back-hander that caved in the head of the nearest guy on my right.

I kicked him in the chest as I readjusted my grip for an overhand. As he fell back, I stepped forward. The guy behind him was struggling under the weight of the dead body. I swung the axe up and over and brought the blade crashing down into his skull. It split open and his brains exploded, showering gore over the table. I wrenched the blade free, still roaring, and stepped forward and to my right. The guy who'd been reaching for his weapon had his arms up over his eyes, struggling to get out from under the man with the split skull. In one fluid motion I brought the axe up and under, shattering his jaw and tearing through his face.

On his right there was another man, scrambling to run from the table. I brought the axe down and to my right and tore open his ribcage. Across the table, the gunman with no hands had collapsed unconscious. His pal, drenched from head to foot in blood, was holding his revolver in both hands, staring around him and saying over and over, "Oh God no... Oh God no..."

I realized I was still making horrific, inhuman noise. I didn't stop. I jumped up on the table, gave a huge swing right to left and tore his head clean off his shoulders. I looked around as it hit the concrete and rolled away. My lungs were going like bellows, my heart was pounding and my brain was roaring like it was on fire. There was somebody missing. Vasco was missing. He should have been at the table. I counted the bodies. There were eight. There should have been nine. I felt my abdomen clench like a fist and I bellowed, "*Vasco! I am coming for you, you son of a bitch! Vasco!*"

I jumped down from the table, threw down the axe and looked at my hands. They were slick with blood. I wiped them on my jeans and picked up the revolver that had skidded across the floor. I walked to the gaping hole in the wall and stepped out. Across the yard, a group of men and women and children stared at me, uncomprehending, fearful, disgusted. I ignored them and looked toward the office building. Vasco was there, standing beside one of the Dodge trucks, staring back at me. I cocked the hammer and took aim.

TWENTY

He had pulled open the door and climbed in before I could get a bead on him. Next thing, he'd swung around and was accelerating across the courtyard toward the track that led back to the road.

I took my time. I knew where he was going. Besides, there was only one stretch of road this side of the mountains that he could use, from the mine to Independence. Without a chopper, he was stuck here. I walked across the yard and went into the office. I picked up the old phone on the wooden desk. It was a landline and it worked. I got the number for the county sheriff in Lovelock and called.

"County Sheriff's Office. Deputy Beltran speaking."

"Do you know the Rochdale mine in the Humboldt Mountains?"

There was a moment's hesitation. "Can't say I do. Who is this?"

"That's not important." I looked at the map hanging on

the wall. "About twelve miles from the I-80, as you cross the Humboldt range on the Independence Road, there's a turnoff to your left. There's a track that leads up to a mine..."

"Well, that ain't the Rochdale, that's the old Henkle mine. That's been closed since the nineteen eighties."

"Well, I have news for you, Deputy. The mine is operational and has been for a while, and they have been using slave labor."

"...say again? *Slave labor?* Is this some kind of...?"

"There are about two hundred and fifty men, women, and children at the mine right now, starving and freezing. In my book, that does not constitute a joke, Deputy. You better get out here."

"But it's gonna take *hours* in this. I can't just...!"

"I'm going to make them as comfortable as I can. But unless you want a hundred and fifty deaths on your conscience, you better make whatever phone calls you need to make and get here."

I hung up, went back over to the long barn, and went inside. The kids were in there with their parents. There was a lot of hugging and weeping going on. Maybe there was some healing, too. I wouldn't know about that. A couple of women and a man came up to me. They kept pointing at my face and saying something, like it was a pity I had such an ugly one. I shook my head. "*No comprende.*"

One of the women turned and called, "*Becki! Becki! Venga, Cielo, venga acá!*"

Becki, a girl of about fourteen, detached herself from the group and approached.

"*Si, Tita.*"

Her mother rattled at her in Spanish, gesturing at me with both hands. The girl studied me with dark eyes, then spoke, "My mom says where is Maria, her daughter? The man took her away."

"Tell your aunt I'm going to get her and bring her back."

The woman listened to the translation, watching me with anxious eyes. Then she clung to me, saying, "*Gracias! Gracias!*" and rattled something else, pointing at my face.

Becki told, "She says thank you, and you have blood on your face and your clothes. You should wash it off..."

I shook my head. "Tell her thanks, but I'm not done yet. I called the county sheriff. They're going to come and get you, but it'll take hours. It may not be till tonight, or tomorrow. You need to go to the main building." I pointed back toward the office. "You can make fires and stay warm in there. Those men won't be coming back."

"What will happen to us?"

I shook my head again. "I don't know, Becki. They'll probably send you home. But anything has got to be better than this, right?"

I said goodbye and left. I went back to the scene of the slaughter and rummaged through several coats until I found the keys to a Dodge. Then I crossed the yard for the last time, pressing the unlock button until one of the trucks bleeped. I clambered in, fired her up, and spun the wheel, headed back toward the farm. As I left the complex, I could see them behind me, filing toward the office building in small family groups, hugging each other.

The snow was holding off, but the sky was still dark and

brooding, promising another blizzard that night. That would slow down the rescue party. They might get to them by the evening, but they wouldn't get to Independence or the farm till the next day at the soonest. I smiled. It couldn't have been a pleasant sight.

I came out of the mountains and turned north through the stark, white wasteland. I was trying to figure out in my mind what Vasco would have done. He knew I was coming for him. So he would do two things. He'd try to find Primrose to use her as a bargaining chip, as well as Abi and Sean, and he would go back to the farm, where he had the support of Al and whatever men he had left behind there.

My mind strayed to Primrose. I wondered where she was and what she had done. Had she gone to the church? Could the reverend be trusted? I had a hunch he and the doc were both good men—Primrose said they were. But I also had a hunch that in this town you couldn't trust anybody—not even the good men.

By the time I came to the intersection, I still hadn't made up my mind. The road ahead was blocked by three feet of snow. The road to the left would take me to Independence, the Pioneer Guesthouse, empty, cold, hung with the angry shrouds of death. And Primrose?

I looked right. The white arch, the broken iron gate, the path. I could still see the red Toyota half buried in the drift. And beyond it, in the distance, the mock Georgian pile. There I knew what I would find. I would find Abi and Sean, and I would find Vasco, Karen, and Al.

I spun the wheel and turned right, accelerating fast up the track. As I approached I saw, parked outside the front of the house, the truck Vasco had taken from the mine. I skidded to a halt just past the Toyota and drove the Dodge into the ditch, where it was half-concealed. Then I climbed out and made my way on foot toward the back of the house, wading knee-deep through the drifts with my feet freezing, numb and aching.

Nobody seemed to have spotted me. I did something that should have been a smile, but was too ugly for that, and told myself there were not many people left to spot me. I came finally to the kitchen door. The glass panes were frosted over. I stood a moment, looking down at the mounds of snow, then stepped over, reached in to a frozen drift, and pulled out my kit bag. All that was left in it was my second Sig Sauer, a couple of boxes of ammunition, and my bow. I took the Sig, cocked it, and hesitated a moment. The house or the lodgings?

I turned away from the house and made toward the lodgings. When I got to the door, I tried the handle. It was unlocked. I stepped through and found myself in a long room. On the far left was an open-plan kitchen with a table long enough to accommodate a dozen men. On the right was a lounge with a TV, a couple of sofas and maybe six or eight chairs.

Separating the two sections was a staircase that rose up to a second floor. I figured that was where the bedrooms were. I could hear men laughing, and a woman crying out. I ran up the stairs and came to a landing. Two corridors branched off, one to the right and one to the left, leading to two rows of six rooms. Down to the left I could see light coming from an open room. I walked toward it and stepped in through the door.

There were three men. Two were standing, leaning

against the wall with their arms folded across their chests. One of them was in his early twenties, clean shaven, with thick red hair and a spray of freckles across his face. The man next to him was in his forties, with dark hair and a moustache which would have been at home in the 1970s. They were looking at me and leering. Directly in front of me there was a bed with a blue duvet. Sitting on that bed, with his back to the window, was the third man. He must have been in his late twenties and also had red hair and freckles. I logged that the two might be brothers. He was also leering. On his lap was Abi. Her face expressed astonishment at seeing me, but also fear and distress, because the man holding her had a Remington .45 pointed at her temple.

He shook his head and said, "Woah! Man, you are a *mess!* Joe said you might be dropping in, so we was looking out for you."

I heard myself speak and my voice sounded dead. "What's your name?"

"Huh? My name?" He looked at his pals and they all laughed. It sounded oddly adolescent, like none of them had ever made it to adulthood. "My name is Sir, because I am holding a gun. And you are going to hand your gun over to my brother over there."

I shook my head. "You don't want to hurt her. I have just killed twelve of your pals up at the mine. Eight of them I slaughtered with a fire axe. If you hurt her, there will be nothing standing between me and you." I plucked at my shirt and showed him the blood. "See this? This is the blood of your friends."

For just a moment he looked worried and glanced at his brother. "I think this feller is a bit crazy, Mike. What do you say?" They started laughing again. "Take his gun from him, Mike."

Mike moved off the wall and stepped over to me. He reached out for the Sig. I stopped him dead with a question.

"Were you going to rape her?"

He looked me in the eye for a second, then grinned his idiot grin again. "Yeah. No. We *are* going to rape her, just as soon as we get through with you."

I shook my head again. "No, you're not."

I angled the Sig down and shot his balls off. He looked down, gawping as blood cascaded onto the floor, draining out of his body and saturating his pants. His brother stood, screaming hysterically, "*What did you do? What did you do? Jesus!*"

He kept aiming the gun at my head, then back at Abi, then at me again. I could have shot him, but the risk to Abi while he was hysterical like that was too great. Now he was screaming, "*You freeze! You freeze! I swear I'll shoot her! I swear it! Freeze! Freeze!*"

Mike sagged at the knees and keeled over. His brother's lip curled and he began to sob. He was losing concentration. Another couple of seconds and I could take him and the moustache. But before that happened, a fist like a boulder smashed into the side of my head and everything went dark.

Consciousness came back to me as I was being dragged by my heels up the frozen path toward the kitchen door. The ox with the moustache had a hold of me and was walking backwards, hauling me after him. Mike's brother was ahead of us, holding the gun to Abi's head as he shoved her forward. The ox spoke over his shoulder. "He's awake."

He dropped my heels and pulled my Sig from his belt. He waved it at me and said, "Get up."

My head was splitting, but I wasn't going to let him see that I was in pain. I sat up, then got to my feet. Mike's brother had opened the door and pushed Abi through into the kitchen. He went in after her and the ox pushed me up the step and inside. Then they both got behind us and pushed us into the hall and toward Al's study.

I looked at Abi. "Any news?"

She shook her head. "Is it true, what you said?" She looked at my shirt, my jacket and my face. "About the blood, is it true?"

I nodded. "Yeah, it's true. Rochdale is a mine. The were using child slaves up there."

"*Shut your mouth, you son of a bitch!*"

Mike's brother slapped me hard across the back of the head, then moved forward and opened the door to the study. He went in, tears were streaming down his cheeks and he could barely talk for sobbing. He stared toward where I knew the desk and the French windows were, and said, "We have him, Mr. Groves. He killed Mike, but we have him."

The ox thrust us into the room. I staggered and stopped, then looked. Al was standing by the fireplace looking at me. He had a Ruger P90 .45 caliber in his hand. I knew it was a reliable, accurate gun, and my guess was that Al was an experienced marksman, and a damn sight more dangerous than Mike's brother. On the sofa was Karen. She also had a pistol in her hand. I couldn't see what it was, but it looked like a .22. Sitting beside her, with his ankles tied and his wrists behind his back, was Sean. And in the armchair, with one leg crossed over the other, was Joe Vasco. He had a Desert Eagle in his lap, and he looked as mad as a wild dog with a hornet up its ass.

He said, "Walker, you are one dangerous, crazy son of a bitch. You have to be put down, and I am going to put you down right now." He cocked the gun and stood up.

TWENTY-ONE

I WAS READY TO DIE. I'VE BEEN READY TO DO THAT for a long time. But I wasn't ready to let Sean and Abi die. I smiled at Al and said, "I called the county sheriff from the mine."

He scowled. "You did *what?* Are you insane?"

Karen looked sick and turned to her husband. "Al...? Aloysius?"

Vasco shook his head and said, "He's bluffing," but he didn't look convinced. He added, "You've as much to lose as we have."

I laughed. "Not if I'm dead, pal."

He turned to Al. "He's a damned liability! We need to get rid of him!"

I looked at Sean, smiled and winked. Then I said to Al, "How're you going to explain the blood on your carpet, Al?"

He looked at me like I'd said something real stupid. "I? *I? Explain?* What about *you?*" He waved his gun at me. "How many men have you *murdered* since you arrived in this village?"

I smirked at Karen. Her eyes were bulging and her mouth was sagging open. "I kind of lost count, Al, but the population of Independence is somewhat depleted now. Tell me something, do you really think the sheriff is going to believe that one man alone accounted for almost twenty of your cowboys? You think they'll believed I wiped out your entire mining operation? When all the evidence points to the fact that you were running the mine illegally, and using slave labor, and child slaves..."

He was shaking his head. Karen had got to her feet and stepped toward me. She said, "It was for their own good!"

He spoke at the same time. "It isn't the way it looks. We had a reason."

Karen interrupted him. "Do you know what would have happened if we hadn't taken them in?"

"It was best all round!"

I silenced them both. "Those children were starving, working with their bare hands in the snow, separated from their parents! Brutalized, beaten..."

Al screamed. It was a horrible sound, like a giant parrot. His face was crimson and his left hand clutched like a claw. "*It was necessary! You don't understand! You can't judge!*"

Joe stepped forward. "Let me finish this."

I smiled at him. "Finish it?" I nodded. "You'll finish it. All of you, under the doctrine of joint criminal enterprise. What do you think the jury will find? Four children raped and murdered. Then their parents, and after that Abi's husband. Then there are the charges of slavery and child slavery? How many of *them* have died, I wonder?" I laughed again. "And then there are all the men that I have killed. Kill me and all of those deaths will be imputed to you. It will be the death penalty for all of you. No question."

Al had gone a sickly gray color and his wife had covered her mouth with her hands. She whispered, "Arnold..."

I nodded. "Yeah, who's going to look after little Arn when Mommy is put to sleep?"

Al rasped, "You're a monster..."

Joe raised the .45. "The hell with it!"

Karen screamed, "*No! Wait!*" Then, "We need to think this through." She stared at her husband. "Think of Arnold. A deal, some kind of deal." She turned to me. "You testify it had nothing to do with us. We had nothing to do with the mine..."

I smiled. "I'm listening. Keep talking. What about the snow plow?"

She hesitated, then stammered, "The... the snow plow?"

I half-yelled at her, "It cleared a path from the mine to your damn doorstep!"

Vasco said, "He's right, goddammit!"

Al said, "Jesus Christ!" and walked to the French doors. He stood looking out at the snow. "The whole thing is unraveling. We need to lose the snow plow." He turned. His face was tight and his eyes were wild. "We need to lose the snow plow. Clear the road down toward Mill City, work through the night if we have to. You and the boys, you clear the road and then dump the plow. We deny everything."

Vasco pointed at me. "What about him?"

"He has as much to lose as us. If we go down, he goes down with us."

I raised an eyebrow. "So what's the deal? Primrose, Sean,

Abi, and I walk away, and we testify that you have nothing to do with the mine. That there was some crazed killer on the loose who passed through with the blizzard murdering most of your men. And whatever happened at the mine is a mystery. We didn't even know the mine was working again."

He stepped toward me, nodding eagerly. "Yes! Yes, that could work!" He looked at his wife. "That could work, Karen. What do you think?"

Vasco snarled, "It's bullshit. You trust this son of a bitch?"

I gave him a once over. "Face it, Vasco. You're out of choices. You need us to fix and corroborate an alibi. We need a truce and you know it. And there's something else." I pointed out toward the kitchen. "You got one dead guy buried in snow outside your kitchen door, and you got another in the lodgings with a gallon of blood all over the floor. You had better get scrubbing and disposing before the sheriff decides to send in a forensics team."

Pat turned to me. He still had tears in his eyes. "Don't talk about my brother like that..."

Vasco was shaking his head. He was losing control of the situation and he was close to panic. "I don't like this. I don't like this, Al. This guy is dangerous. The only way this guy is not dangerous is dead!"

Karen was staring at me like she was hypnotized. I held her eye for a long moment, then looked at Al. I said, "He's right. I am. I am a very dangerous man to have as an enemy. But ask Abi, ask Sean. What am I like as an ally? I am as loyal as an ally as I am dangerous as an enemy. You want me on your side."

Vasco started laughing. It was an ugly, braying noise.

"Oh, this is priceless! The lone fucking ranger just rode into town. Now he's going to be our best friend. Halle-fucking-lujah!"

I gave Al a lopsided smile and gestured at Vasco. "This from the man who wanted a bigger bite..." I turned and looked at Karen. "...of the cherry."

Vasco spun and advanced on Al. "If we give up our hostages we will be defenseless against him!"

Al swallowed. I could see he was trembling. I spoke quietly, reasonably. "What are you now, Vasco? This place will be crawling with Feds within twenty-four hours. If the sheriff can get hold of a chopper you'll probably have him here before that. Right now you have two bodies to dispose of in several hundred miles of snow. And you have any alibi we care to come up with, plus independent witnesses to corroborate it. Do something stupid now, and you will have five bodies to get rid of, plus all the forensic evidence—and you'll have to explain the damage at the guesthouse as well as the mine. Your choice."

I turned to the ox with the moustache and held out my hand. "Give me my gun, big guy. And you two had better get scrubbing. It is going to be a long night for you." I turned to Vasco. "And you? You had better get busy with the plow. Me, Abi, and Sean have got a lot of work to do back at the guesthouse."

Al turned and stared at Vasco. "I'm sorry, Joe. He's right. It is the only option we have."

I showed Vasco an expressionless face. "I'm facing a lethal injection myself, Joe. We all are. It's in all our interests to play ball. As long as we keep our story straight, we're OK. And we are running out of time."

He turned savagely on me and thrust out his arm, pointing his weapon at my head. I held his eye.

Karen said, "Joe, if you pull that trigger you sentence us all to death."

He lowered the gun.

I said, "Go plow, Joe. We're going to fix up the guesthouse. We meet again before the snow starts to agree our story."

Joe turned and stormed out. The front door slammed. I turned to the ox. He handed me my Sig. I said, "Get scrubbing, boys."

Pat's face was constricted. He said, "...my *brother!*"

I snarled, "You want to join him?" He swallowed. "So get scrubbing!"

They looked at Al. He nodded and they left. I jerked my head toward Sean. "Cut him loose, Al." As I said it, I slipped my gun into my waistband behind my back to show there was no threat.

He looked at his wife. "Untie the boy, Karen."

She did as he told her and a moment later Sean and Abi ran to each other and embraced, holding tight like they never wanted to let go. I met Karen's eye. "It's a sacred bond, Karen, between a mother and a child."

She looked away. I turned at Al.

"There is a weak link in this chain, Al."

"I know."

"Vasco is out of control. His prints are all over the plow and all over the mine. Plus the Mexicans will identify him. Worse than that, he has no strength of character. If the Feds go to work on him, he'll break and make a deal. If he does that and tells them about the depot, you are sunk. And if you go down, like you said, we all go down."

He frowned. "What are you suggesting?"

I shrugged. "One of three things. Either he takes the fall; we frame him so it looks like he was running the mine behind your back, and some kind of gang war broke out between him and some of the hands. Or we kill him." I paused a moment. "Or better still, we do both."

Karen was staring at the door. Al was staring at the fire. They were both working out the details in their heads.

She said, "It's the only way. Will you take care of it?"

Al looked at me. "You're right," he said, though whether he meant me or Karen was unclear. "He has been a problem for a long time, attracting attention, making demands..."

I said, "I'll take care of it. I'll get to him before he gets too far on the plow. I'll kill him and take him up to the mine with the others. But I need to know something. Are there any papers or documents connecting you to that mine?"

He thought about it. "Yes," he said at last. "It belonged to a friend of my father's. My father was a non-executive partner. The mine in those days was just the quarry at the back. It stopped producing..."

I said, "Gold?"

He nodded. "Without the gold, the land was practically worthless. When old Henkle died, he left the land to my father, who left it to me. I was always curious about the land to the west, where they are mining now. I did a private survey and found there was gold there, not a lot, but enough. And when..."

He stopped dead and Karen turned to stare at him. He took a deep breath.

"Anyway, I have friends and we made a deal. I hadn't the capital to start a whole refining process, but I could sell them the crude ore. With the Mexican kids, it cost me practically nothing and we made a very substantial profit."

I nodded. "I want a cut. We let the whole thing cool off for a few months. Then we start it up again. You have someone who can get you the labor from Mexico?"

Abi and Sean were staring at me with horror in their eyes. I ignored them. I was too busy watching the expression on Al and Karen's faces. They were confirming what I had suspected.

"Yes!" It was Al. He was thinking all his Christmases had come at once. "Yes, that isn't a problem."

"Good. We'll discuss percentages later. Right now, I need my knife and my gun back. I'll have a word with the boys and then I'll go and deal with Vasco. I need to move fast before the sheriff gets there."

He nodded. "Yes, yes, quite so. Of course." He moved to his desk, unlocked a drawer and extracted my Sig and my knife. I went over and took them from him. I put the Sig in my pocket and slipped the knife into its sheath in my boot. Then I turned to Abi. Her eyes were begging me to tell her it wasn't so, that I wasn't like all the rest.

"I need you to get Sean home. When Primrose comes in, get her up to speed. I'll take care of Vasco, then I'll come and collect you." I turned to Al. "We'll have dinner, discuss the details, get our story straight."

His face was eager. Even Karen was looking at me in a new way. "Yes," he said again, smiling. "That will be nice. Bring the kids. You can stay over. You don't want to go back in this weather."

It was all very civilized. I smiled. "Fine. Can you lend Abi a truck for an hour or so?" I turned then to Sean and looked him straight in the eye. "Remember what I told you about discipline?"

He nodded.

I smiled. "Good man. I'll see you later."

And I walked out, to go and deal with Pat and the ox. Behind me, I could hear Al and Karen talking to Abi like she was an old friend and they were arranging a nice social gathering. They were like voices coming from a parallel reality, where what was normal was the insane, the ghastly, and the grotesque. I blocked them out and kept walking.

I went out into the snow and followed the path to the lodgings. In a strange replay of what I had done earlier, I opened the door and stepped inside, closing it behind me. I glanced at the kitchen. Now several cupboards stood open, but there was nobody there. I waited a moment, listening. I could hear voices upstairs, sullen, griping. I climbed the steps, feeling a momentary weariness in my mind and in my heart. For a moment I longed for Marni, for her sanity, for the hope she gave me that I could be a better man: a better human being. I pushed the thoughts away and walked down the passage once again to the room where Pat and the ox were on their knees, scrubbing the floor with bleach. I wondered what they had done with Mike's body, then decided I didn't care.

I stood in the doorway. They looked up at me. I put a single round into each one of them, in the center of their foreheads. All their scrubbing was for nothing. I turned and walked away.

TWENTY-TWO

I took the Audi Q7 down the track, back toward the road. I could see the plow through the windshield. It was on the road, but it was motionless. I pulled up outside the broken gates, swung down, and walked across the cleared blacktop toward the cab. The door was open, the key was in the ignition, but Vasco wasn't in the plow. He'd driven up, positioned the vehicle ready to start shifting work, and then he'd climbed down and disappeared.

I scanned the area. It was no more than three in the afternoon, but already the sky was casting a menacing darkness over the plain. The empty miles of featureless white would have made a man's silhouette stand out. But there was nothing: no tracks, no tell-tale humps in the snow, nothing but a white wasteland and the freezing, desultory wind lifting occasional ghosts and drifting them across the empty landscape.

Empty but for one, singular feature. I stood staring at it for a moment. A sudden twist of anxiety told me I had just found Primrose, but Vasco had found her before me. I pulled the Sig from my pocket and ran toward the depot. I hit the snow and started wading like a man running through deep surf. It dragged at my feet, made me stumble, was agonizingly slow. My breath tore at my lungs. I finally made it around the palisade fence to the main gate and, with a sickening jolt, I saw the SUV that Abi and Sean had taken to return to the guesthouse. They had had the same realization. I ran, skidded and fell on the frozen ground. Scrambled to my feet and made it around to the door. I cocked the Sig, wrenched the door open and went in.

It was dim. The only light came from a small fire that was burning in the corner, where a pile of blankets formed a makeshift bed. Primrose was there. So were Abi and Sean, and so was Vasco. Abi and Sean were sitting to one side, on a couple of drums. I couldn't see Vasco clearly enough to take a shot, because he was standing behind Primrose. She was standing in the middle of the floor, with her arms stretched up above her head. She had a rope tied roughly around her wrists, slung up over one of the rafters and attached at the other end to one of the drums of gold ore. Her face was pale, her breathing was shaky, and despite the cold she was sweating. I could see his left hand on her left shoulder. Both Abi and Sean were watching me from where they were sitting. They looked as terrified as Primrose. Joe Vasco spoke.

"Well, lookie who just came in. The Lone Stranger..." He laughed like he'd said something funny.

I closed the door and took a step closer.

He went on. "You know what I got back here? You being a fighting man, a man of weapons, you'd be interested." His voice changed suddenly, became menacing. "Don't come any closer, friend. I'll tell you all about it."

"I thought we had an arrangement, Vasco. What are you doing?"

He laughed. It was an ugly sound that seemed to creep among the shadows. He leered at me and rested his chin on Primrose's shoulder. "You want to take a shot? How good are you? Light ain't great. Be a shame to miss and hit this pretty little lady. Especially before I've had my bit of fun with her." He narrowed his eyes. "We didn't have no arrangement, Walker. You made your arrangement with Mr. and Mrs. Stupid. You think I didn't realize the little game you was playing? Well, now we're going to play my game. My game is called..." He grinned and slid his right arm around her waist. Clutched in his hand was a hunting knife with a broad, six-inch blade serrated along the back. He repeated, "My game is called, where do we put the knife?"

I kept my voice steady. "Do you know what I will do to you if you hurt her, Vasco?"

"Do you know what I will do to her if you don't put down your gun and your knife?"

I bluffed. "We have a stalemate."

He shook his head. He was still resting his chin on her shoulder. "Uh-uh. 'Cause, see? I don't have to kill her. I can take my sweet time. I can cut open her shirt and I can cut slowly into..."

"All right! You made your point." I bent down and laid the Sig on the floor, then stood.

He chuckled. "And the knife, Mr. Special Ops. Next to the pistol."

I pulled the knife and laid it next to the gun. "OK," I

said. "Now what? This is between you and me. Let them go."

"Are you kidding me?" He stood erect and turned to Sean. "You, pick up the gun and the knife. Put them over there, by the wall, where I can see them. Do anything stupid and I'll skin your sister like a mule deer."

Sean walked to me. Our eyes met for a second in silent communication. He picked up the weapons and carried them to one side, as Vasco had instructed him. Then he returned to his mother's side.

"See, Walker, the big difference between me and Al and Karen, is they're stupid, and I am not."

I gave a small laugh. "You look pretty stupid to me, Vasco. How are you going to explain all this to the Feds and the sheriff? Do you realize that Al wants to frame you alone for everything—from the mine to the girls who were murdered? You're playing right into his hands."

He was laughing again, waving the blade in the negative. "Uh-uh, see, there it is. I don't believe you are stupid enough to call the sheriff. I figure you for a poker-playin' man, and that was all one big bluff. I have to hand it to you. It was smart and you wrapped them around your little pinkie just like you wanted. But I ain't as stupid as they are."

I nodded and gave a little snort. "So what's your big plan, Einstein?"

He put his elbow on Primrose's shoulder and pointed the big blade at me like a gun. He narrowed his eyes, like he was aiming that gun. "See?" he said. "I got you figured out."

I laughed quietly. "Really?"

"You're tough. I got to hand you that. You're one tough son of a bitch, and you are dangerous. You are without doubt the most dangerous man I ever knew. But you got one, big weakness."

"What's that? Enlighten me."

"You got a soft spot for a pretty woman. Me? I'm happy to kill you and the kid and then have my way with momma here and the girl. Then I'll kill them too, and walk away a happy man. But you, you think you're some kind of hero: Captain America, the Lone fuckin' Ranger, some knight of the fuckin' round table. You..." He wagged the knife at me again. "You want to be a good man. And *that*, friend, is your weakness. You know why?"

He slipped his left hand over her left shoulder and changed the knife from his right to his left. Then his right hand disappeared and came back holding his Desert Eagle. Primrose's eyes were wide and wild. Her breath was shaking badly. Abi stifled a sob, and Sean said, "Don't let him see you're scared, Mom!"

Vasco pressed his cheek against Primrose's and pressed his body up close against her back. He slowly brought the knife around, so that his elbow was poking out and the point of the knife was pressing against her chest at the height of the fifth intercostal. Then he aimed the pistol straight at my gut. He was six paces away and could not miss.

"They say," he drawled into her ear, "that a shot in the belly is the most painful way to die. Now I'll tell you what my plan is, Mr. Hero, you're going to stand there and allow me to shoot you in the gut. Because if you move, I am going to ram this big old cock of a knife right into her heart."

"And if I allow you to kill me, what guarantee have I that you won't then rape and kill her?"

He was enjoying himself, having a great old time. He

leered and drew breath to answer. I didn't hesitate or change the expression on my face. I just slipped my left foot back and around behind my right one, so my belly was no longer in his line of fire. In the same fluid movement, with my right hand, I pulled the second Sig from my waistband, behind my back, and took the shot of my life. I put a 9 mm hollow tip right through his left elbow. It shattered the joint and at the same time, the sheer force of the slug violently levered his hand away from her chest. He staggered back, screaming, "*Oh shit! Oh shit!*"

I aimed up at the rafter and shot the rope where it lay against the wood, and Primrose ran staggering toward her mother. With her out of the way, I took aim at Vasco where he lay on the floor. Maybe it was because I didn't want Sean to witness a killing. Maybe it was because I was exhausted. Maybe it was both. Whatever the reason, the shot was not instant. I took maybe a quarter of a second to line him up, and by that time, in his pain and his rage, he had fired. He didn't aim, but he got lucky, and the slug hit my gun, dented the barrel and ricocheted across my hand. There was no permanent damage, but the pain was excruciating and my gun was unusable.

I swallowed the pain and moved toward him to finish him with my bare hands, but he had staggered to his feet. He was strong, and what was worse, he had a strong mind. He must have been in agony. His left arm was hanging limp by his side, bleeding profusely. He was still screaming, making inarticulate noises, but his eyes were fixed on me and he was walking toward me, with the gun held out in front of him.

For a moment, his eyes glazed and seemed about to roll back in his head. He let out an animal groan and doubled up. I took a step toward him, but he yelled then screamed. He flushed red and took another step, staring hard into my face. I started dancing like a boxer, making a moving target. His gun wavered. I danced toward him. He thrust the weapon forward, I danced away and he fired. He missed and I heard the slug thud into one of the drums of ore. I rushed him and saw the black hole of the muzzle loom into my face. There was an explosion that made my ears ring and I danced away again, shaking my head.

He had five rounds left in his magazine. It was too many, and I couldn't keep dodging forever at this range. I had to attack. I lunged in a scissor kick aimed at his gun hand. He pulled it back and I missed. When I landed, I was just two feet away from him and he smashed the heavy steel gun into the side of my head. It was like being kicked by a mule. I staggered back, stumbled, and fell, cracking my head a second time on the concrete floor.

I was stunned and numb, and not thinking, but some instinct, or maybe the years of training, made me roll and I heard a slug smash into the floor a couple of inches away. I staggered to my feet. By the wall I saw a shovel. It was seven or eight feet away. I lunged for it. My head was still ringing and I had no coordination. I stumbled and fell, with my fingers clawing at the blade. Another explosion and another slug hit the wall behind me. The shovel fell across me. I got to my knees, grabbing it like a spear. His face twisted with hatred. He aimed straight at my head. He was not going to miss. There was an explosion. I roared and hurled the shovel. I saw the muzzle of the Eagle erupt in flames. I felt a searing, burning pain in my head. I saw Vasco's head wobble and the right side of his skull erupt in blood and gore, and at the same moment the blade of the shovel embedded itself in his chest and he went down.

I turned and looked. Abi was standing, holding my Sig in both hands. She was trembling violently, staring at the twitching corpse on the floor. I struggled to my feet. A couple of times, my legs gave under me and I had to support myself on the drums stacked behind me. I took one step, and then another and finally made it to her side. She looked up at me as I took the pistol from her hands and slipped it into my waistband, behind my back. Suddenly, violently, she flung her arms around me and squeezed, sobbing into my chest. I held her tight and kissed the top of her head. Then Sean and Primrose were there, with their arms around both of us, and all three of them were sobbing.

I heard Abi's voice, muffled by my jacket: "It's over, please tell me it's over, Lacklan. Tell me it's over..."

I kissed the top of her head again and rested my chin on the soft cushion of her hair. "Nearly," I said. "Very nearly."

TWENTY-THREE

SHE LIFTED HER CHIN AND SEARCHED MY FACE
with her eyes.

"What? What else?"

I shook my head. "You three have been through enough.
Take the kids home. You need to clean the living room.
Leave no trace, Abi. You understand?"

She nodded. "Will you...?" She stopped, searching my
face again. "Will you come back to the house?"

"Yes. I'll try to get there before the storm starts up again.
Go now."

I walked them out and watched them climb into the
truck and drive along the road to Independence. Then I
went back inside, collected the weapons, including the
shovel, and dragged Vasco's body out to the yard. I went and
got the Q7 and drove it to the depot gate. There I loaded
Vasco into the back seat and drove him back to the plow
where, with extreme difficulty, I put him in the driver's seat.
I put his knife in its sheath on his belt and put his Desert

Eagle in his right hand. The shovel I dropped on the blacktop beside the plow. I was wearing woolen gloves, so I had left no prints. It would be a nice mystery for the Feds.

I inspected the back seat of the Q7 and found traces of Vasco's blood. I smiled. That was fine. I drove back to the farmhouse and parked out front. Then I walked inside, crossed the tiled hall with echoing footsteps, and found Al and Karen sitting silently in front of the fire. They looked up as I came in, each with an anxious, hopeful face. I gave them two-thirds of a smile and walked to the tray of decanters on the credenza. I poured myself a large whiskey, fished a pack of Camels from my pocket, shook one free, and lit up with my battered old Zippo.

Al said, "Did everything go OK? Did you take care of Joe?"

I took a drag, inhaled deep, all the way down, let it out slow, and pulled off half the glass of Irish. Then I went and lowered myself into an armchair in front of the fire.

"Vasco is dead," I said, and followed up with a lie. "I made it look like suicide."

Al nodded. "Oh, good. Yes. Good idea. It all became too much for him."

I studied his face a moment. "Pat and the other guy are taking care of things in the lodgings."

"Good, good."

I turned to Karen, who was staring at me with no expression. I said, "Abi, Sean, and Primrose have gone back to the guesthouse. They're cleaning that up."

She said, "Primrose..." with no inflection. It was just a statement.

"She was hiding out at the depot."

She turned to Al. "Nobody thought to look there."

He blinked a couple of times but didn't say anything. I took another drag and another drink, let the smoke out slow through my nose. "I don't want Primrose hurt. I don't want anyone in that family hurt. I will respect and protect your family, Al. I want the same in return." I gave Karen a once over, trying to read her. It wasn't easy. I turned back to Al. "I know you're a man who cares about family, Al. I want you to think of Abi, Primrose, and Sean as my family. Have we got a problem there?"

"No, no, not at all."

I looked at her. "Karen?"

"No. No problem."

I stared into my drink for a moment. "You brought a Mexican kid back with you this morning."

Al turned away and looked into the flames in the fire. "A friend for Arnold."

"She was filthy, skinny, starving…"

Karen sat forward, smiling. "Oh, she's had a bath and combed her hair. She had something to eat, and she has a nice dress now. She looks quite lovely. They're getting on very well. They seem to have taken to each other." She laughed. "She's Mexican, but she's only a playmate. It's not as if they're getting engaged or anything!"

I shook my head. "Why?"

Al wouldn't meet my eye. I turned to Karen.

She shrugged. "I don't know what you mean."

"Why do you need to pick his friends from among slave children? Why doesn't he make friends in the normal way?"

She looked impatient. "You've seen him! He's ill. I have

to keep him at home where I can look after him. You said yourself, family…"

"Karen is very," Al hesitated, then said with emphasis, "…*protective* of Arnold. She feels only she can really look after him."

"What's wrong with him?"

He shook his head. "We don't know. He seems to be weak, a little sickly…"

"What do the doctors say?"

Karen flashed a glance at Al. "We haven't taken him to the doctor. We thought it was better to care for him ourselves. Nobody really understands Arnold the way we do. We are his parents." She gave me a long look, then added with heavy meaning, "We don't like outsiders prying."

I snapped, "Well, get used to it. I'm a hands-on kind of guy. I like to know what goes on with my business partners."

Her eyes went hard. "Arnold is none of your concern."

"I'll decide that."

Al stared at his wife, chewing his lip. "Karen, Mr. Walker, *Lacklan*, is our friend now…"

I interrupted him. "So what happens? He makes friends with them. Then what? He has sex with them, too?"

Karen cried out, "No! Of course not! They talk! They spend time together, it's soothing for him…"

"He wanted to be friends with Primrose."

She gasped. "How did you know that?"

"I know things. Why couldn't he be friends with Primrose?"

"She was too old for him. Why this interest in our son?"

"Who decides if she's too old? He liked her."

Her face flushed and she shouted at me, "*I decide! Will you stop this interrogation!*"

I shook my head. "No."

Al interceded, "Really, Lacklan, I don't see what this can have to do with you."

I sipped my whiskey and took another drag on my cigarette. "I'll tell you what it has to do with me. Vasco had a bigger hold over you, Al, than just the mine. He abused you and disrespected you and blackmailed you and there was not a damned thing you could do about it. He had found your Achilles' heel and he was screwing you..." I turned and raised an eyebrow at Karen. "Both of you, for everything he could get." I looked back at Al. "And there is only one thing that I can see that could make you that vulnerable. And that's your son."

He wouldn't meet my eye. He stood suddenly, moved to the drinks tray behind his chair, and poured himself a drink. When he spoke, he addressed his words to the his glass. He said simply, "What you're saying makes no sense. How could Arnold's illness make me vulnerable?"

I shrugged. "I don't know. But I do know that it does." I smiled at Karen. "Tell me something, Karen. What happens to Arnold's friends when the visit is over?"

Neither of them answered. Al remained staring down at his drink. Karen's mouth became a thin, obstinate line and she turned her face away from me.

I gave a small laugh. "Let me guess. Let me see if I can guess. Do you send them back to their families? Well, you don't want this kid going back. Because if she goes back, she has something on you, she can identify you, and if she or her parents should escape, she can put her finger on the owner of the mine, who not only uses child slaves, but takes those children home for his son to..." I paused and labored the word, "...*play* with."

Al said, "That's not what happens."

I ignored him and went on. "And, however remote the possibility of escape, you are not a man who likes loose ends. That was one of the reasons you did not like Vasco. He was a man liable to leave loose ends lying around. So it is much easier, when the nice little girls finish their visit, to simply have them disappear. And you had a man in your household who was more than willing to do that job for you: Vasco. Only trouble was, once he'd done one job, he had you over a barrel."

I was talking, working my mouth, but I knew there were more holes in my theory than in a self-medicating hypochondriac acupuncturist. That didn't stop me. I kept going. "Or are you going to tell me that Vasco didn't have a taste for killing young girls?"

The silence was a palpable thing. Finally, Al said, "He did, yes. He was sick in that way; in many ways."

I felt a hot flush of anger and fought to control it. "Yeah, he was sick. You're just pragmatic."

"I do what I have to do to protect my family."

I stood. "Well, call me sentimental, Al, but this kid goes home."

Karen said, "That's not possible."

I snapped, "Why not?"

She stood and came toward me, reaching for me. "He needs to be with her. Then I'll see to it. Then I'll take care of it. I'll see that she's... that she..."

"*Karen!*" It was Al.

I turned to look at him.

His face was flushed with anger. "*Be silent!*"

She clamped her mouth shut.

He glared at me. "It is impossible. How would you get her there?"

"I'll drive her."

"You'll never make it there and back before the storm sets in for the night."

"Then she comes with me."

"Don't be stupid, man! What do you think will happen when the sheriff gets here? Or the FBI?"

I stared at him. "So what do you propose?"

It was Karen who answered, with her fists clenched and her face crimson. "*She must be eliminated! They are always eliminated! It is the only way!*"

I thought of the two pathetic kids upstairs: her, a child of fifteen, robbed of her innocence, ripped from her family, enslaved, brutalized, and now abducted and sentenced to death—why? Because she looked nice, because she was selected by this maniac to talk to his son for a few hours. And the boy, an emaciated wreck who despite his twenty years had never made it to adulthood, sentenced to be smothered by his mother, fed little girls to talk to in some ghastly Freudian nightmare, and then have his 'friends' taken from him and slaughtered. It was insane.

But even as I thought about it, I knew I was missing something. I knew there was more to it than that. I had always known, since I'd seen them in the church, that there was something deeper, darker, about this family; something crucial that I was missing. I turned and walked out of the room, crossed the hall, and climbed the stairs. Karen came running after me, screaming, *"What are you doing? Where are you going? What are you going to do? Stop! Stop!"*

She clawed at my back. I turned, put my hand over her face, and shoved. She stumbled back, tripped over her own feet and fell, sprawling on the cold floor. Al hurried out of his study and went to help her up.

I ran up the stairs and made my way along the corridor to Arnold's room. The key was in the lock on the outside, and the door was locked. I unlocked it and went in.

The sight that met my eyes was sickening. The girl was on his bed. She was dressed in a pretty frock. She had been bathed and her hair washed. She looked pretty, almost unrecognizable from the girl I had seen that morning. She was staring at me and her eyes looked close to terror. Next to her, Arnold was curled in the fetal position, dressed in his pajamas. His eyes were open, but he didn't look up. He didn't react at all. He just lay there.

I looked at the girl.

"Te llamas María?" Was her name Maria.

"Si, soy María."

"Sabes manejar?" I asked her if she knew how to drive. Mexican kids learn young. She nodded. *"Si."*

I jerked my head. "Come on!"

She hesitated.

I said, "Do you speak English?"

She nodded. "A little."

"Well if you want to live, come with me. Your family is waiting. *Hurry!*"

I guess she figured she didn't have much to lose. She jumped off the bed and ran to me. I grabbed her wrist and we moved along the landing. At the top of the stairs, I saw Al and Karen halfway up.

"Get back in your study or this story ends right here."

He was unarmed and he backed down a few steps. Karen reached toward the girl and climbed another step, smiling, appealing, "No, honey, you can't leave. You have to stay. We still have so much fun to have. We'll have a party, I'll bake a cake..."

I stepped in front of the girl and rushed the half-dozen steps between me and Karen. I thrust the Sig in her face and snarled, "I am serious, Karen. I swear I'll throw you down the stairs. You get your damn kicks somewhere else!" She backed down to the hall and I shouted at her, "*In the study!*"

She ran sobbing to her husband. He took her in his arms, stared at me shaking his head, and they went inside and closed the door. I grabbed Maria's arm and said, "Run, fast!"

We went out the door and ran down the drive. The sky was turning black again, the wind was beginning to rise and there were snowflakes drifting in the air. I ignored the Q7. I wanted the Feds to find it there, and in any case, if weather conditions got tough, she would need something with real grunt. We made it to the Dodge RAM I had ditched earlier. I climbed in, backed it out of the ditch and swung it around. Then I climbed out and held the door open for her. She looked at me a moment like I was crazy. I smiled.

"Go back to the mine. All the bad guys are dead. *Los malo están muertos.* Your parents are waiting for you. Tonight, maybe tomorrow, the sheriff will come. He will help you. *Comprende?*"

She nodded. Her eyes flooded. "Thank you."

Next thing, she'd clambered in. She slammed the door and took off like a greyhound with a Carolina reaper up its ass. I watched her corner onto the blacktop at the end of the drive and head toward the mine doing eighty and climbing.

I stared toward Independence. The red Toyota with the broken windshield was there, beside me. I could probably make it work. Hell, I could probably walk it before the storm started in earnest. But I looked back at the farmhouse. There was unfinished business there, with Al—and Karen. But I didn't know what it was, or how to finish it. So I just stood and stared as the darkness crept in around me.

TWENTY-FOUR

I DIDN'T KNOW WHAT IT WAS, OR HOW TO FINISH it, but I did know where. So I turned and I walked along the frozen path, under the darkening sky, toward the farmhouse. The door was still open. It swung on its hinges, beating the wall in a broken tattoo, like a madman trying to beat memories out of his mind.

I stepped inside and closed the door behind me. The big marble hall with the sweeping staircase was silent. There had been so much death in this house, what could you expect but silence? I looked down at my hands. They were still smeared with dry blood. They were the same hands that had held Marni; the same hands that had handed Maria the key to the Dodge. They were the same hands that just a few hours earlier had cut down eight men with an axe. Were they the hands that were responsible for this silence of death?

I looked at the study door. It was closed. I wondered what I would find inside, and instinctively glanced up at the landing: the dark corridor that led to the right, towards Arnold's room. What would I find up there?

I crossed the hall and my heels echoed, loud, sharp ricochets like running feet going up the walls, and into the shadows beneath the ceiling. I took the cold, brass handle in my hand and pushed open the door, stepped inside.

He was sitting in his chair, staring at the flames in the fire again. In his hand he held a glass of whisky. He didn't look up. My glass was still on the mock Queen Anne occasional table beside the chair where I'd been sitting. I picked it up and crossed behind him to the sideboard, refilled it, and went to sit in my chair. I felt exhausted. I closed my eyes for a moment and tried to find somewhere in my body that didn't hurt; somewhere in my mind where there was no ache. I found nowhere.

When I opened them again, he was watching me. When he spoke, it was the voice of a man preparing to depart, attempting to leave behind at least some kind of explanation, a justification for his life.

"You can't understand," he said, "unless you've had children."

"The families at the mine," I replied, "had children. Did you understand them?"

He looked away from me, at the wavering flames, at the logs being steadily consumed. "You think differently when you have children. They come before everything. Even before God."

"Are you speaking for yourself, or for Karen?"

"She's his mother." He said it like it was an explanation, like it told me something I didn't know. "He was everything to her." He sighed heavily. For a moment he looked to me like a very old man, laying his head down upon a pillow for the last time. "I don't know if you can begin to understand. I don't know why God has chosen you as my judge, if you can have no understanding of what happened, of how it was." He shook his head. "She did not live, she had not lived until he was born. And then..." For a second his face showed some animation. "Then it was as though she were born when he was born." He turned to me. "I saw her that first day, holding him in her arms, and she was alive! She loved... him..."

He turned back to the fire, and the flicker of flame I had seen in his face drained away again. I asked, "What happened?"

He didn't respond for a while. Then he shrugged. "Life happened. For almost fifteen years we were happy. Maybe that's not such a bad run in this world. I ran the farm, grew crops, did the work a man is supposed to do in this world. I lived..." His face darkened with bitterness. "I lived an *honorable* life. And she cared for our son. He was never strong. At the age of ten or eleven he began to show signs of being sickly. He wasn't stupid." He looked at me as though I might challenge that statement. I didn't and he turned back to the fire. "He was just different. It was as though, where the rest of us look out into the world, he looked within instead. It made him a lonely child."

I pulled my cigarettes from my pocket, extracted one, and lit up. I inhaled and took a long sip of whiskey. "What about school?"

He shook his head. "She wouldn't have it. She wouldn't be parted from him. We tried to take him to a nursery school when he was just a small toddler. They both became inconsolable. He was hysterical and so was she. So we opted for home schooling. We briefly employed a home tutor. But that was impossible, too. Karen made it impossible."

"She interfered in the classes."

It wasn't a question. He nodded. "After a week, she left and Karen took over the lessons."

I took another drag and breathed the smoke deep into my lungs. "So he never made friends. Never learned to play with other kids."

He shook his head. "Karen said he was not like other children. They did not understand him. He was sensitive. She said he was fragile. All he needed was his mother."

"You didn't agree."

"No. I believed that he needed friends, albeit sensitive friends, intelligent children who would not victimize or torment him."

"Not easy in a community with barely twenty families."

He gave his head a small shake. "You'd be surprised. This is not the wild west anymore, Lacklan. There are no more gunfights, no more Indians. This is..." He trailed off. "This could have been an idyllic community. It was. The children in Independence were happy and healthy. Wholesome. They were reared in the tradition of Christian kindness, tolerance, family..." His face twisted with grief. "If I had...." He threw back his head and looked at an empty spot in space. The flames washed his face and reflected like wet fire on his tears. "If I had only shown a little strength. If I had only cared enough to do something. The teacher and the children at the local school, all those good people in the village, they would have loved and nurtured him."

"But Karen wouldn't have it."

He nodded.

I added, and watched his face carefully as I said it, "The sickness was hers, not his."

He went very still. After a moment he took a deep, wet breath. "The sickness was hers, not his, and she passed it to him through the milk from her breast. And I stood by and watched it happen, may God forgive me."

"When did it start?"

"Predictably, as he started to approach puberty. He would see the little girls of his age."

"See them how?"

He smiled. "Through the windows of the car. He began to develop crushes. As we all did at that age. He would fall in love with this girl, or that girl..."

"Rose Gordon...?"

His face went gray. He sagged. Stared down at his hands in his lap. "Rose and Sally Gordon. Sweet, delightful girls. He loved them both. Who wouldn't?"

He fell silent.

I smoked and drank for a moment, watching him, waiting. Finally, I asked: "What happened? They came to visit?"

He took another deep, shaky breath. "I suppose it must be told. She wouldn't have it. She was adamant. They would not cross our doorstep. She would not have them in our house. They were not suitable, they were the wrong class, the wrong kind of people. You name it, she came up with every reason and every excuse in the book. But the more she said no, the more he cried, the more violent his tantrums became, until in the end he had a fit."

I frowned. "A fit?"

He nodded. "It is hardly surprising. God alone knows

what kind of Freudian nightmare was going on in that poor child's mind. Every kind of emotional repression and blackmail you can imagine. The only emotion he was allowed was the adoration of his mother. Everything else, *every other emotion* was..." He held out his hand and clenched his fist. "...*crushed*! He was emotionally blackmailed into remaining a four-year-old, Lacklan. And finally, when he was about twelve, he snapped, broke under the strain. He became what you see today. He started to have fits, he would go into hysterical paralysis for days on end. Finally, she relented and asked the Gordon girls if they would like to visit with us. They were extremely kind to Arnold. They mothered him and spoiled him. They baked brownies with Karen and fed them to him, they read him books..."

Again he trailed off.

"How did Karen take that"

He snorted. "It was the happiest we had seen Arnold in *years!* And of course he was hopelessly in love with both of them. He demanded that they come back the following weekend, and the weekend after that."

"How old was he by then?"

"Fourteen, fifteen."

"How long did it go on?"

"From fourteen to fifteen."

"So when the Gordon girls were raped and murdered..."

"They were visiting Arnold, yes." He leaned back in his chair and closed his eyes. "Karen had become increasingly unhappy with the girls visiting so often. It was practically once a week. Arnold lived for those visits. His focus of affection had shifted, as a teenage boy's must, from her to the girls. She had become morose, bitter, unreasonable to the point of being irrational." He opened his eyes again, stared into his drink and took a sip. "One day, out of the blue, she decided we had to promote a young hand we had recently employed."

"Joe Vasco."

"Yes, Joe Vasco."

"And that was when it started."

"Two weeks later, the Gordon girls were killed and their family disappeared shortly afterwards." He paused, staring at his hands in his lap. I had the impression he was fighting back tears. Eventually he raised an eyebrow, drew breath, and went on, "The sheriff came over from Lovelock. He investigated, but there was no evidence. It was as though their parents had vanished off the face of the Earth. The sheriff went away and things returned to normal for a while. But pretty soon Arnold started hankering for a friend again. He had fallen in love with another little girl."

He raised a hand and wiped a tear from his face.

I said, "Sally."

He nodded. "Little Sally Ibanez. A ray of sun. She lit up the house. Her laughter...!" He laughed himself, but it was chocked off into a sob. He shook his head, barely able to talk, but needing to go on. "She couldn't walk anywhere. She had to run. Run and laugh. She filled the house," he waved his hand in an extravagant gesture, "she filled the house with noise, the way Arnold should have done, but never did... was never able. Was never allowed..."

"Then she was killed, too."

"Then she was killed, for being pretty and lovable, and full of joy. Arnold adored her. So did I. And Karen detested her. I don't know the details. I never want to know the details. I barely hold on to sanity as it is, Lacklan. I cannot escape the reality that I am as responsible for what happened to those children as Karen and Joe Vasco. But I cannot bear to know the details."

I took a sip and flicked the butt of my cigarette into the flames. The horrific reality was clear, even if, as Al said, the particular details were missing. I had as little desire to know them as he did. But there was another, equally disturbing level to this story. I reached for my Camels and pulled another from the pack. I flipped the Zippo and sparked the flint, leaned into the flame, and sucked. I flicked the lid closed and stared at the battered brass in my hands, turning over in my mind how one thing led to another. It was barely credible. I looked at him and shook my head.

"So the mine. The mine was not about the gold."

He glanced at me and the flames danced in his wet, swollen eyes. "No. Never. Not for me. I knew there was gold there. I didn't know how much. It was in my mind to make a deal with one of the big Nevada corporations before I died, to secure Arnold's future after I was gone. But Karen and Joe came up with another plan." He shook his head. "I am not shirking my responsibility. I colluded. I am as guilty as they."

"Joe had the contacts in Arizona?"

"Yes. He was from Arizona. Most of the hands you met and disposed of were from Arizona or New Mexico. They had all done time. They were all involved one way or another in trafficking Mexicans across the border. He had this brilliant idea, bring in families to work the mine. It was an idea that was easy to sell to the Mexicans! No need to leave your wife and kids. Bring the family. We'll look after you all. It's a gold mine! Good pay and you all stay together."

I finished for him, "But when they get here, you separate them. You feed them and house them, at a minimal cost, and force them to work the mine. The threat that keeps them going, and stops them escaping, is what will happen to the kids if they do."

"And for the kids, what will happen to their parents."

"And meanwhile you have an unlimited supply of girls for Arnold to fall in love with. And when the time comes to get rid of them, nobody is going to be asking any questions. As far as Mexico is concerned, they left the country illegally. As far as the U.S.A. is concerned, they never arrived. They don't exist."

He nodded. "That is correct."

"And meanwhile, you clean up at the mine." I gave a small laugh. "This is Nevada! Home of Las Vegas, Reno, the Mafia! How hard could it be to find a sympathetic partner to take tons of gold ore off you on the quiet, no questions asked. You mine it at practically no cost, they buy it, process it, and sell it. Everybody wins, excepts the Mexican families and the kids who do the mining. But who cares, right? They are expendable."

"I am not proud of what I have done. I believed it was best for my son."

"And that's your excuse?"

He shook his head. "There is no excuse. It's my reason."

"What happened to Peggy?"

He stared at me for a long time. His face twisted, his bottom lip trembled. When he finally spoke, his voice was ugly with tortured emotion. "He wanted little blonde girls, with blue eyes. Karen hates Mexicans... So he hates Mexicans!"

I snarled at him, "She didn't want him with any girl. But if he had to have one, she had to be blonde and blue-eyed. Only an Aryan was good enough to die for her son."

He fell back in his chair and sobbed.

"How many little Mexican girls died before you decided they weren't good enough?"

"Five."

"Where are they buried?"

"Behind the lodgings."

"You son of a bitch. What about the other families?"

"After a year, they were returned to Mexico, and a fresh lot were brought in. Threats of retribution if they spoke were enough to keep them quiet. Not that any officials over there would care, or take them seriously, if they did speak out."

I stood. "Where is she?"

"Upstairs, with the boy."

I left the study. I climbed the stairs feeling like I was in some kind of surreal nightmare. I walked down the long, dark, narrow corridor to his room and opened the door. I stood on the threshold. He was alone on his bed, still curled in the fetal position. He gazed at me with empty, hungry eyes.

"Did you bring Primrose for me?"

I stepped into the room, gazed down at him and shook my head. I could hear Al's feet, weary on the stairs. I said, "No,"

And then there was a sudden, terrible explosion of pain in my head.

TWENTY-FIVE

I could hear screaming. My mind told me it was Primrose screaming. But as I surfaced from the darkness, I became aware that it wasn't. It was the gale. It was hurtling off the plain to the north, breaking around the house, screaming in the pylons and the trees, and then groaning around the building. I groaned, too. There was a terrible pain in my head. I felt sick, and as I tried to raise myself to stand, I felt dizzy. By degrees, I got myself to a kneeling position, then leaned over and retched sour whiskey onto the carpet. I leaned against the foot of the bed, closed my eyes, and waited for the pain and the nausea to pass.

Memories filtered back. I had come up to the room. I had seen him on the bed. He had asked me about Primrose. I had said that I had not brought her for him. And then the explosion of pain that had ripped at my skull.

I opened my eyes and looked down at where I had been lying. The poker was there, on the floor. There was blood caked on it. I felt the back of my head. The hair was matted, sticky. Maybe one day I would learn to live by my own creed. Be in the moment. React in the moment.

I forced myself to stand. Another wave of nausea. The black glass in the window showed flurries of snow. That and the wind told me I had been out for a long time. Too long. An hour at least. I tried the door. It was locked. I reached for my gun. Naturally they had taken it, along with my knife. Sergeant Bradley looked at me from within my mind and shook his head. I told him to shut up, took my Swiss Army knife from my pocket, and started removing the hinges from the door frame. People always focus on the lock, but too often forget about the hinges.

After a couple minutes, I wedged the screwdriver into the crack, levered the door enough to get a hold of it, and ripped it out of the frame. Then I was running down the stairs, trying to ignore the blunt hatchet in my skull. The front door was open, like the last person to leave had been in a hurry. The gale was blowing snow in across the cold marble floor. I stepped out and needles of ice lashed my face and drove through my jacket and my shirt to tear at my skin.

There were no vehicles. The Q7 was gone, the Jeep was gone, the Dodge was gone. They were all gone. It was almost three miles to the guesthouse. There was no doubt in my mind that three miles in a blizzard, while suffering from a concussion and exhaustion, was more than enough to kill you. I thought of the red Toyota with the smashed windshield. I might be able to make that work. Toyotas are pretty much indestructible.

I set off down the track at an unsteady, sliding run, trying not to slip and fall on the freezing road. After a minute I came to the Toyota, and a knot of anxiety twisted my gut. The hood was up and, when I looked, the battery had been riddled with gunshots.

That left only one way to get to Abi and Primrose, and Sean. I had to go on foot. I didn't hesitate. You don't hesitate in the face of the things you know you have to do. You just do them. I put my hands in my jacket pockets and started to walk. There are no good ways to die. But nobody gets out of here alive either, and this was as good a way to go as any I could think of. I summoned up the memory of Sergeant Bradley again, smiling at me with his big, bearded Kiwi face, taunting me with his weird Kiwi accent, "Come on, you big girl's blouse! Couple of miles in the snow—do you good! Make a man of you!"

The fact was, the storm was not as bad as it had been the night before. The wind was fierce and the temperature was well below zero, but the snow was not so heavy, and because what had already fallen had frozen, it was not being whipped up into clouds by the gale. At least, not much. Visibility was not too bad, and pretty soon I could see the icy twinkle of the lights in Independence. I was shivering badly, but I picked up my step, telling myself it was not so bad. I could make it.

I came at last to the road and stopped. On my right, I could see the black hulk of the snow plow. That would get me to Independence in a matter of a few minutes. It would deprive me of the element of surprise. It would give Al and Karen advance warning of my arrival and give them the chance to escape. But it might also save Abi, Primrose, and Sean's lives. But even as I was thinking it over, I heard, among the howl and groan of the wind, another sound: the sound of a straining engine, the sound of tires spinning, trying to grip onto ice. I ran.

I sprinted, heedless of the possibility of sliding and falling, not giving a damn if I did or not. I had to get to that vehicle before the tires bit into the earth under that layer of ice. I sprinted across the blacktop, hit the dirt road on the other side, lost my footing and sprawled facedown on the frozen ground, skinning my hands and my knees. I didn't pause, I got up running and hurtled forward, pounding the ground with my boots, digging deep, finding reserves of strength and energy I didn't know I had. And then it was there, twenty yards ahead of me, the Audi, with its back wheels stuck in a drift, all four wheels spinning ineffectually, achieving nothing.

Then the driver's door opened and Al climbed out. He took two steps toward me, his face twisted and distorted with rage. He raised his hand and I saw he was holding my gun. With the momentum of my run and the frozen ground, I could not stop. I couldn't change direction. I had no control. All I could do was hurl myself in a dive at his feet. The Sig spat and I heard the bullet zing past my ear. Then I was smashing into his legs and he slammed onto the road, sprawling across my shins. I heard the gun clatter onto the road.

I scrambled to my knees, turning as I did so. I could hear him gasping, "Oh God... Oh God..."

I stood, grabbed him by the collar, and dragged him to his feet, shouting at him, "*Enough, Al! Enough!*" As I did, I saw his right arm flash and I knew he had my Fairbairn & Sykes fighting knife in his hand. I didn't think. My left hand flashed to his inside elbow as I stepped back. My right grasped the outside of his wrist and I shoved, turning the blade inward, guiding it into his heart.

We were just inches apart. We stared into each other's eyes. He looked astonished, frowned. I have little time for philosophy, but sometimes when I look into the eyes of a dying man I remember what the Buddhists say: that your dying thought conditions your next becoming. Aloysius Groves had become a monster, had conspired in the murder and enslavement of children, yet in that moment, a pale flame of compassion burned inside me; maybe because I knew that he hated himself for what he had become.

I heard my voice rasp, in spite of myself, "Wherever you're going, Al, whatever awaits you there, you can be better than this."

Let that be his dying thought. His eyes glazed and his life left his body. I reached down and picked up my Sig. Then I dragged his empty carcass by his ankles to the front of the Audi and wedged his legs under the front wheels. I climbed in, put it in drive and accelerated slowly. The tires bit into the legs and slowly pulled the SUV out of the drift.

I kept it steady at fifteen miles an hour. I half expected to find Karen buried in a drift too, but there was no sign of her. There was no sign of her on the road, or in the village when I finally arrived. I parked the SUV beside my Zombie, climbed out, and trudged through the deep snow in the front yard up to the door. I rang on the bell and hammered on the wood. I heard a door open and close inside, then silence. I rang again and hammered again, and shouted, "*Abi! It's me! Lacklan! Open up!*"

Then there was the rattle of a lock, the door wrenched open, and Abi was there, reaching for me with both hands.

"Oh, thank God! I was so worried!" She held me close and I held her back, but only for a second.

I said, "Abi, there is no time. Get inside. Where are the kids?"

She let me go and stepped back. I closed the door. "Abi, the kids, where are they?"

She frowned. "Upstairs, in bed. They were exhausted. Why...?"

"I can't explain now."

I turned and sprinted up the stairs, moved swiftly along the landing until I came to Primrose's door. I opened it quietly and went in. The room was dark. The drapes were closed. I could hear the soft, steady flow of her breath. I moved to her side, hunkered down, and folded back the duvet. She was sleeping peacefully. I stood and moved to the window, pulled back the edge of the drape and peered into the garden. The window was closed and locked. The back yard was empty. There were no prints in the snow.

I turned. Abi's black silhouette was framed in the doorway. I moved to her, we stepped out onto the landing, and I closed Primrose's door behind me, then went to Sean's room.

He was out cold under his bedclothes. I folded them back. He was sleeping soundly, breathing deeply and slowly. I checked his window. It was securely closed. I could see down into the small square, my Zombie, the Audi, the doc's house and the dark plain beyond. There was nothing, nobody. Where was she?

I stepped out onto the landing. Abi took hold of my lapels, staring up into my face. "What is it, Lacklan? What's going on? Tell me."

I looked into her face for a moment, then pushed past her and ran down the stairs and into the kitchen. She was close behind me. I checked the kitchen door. It was locked. There was a deadbolt at the bottom and another at the top. They were both driven home.

I turned. She was standing at the table, watching me, her face tight with anxiety.

"Lacklan...? You're hurt. You have blood on the back of your head."

I ignored her comment. "There's no deadbolt on the front door?"

She shook her head. "No... Please tell me what's going on."

A wave of nausea flooded over me. I moved to the big pine table. I took off my jacket, pulled out a chair, and sat. "Make some coffee, would you? Very strong, and sweet." I put my head in my hands. Where did you begin to explain?

"Al is dead."

She was opening a coffee percolator, watching me. "Did you kill him?"

I nodded. "In self-defense. He was on his way here. Karen is here, somewhere. Abi, she's crazy. She is behind all of this."

She finished preparing the coffee and put it on the cooker to brew. The wind rattled the kitchen window. She came to the table and sat, took hold of my hand. "Are you sure?"

"Oh yeah, I'm sure. If it weren't for the gash on the back of my head, I might think I was out of my mind and had imagined it all. But that crazy bitch hit me with a poker."

She frowned at me like she herself was wondering if I

had lost my mind. I started to talk, to tell her about my conversation with Al, and the more I talked, the less skeptical she looked. The coffee percolator began to gurgle. She rose and crossed the room to pour the hot, black brew into a mug. As she did it, she said, "It was Karen's idea for the girls to go over and visit. I remember because Pamela Gordon, that was their mother, talked to me about it. She wasn't sure what to do. Everybody knew that Arnold was a bit... *odd*. But she didn't want to offend the Groves. They carried a lot of weight. It was the same with Sally's Mom. It was Karen who asked for Sally to visit."

She returned, handed me my mug, and sat. And it was in that moment that the terrible, tortured shriek split the night, and something big and heavy smashed against the kitchen door. It pounded again and again, and the scream wouldn't stop.

I went to stand but Abi was clawing at my arm, screaming, "*Oh dear God! Don't leave me! Don't leave me!*"

I yanked my arm free, pulled my Sig from my waistband and ran across the kitchen floor. I crouched, slid back the bolt at the bottom of the door, and reached up and slid the one at the top, feeling my fingers were made of lead. I turned the key and pulled the door open, aiming the gun straight ahead of me.

There was nothing there.

I took the gun with both hands and stepped into the snow, scanning left and right. There was nothing, only the deep tracks that led across the snow to the plum tree. I stepped out and scanned the wall of the building. There was nobody hiding there. I waded to the tree, pulled myself up, and looked over the fence.

Nothing.

Abi was silhouetted black in the open kitchen doorway. I could see the warm light coming through the window from the inside. I could see the kitchen table, the blue iron range, the chairs where we had been sitting. She had seen all that too, from up here. It had been a distraction. A distraction from the only other point of entry.

The front door.

TWENTY-SIX

I leapt down from the tree and tried to run through the deep snow. Each wading step took a whole, interminable second. Abi stood staring at me, her eyes wide with fear. She kept asking, "What? Lacklan, what is it? You're scaring me!"

I got to the door and ran, slipped on the snow on my boots and fell, scrambled to my feet, and took off through the living room toward the reception. Abi was just behind me. I ripped open the door. Freezing wind fingered my face. Snow swirled at my feet. I stared out at the black night, because the front door was open.

I swore violently and ran up the stairs, taking them three at a time, screaming, "*Primrose! Sean! Wake up! Wake up!*"

I hit the landing and ran for Primrose's room. The door opened as I got there. Primrose was staring at me, wide eyed and sleepy.

"What is it? What's going on?"

I said, "Sean!" and turned. Abi was already opening his

door. I shouted, "*Abi! No!*" But it was too late, she'd pushed it open. I threw myself at her as Karen lunged. Abi fell sprawling on the floor. For a second I saw Karen's face, twisted with frenzied hatred. Then I felt the hard blade of a kitchen knife slash deep into my arm. The Sig fell from my hand. I grabbed her wrist and tried to twist her arm, but her strength was terrifying and she clawed at my face with her free hand. We staggered back toward the banisters. I felt my foot knock my gun and heard it clatter through the rails and down the stairs. I tried to kick at her legs, but she was rushing forward and I was off balance.

I fell and she fell on top of me. I felt the warm blood oozing down my arm. She put all her weight on the knife. The big, silver blade was just inches from my face, smeared with my blood.

Was it just my blood? Past Karen's frenzied face, I saw Abi reaching down for her. I shouted, "*Sean! Check Sean!*"

She hesitated a moment, then vanished, running for Sean's room.

Everything had happened in a few seconds, and suddenly I knew, either I could do something now or in the next couple of seconds, Karen would kill me. All I could do was go as crazy as she was. I roared in her face and bucked my hips like a bronco, wrenching her arms to one side. She fell. I struggled to get to my feet but she was thrashing like a hooked fish, trying to slash at my hand where I still held her wrist. She gashed me. I let go and stood back.

I was at the top of the stairs. My arm was bleeding profusely. She switched the knife to underhand, screamed like a banshee and rushed me. I grabbed her arm, felt the blade cut into my chest and we both fell. As we went down, I yanked her around so I landed on top of her, keeping the knife away from my body. I heard her groan and her eyes rolled. I grabbed her baby finger with my right hand and forced it back, trying to release her grip on the handle. She started to thrash and kick and scream again. A voice somewhere shouted, "I can't get past you!" But before I could make sense of it, we had started to slip and slide down the stairs.

We hit the bottom. And I felt a body move past me. Vaguely, I was aware of Abi having jumped over us. I pinned Karen's right hand to the floor with all my weight. She wriggled her hand, sawing at my arm with the blade. I ignored the pain and tried to pound at her face and body with my right fist, but she gripped my arm, sinking her nails into my flesh.

I managed to maneuver my body around until I could plant my right foot on her arm. I knew the Sig was down there somewhere, and now I had a chance to look for it. Abi was standing there, in front of the reception desk holding it, trying to aim it at Karen. I snapped, "Don't!"

She glanced at me. I stood and made a big stride toward her, took the gun from her hand and turned. Karen was scrabbling to her feet. She still had the knife in her hand. She lunged and I fired, double tapped right into her forehead. Her head rocked and a big plume of gore sprayed from the back of her head. She stood for a moment, looking like she'd just received some shocking news, then keeled over backward, like a dark parody of a slapstick faint.

I stood looking at her for a moment. I was lightheaded and realized I was losing blood. I shouted up the stairs,

"Don't come down! Stay there..." Then to Abi, "They mustn't see this."

She was staring at me. I knew she was in shock. A voice in my head was telling me this was all wrong. I needed to get Karen out of the house. I had to protect the kids from the horror. It was imperative to protect the kids. I stepped over to what was left of Karen. I bent and took hold of her ankles. My head swam and I took a moment to steady myself. I heard Abi's voice. "Lacklan, you're bleeding. You're bleeding badly. You need a doctor..."

"Not yet..."

Somehow I found the strength to drag her body out and dump it in the snow. I went back in and closed the door. Abi came to me. Her face was drawn with anxiety.

"Lacklan, you're very badly hurt. Look at you! I have to stop the bleeding. Come into the kitchen."

She led me through the living room and back into the kitchen. I sat while she found the first aid kit. I heard myself say, "Stop the bleeding first, then we'll clean the wounds."

She stripped off what was left of my shirt. I had a three-inch gash on my right lower arm that was bleeding profusely. She tied a tourniquet just below my bicep, then bound the wound. "You'll need stitches. I'll have to get the doctor."

I shook my head. "Not yet. I'll go to him, but not yet..."

I still had the feeling that something was wrong. Abi was kneeling beside me, patching up the cut in my side. "It's not as bad as the one on your arm, but your hands..." She stood and took my hands. I looked at them. She was shaking her head, fighting back the tears. "Your poor hands."

Something was wrong. The nagging sensation in my

mind was getting worse. I stood. The adrenaline was pumping hot in my belly. I said, "Abi, where are the kids?"

She frowned. "You told them to stay upstairs. Sit down, Lacklan. I'll call them."

"No." I grabbed my gun and went out to the reception. I stared up the darkened stairs and shouted, "Primrose! Sean! Come down!"

There was no response. Abi came up by my side. "Lacklan, for God's sake, what is it?"

I looked into her face. I knew what was wrong. I ran up the stairs. Sean was lying face down on the landing. I knelt, felt for a pulse. He was alive. I could hear Abi running up after me. I moved quickly to Primrose's room. Behind me, I heard Abi scream, "*Sean!*" and a rush of feet. I pushed open the door and froze.

She was lying motionless on her bed. Her eyes were open and staring. Arnold was lying curled up next to her. He was naked. His skin was very white and strangely luminous in the darkened room. He had one leg across both of hers, and he held a long, slender blade to her throat. He didn't look at me, but he hissed in his throat, "Get out..."

I had no shot to his vertebrae. I had no way of disarming him or killing him without risking her life. I spoke quietly. "Give me the knife, Arnold."

I saw his eyes shift. He looked at me sidelong and there was contempt in his face. He said again, "Get out. I am not done."

Primrose was staring at me. I met her eye. "Has he hurt you?"

She whispered, "No, but I am very scared... Please stop, Arnold..."

He smiled. "Shshshsh... We're going to play. It's a nice game. You'll like it. It's my special game with Mommy."

I spoke more loudly, "You can't play that game anymore, Arnold."

This time he turned his head, lifted it off the pillow. His expression was ugly. I forced myself not to look at the knife.

He said, "I told you to *get out!*"

"What will you do to me if I don't?"

"I am *not done here!* I am *playing my game!*"

He was a four year-old having a tantrum in the body of a twenty year-old. And whatever his hysterical paralysis did to him most of the time, right now he didn't look emaciated or weak at all.

"Your mommy is downstairs, Arnold. She wants to see you."

He sneered and shook his head. "No, she doesn't. She likes it when I play our game."

"I can hear her calling. She says she wants you to go downstairs."

He shook his head again, raising it a little more off the pillow. "You're *lying!* She said I could play with Prim! She said I could! And you can't stop me!"

"Your mommy says you can't now."

"I'm not *done!*" His voice was changing, becoming petulant, whining, "Get *out!* I wanna play with Prim. Leave us *alone!*"

I took a step into the room as I answered him. "I'll tell you what, Arnold, how about this? You come downstairs with me, we talk to your mom, and Prim waits right here. If your mom says it's OK, then you come right back up and finish your game."

His head flopped back on the pillow. He pressed up closer to Primrose and hugged her tighter. The blade nicked her skin and I saw a tear of dark blood run down her neck and onto her nightdress. I saw her tense and heard her whimper. My heart was pounding hard in my chest. I was as close to panic as I had ever been. But I smiled, snorted, and shook my head.

"She's going to be mad at you, Arnold. She won't be happy."

"I don't *care!* I don't *believe you!* Leave us alone!"

"I can't do that."

"Leave us *alone!*"

"Your mommy won't let me."

His voice was becoming shrill. "*Leave us alone!*"

"Mommy won't let you!"

He sat up. His face was crimson with rage. The tendons in his neck stood out like rigid cords. His veins bulged. He screamed at me, "*Leave us alone! Leave us alone! Leave us...*"

The double crack of the Sig silenced him. I put both rounds through his throat and shattered his vertebrae, paralyzing his body from the neck down and killing him almost instantly. Primrose screamed and covered her face. I stepped forward, grabbed him and yanked him from the bed before he could fall back beside her. Then I picked her up in my arms and carried her, weeping and trembling, to the door. Abi was there, reaching for her. "Oh God, please say she's all right. Please tell me she's all right."

"She's safe. She's unhurt." I pushed past her. "Get Sean. Bring him downstairs. It's all over now. Now it's all over." I carried Primrose down the stairs to the living room, where I settled her and Sean on the couch and made a fire, while Abi brought down blankets and made strong, sweet tea.

While the three of them sat, huddled together on the sofa, holding each other, I got dressed. Then I went and got Arnold's body, carried it down, through the snow and the screaming wind, to the Q7 and put it in the back. Then I returned, got Karen's body, and put it next to his. Finally, I set off toward the intersection. On the way, I collected Al and drove all three of them to the snow plow, where I dumped them on the road. Like I said before, it would be a nice mystery for the Feds, but there would be no suspicion on Abi. She and the kids would not be involved. Now, nothing pointed to them.

After that, I started the long, freezing, two and a half mile walk back toward the Pioneer Guesthouse. It would be almost an hour's walk in good weather, double that in the storm. I was pretty sure I wouldn't make it. I had tapped and exhausted the last reserves of strength I had. I would walk as far as I could. At some point, I knew I would start to hallucinate, then I would grow very sleepy, and finally I would pass out. And I wouldn't wake up.

The hallucinations started sooner than I had expected. I told myself it was because of the loss of blood. I could see the lights of Independence flickering through the falling snow up ahead of me. They started to move and shift, like a UFO through the drifting flakes. An agreeable sleepiness was creeping over me. I thought maybe checking out now was not such a bad thing. I was tired. Tired of the killing. Tired of man's inhumanity to man, and woman, and child. I could check out of the Pioneer and lie down to sleep in a drift, and drift, drift away into peaceful, dreamless slumber. Check out.

Still I walked, in a trance, putting one foot in front of another, just one more time before lying down.

The lights grew and I wondered if I was seeing that light at the end of the tunnel that some people report. Through the howl and wail of the wind, I heard a grinding, whining, and then I began to laugh. Because I was not dying. I was not checking out just yet. It was the Dodge RAM, and Abi, Primrose, and Sean had come to get me.

EPILOGUE

THE SHERIFF DIDN'T ARRIVE UNTIL LATE afternoon the next day, and the Feds arrived the day after that, and by then the storm had abated and the snow had started to thaw. We had plenty of time to wash and bleach the bed linen and the floor, and to remove the spots of blood from the carpet, along with any trace of the drama that had unfolded in that house.

The sheriff and the Feds had no reason to link what had happened at the farm and the mine to Abi, the guesthouse, or myself; plus there was not a witness left alive to make that connection for them. So they didn't call until late on the second day. They didn't expect to discover anything from us, and they didn't. I was a guest at the Pioneer, trapped by the storm, and hadn't left the place for the last five days. None of us had. And we all corroborated each other's stories. The village was, as it had always been, closed and silent about its pain and its traumas. They told the agents nothing.

I have no idea if they ever closed the case. It must have

looked to them like a war had broken out between Al and Vasco, and they had all killed each other, though the details of how it had happened would be forever a mystery, to be written up in the *Fortean Times* and no doubt attributed to aliens or an avenging ghost.

It was after the Feds and the sheriff had finally packed up and left, and Abi and I were sitting over coffee after dinner, that she asked me, "How could he do it? He was so weak. Most of the time he could barely walk."

I nodded. "I am no psychologist, Abi, but my guess is that Karen, who was herself deeply neurotic, drove him into a state of hysterical paralysis. She denied him every natural desire and emotion, especially sexual and romantic ones. She put him in a kind of double bind. If he wanted his mother's love and approval, he had to deny himself his natural desire for love and approval from other women. In the end, his internal conflict was so severe he literally paralyzed himself and became all but a cripple.

"But by the time he was fifteen, when she finally allowed him the company of girls, it triggered a kind of Jekyll and Hyde split personality in him. Because his weakness was mentally induced, when he was with girls he liked, driven by his emotional and sexual frustration, he was overcome by his desires, drew physical strength from those desires, and raped and killed them."

She frowned. "Did he kill them, or was it his mother? Or Vasco?"

"I think what he was telling us when he said it was their game, was that he was allowed to be with the girls and rape them, but the girls had to die afterwards. With the Mexican girls, I think that was Vasco's job."

"Why?"

"It's sickening," I said, "but the fact is that he didn't enjoy the Mexican girls as much. He liked blonde, blue-eyed girls, like his mother. Serial killers often have a particular, preferred victim. And that's just what he was, a serial killer." I sighed. "But the problem was that the girls he liked were high risk, and not only that, Karen was jealous of them, because he liked them too much. Things went to pieces when, just before the storm, he escaped and went after Peggy. Vasco was ordered to clean it up, but he was lazy and careless. He didn't want to go digging a grave in the storm that was coming, so he dumped her by the road, probably hoping it would look like she'd been hit by a truck. If I hadn't happened along, he might have got away with it."

She nodded. "Probably." She reached across the table and took my hand. "I'm glad you did happen along." She hesitated a moment. "Will you stay for Peggy's funeral? It's in a couple of days."

"Yes, I'd like that."

"Then I guess you'll be going on, back to Wyoming."

"Yes."

She looked out the window, at the small square where the snow glowed blue under a luminous moon. She was still holding my hand, and I was holding hers. "I don't know anything about you, who you are, what you do... if there is anyone in your life..."

I placed my other hand on top of hers and was quiet for a long while. Finally, I sighed and shook my head. "I'm not sure I know the answer to those questions myself, Abi. My life is more complicated than you can imagine. It's no accident that I killed all these men. It's what I am trained to do."

She smiled. "I had worked that much out."

I hesitated a moment, then said, "I don't know what happens next. I can't explain, but I have a job I have to do." She nodded that she understood, but her face was not happy. I went on, "Let me help, Abi. Let me help to put Primrose through college, and when the time comes, Sean, too. Let me be an uncle or a godfather."

She smiled and stroked my face. "And to me, Lacklan, what will you be to me?"

I thought of Marni, in Oxford. I thought of my unending pursuit of her, holding her only for fleeting moments just so that she could slip through my fingers again. I thought of the unending, unwinnable war against Omega; and I looked at this good, beautiful woman, with her beautiful home: a place where I could be useful, a place that was wholesome, where I could stop killing. I took hold of her hand and kissed it. Then I stood, but I didn't let go of her hand. Instead I led her upstairs to her room.

Don't miss TO RULE IN HELL. The riveting sequel in the Omega Thriller series.

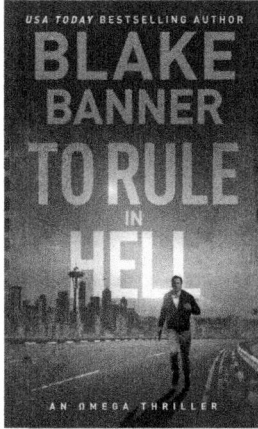

Scan the QR code below to purchase TO RULE IN HELL.

Or go to: righthouse.com/to-rule-in-hell

NOTE: flip to the very end to read an exclusive sneak peek...

DON'T MISS ANYTHING!

If you want to stay up to date on all new releases in this series, with this author, or with any of our new deals, you can do so by joining our newsletters below.

In addition, you will immediately gain access to our entire *Right House VIP Library,* which includes many riveting Mystery and Thriller novels for your enjoyment!

righthouse.com/email

(Easy to unsubscribe. No spam. Ever.)

ALSO BY BLAKE BANNER

Up to date books can be found at:
www.righthouse.com/blake-banner

ROGUE THRILLERS
Gates of Hell (Book 1)
Hell's Fury (Book 2)
Ice Burn (Book 3)
Judgement by Fire (Book 4)

ALEX MASON THRILLERS
Odin (Book 1)
Ice Cold Spy (Book 2)
Mason's Law (Book 3)
Assets and Liabilities (Book 4)
Russian Roulette (Book 5)
Executive Order (Book 6)
Dead Man Talking (Book 7)
All The King's Men (Book 8)
Flashpoint (Book 9)
Brotherhood of the Goat (Book 10)
Dead Hot (Book 11)
Blood on Megiddo (Book 12)
Son of Hell (Book 13)
Merchant of Death (Book 14)
Extinction C-14 (Book 15)

HARRY BAUER THRILLER SERIES

Dead of Night (Book 1)
Dying Breath (Book 2)
The Einstaat Brief (Book 3)
Quantum Kill (Book 4)
Immortal Hate (Book 5)
The Silent Blade (Book 6)
LA: Wild Justice (Book 7)
Breath of Hell (Book 8)
Invisible Evil (Book 9)
The Shadow of Ukupacha (Book 10)
Sweet Razor Cut (Book 11)
Blood of the Innocent (Book 12)
Blood on Balthazar (Book 13)
Simple Kill (Book 14)
Riding The Devil (Book 15)
The Unavenged (Book 16)
The Devil's Vengeance (Book 17)
Bloody Retribution (Book 18)
Rogue Kill (Book 19)
Blood for Blood (Book 20)
The Cell (Book 21)
Time to Die (Book 22)
The Reaper of Zion (Book 23)

DEAD COLD MYSTERY SERIES
An Ace and a Pair (Book 1)
Two Bare Arms (Book 2)
Garden of the Damned (Book 3)
Let Us Prey (Book 4)
The Sins of the Father (Book 5)
Strange and Sinister Path (Book 6)

The Heart to Kill (Book 7)
Unnatural Murder (Book 8)
Fire from Heaven (Book 9)
To Kill Upon A Kiss (Book 10)
Murder Most Scottish (Book 11)
The Butcher of Whitechapel (Book 12)
Little Dead Riding Hood (Book 13)
Trick or Treat (Book 14)
Blood Into Wine (Book 15)
Jack In The Box (Book 16)
The Fall Moon (Book 17)
Blood In Babylon (Book 18)
Death In Dexter (Book 19)
Mustang Sally (Book 20)
A Christmas Killing (Book 21)
Mommy's Little Killer (Book 22)
Bleed Out (Book 23)
Dead and Buried (Book 24)
In Hot Blood (Book 25)
Fallen Angels (Book 26)
Knife Edge (Book 27)
Along Came A Spider (Book 28)
Cold Blood (Book 29)
Curtain Call (Book 30)

THE OMEGA SERIES
Dawn of the Hunter (Book 1)
Double Edged Blade (Book 2)
The Storm (Book 3)
The Hand of War (Book 4)
A Harvest of Blood (Book 5)

ABOUT US

Right House is an independent publisher created by authors for readers. We specialize in Action, Thriller, Mystery, and Crime novels.

If you enjoyed this novel, then there is a good chance you will like what else we have to offer! Please stay up to date by using any of the links below.

Join our mailing lists to stay up to date -->
righthouse.com/email
Visit our website --> righthouse.com
Contact us --> contact@righthouse.com

facebook.com/righthousebooks
x.com/righthousebooks
instagram.com/righthousebooks

EXCLUSIVE SNEAK PEEK OF...

TO RULE IN HELL

CHAPTER 1

I WAS IN THAT PLACE BETWEEN WAKING AND SLEEP, where everything is feeling. You do not imagine in pictures: Your mind is dark. There are no voices: your mind is quiet. And in the dark silence, you feel. I could feel Abi's back, pressed close against me. I could feel her hair on my face. I could feel the fresh linen of the bed, a cool breeze from the window on my face. For the first time in my life I felt I was home and safe. So I kept my eyes closed and held on to the feeling.

Slowly sounds began to filter in. Outside, March was melting the winter snow and the birds were celebrating loudly. A transmission complained in low gear as a truck moved down Main Street toward the farm. Across the road the doc told somebody it was a fine morning—if you wanted to freeze to death. There was laughter and that made me smile. I felt Abi chuckle and I opened my eyes, raised myself on one elbow to look down at her. She was smiling but still had her eyes closed and spoke in a sleepy voice.

"He's such a grouch."

I kissed her shoulder. "You seen the time?"

"It's Sunday."

"Tell that to my stomach."

She opened one eye to look at me sidelong. "Your stomach?" She began to turn. "Come here and let me explain something to your stomach..."

I should have ignored it. I should have let it ring. But it had been too many years of training and conditioning and I had turned and reached for my cell before I knew what I was doing.

"Yeah..."

Marni spoke and I went cold inside. "Hi Lacklan, it's been a long time..."

For a moment I felt sick. I could feel Abi's eyes on me, curious. I said, "Yeah, where are you?"

"Not on the phone. I'm where I was." She was still in Oxford then. A wave of relief, then shame. She went on, cold and efficient. "I'm afraid this isn't a social call. I need to be quick."

"Sure, yeah."

"I need you to do something."

A spot of anger and resentment in my gut. "What?" I felt the bedcovers move, looked and saw Abi walking to the bathroom. Marni was talking again.

"I'm on a secure line, but I can't stay on long, so I need you to trust me and not argue, OK?"

I took a moment to answer. Finally I said, "Yeah, OK..."

"I need you to go to Seattle, 5508 B, 26th Avenue South, Beacon Hill. There you will collect something."

"Collect what?"

"Shut up. When the guy, you can call him Ernst, opens the door to you, you'll tell him you need an extension. He'll tell you to come in and look at some drawings."

"Are you serious?"

"Shut up, Lacklan! He will give you some items and some instructions. Have you clearly understood everything I have told you?"

"Yes, of course I have. But, Marni...?"

"Be quick. I'm running out of time."

"When this is over, we need to talk."

A moment's silence, then. "Yeah, when it's over."

The line went dead.

I sat a moment, staring out at the snow melting on Main Street. I could hear the shower going in the bathroom. The hot pellet of anger in my belly turned into a wave of rage and frustration. It welled up to a peak inside me. I closed my eyes and breathed. It passed, and I swung out of bed and joined Abi in the shower.

Downstairs we made breakfast together in silence. We were alone. I had got Primrose an apartment in Boston, where she was applying to universities, and Sean had joined her there for Easter. Abi and I had been going to spend the Easter on our own together. It was the first time we had been alone.

I put the coffee pot on the table, she set down two plates of bacon and fried banana, and a dish of pancakes. We sat and I watched her while she stared at her plate for four long seconds.

"You're leaving, aren't you?"

"I have to go to Seattle."

"Will you come back?"

"Yes. I don't know how long. It may be a couple of days, or it may be a week. I won't know until I'm there. But I have told them I need to talk to them. This is my last job, Abi."

"Please don't lie to me."

I shook my head. "I am telling you the truth. I've had enough. I'm through."

She reached over and took hold of my hand. Her eyes told me she wanted to believe me. They also told me that she didn't.

After breakfast I packed up the Zombie, kissed Abi and told her I would call her from Seattle, and drove down the long track to Blood Canyon Road. There I turned north. I picked up the I-80 at Mill City and settled down to a thirteen hour drive. The Zombie was actually a 1968 Ford Mustang Fastback. But it had been modified by some crazy geniuses in Texas. Now the twin electric engines delivered eight hundred bhp and one thousand eight hundred foot-pounds of torque direct to the back wheels. It could do 170 MPH over a mile without breaking a sweat, went 0 to 60 in just over one and a half seconds, while spreading your face across the back of your seat, and did it all without making a sound.

I settled at a steady eighty, shook a Camel from my pack, lit it with my battered, brass Zippo and put the Eagles on the sound system. Desperado seemed somehow appropriate, as I thought about what I was leaving behind me and wondered about what I was heading for.

Marni had made it clear it wasn't a social call. That meant just one thing. It was about Omega, and that meant that after the near catastrophe at the United Nations in New

York[1], they were done licking their wounds and now they were ready to join battle again. I knew that while I'd been trying to live a normal life with Abi and her kids in Independence, Marni and Professor Gibbons had not been sitting on their laurels. They had been planning, preparing for when Omega resurfaced. It had always been a matter of time. Now that time had come. They were back, and so were we...

We?

I thought about the word.

All my life there had been two constants: my love for Marni and my hatred for my father. On his deathbed he had made me promise that I would protect Marni in her mission to bring down Omega. It had not been a hard promise to make, back then. But now things had changed. Marni had walked away, and she had not looked back. I had found Abi, and a home in Independence. Now it was a promise I was preparing to break.

If they wanted me to collect something in Seattle, then they would want me to deliver it somewhere too. I would do that. And then I would tell Marni and Gibbons that it was over. I had no future with Marni, that much was clear, and the only future I had fighting Omega was more killing. Killing was something I was good at. I was the best of the best. But nothing wearies, destroys you, nothing drains your soul as much as killing. And I had had enough.

As Don Henley kept telling me, I wasn't gettin' no younger.

I crossed into Oregon as the sun hit noon. I crossed the Black Rock Desert at speed and stopped for a late lunch at

---

1. See *The Hand of War*

Prineville. Then I took US Highway 26 toward Portland, and as evening began to close in, I started to climb, through ever denser pine forests, toward Mount Hood. Finally, at shortly before eleven that night, I stopped at Tanglewild, outside Seattle, because I liked the name, and booked into a Best Western for the night.

As I lay, staring at the dark ceiling, preparing myself for sleep, Independence, the Pioneer Inn and Abi seemed suddenly to be a very long way away.

———

BEACON HILL IS NOT the most exciting place in Seattle. It is a dormitory for the people who work downtown and in the Eliot Bay area. There is nothing there but houses, thousands of them—not quite identical, but close enough—in endless, almost identical rows.

26th Avenue South was not hard to find. I came in on the I-5, followed Beacon Avenue north to South Orca and turned left into 26th. The house I was looking for was on the right, about halfway up, and about as boring and inconspicuous as Beacon Hill itself. I pulled up, climbed out and slammed the door. It echoed down a street with no people in it. I took a moment to look at the house. It was a red brick with very straight, modern lines and a path that wound up through a huge rockery, covered in pines and cypress trees. The path ended at a front porch that was more like a terrace.

I climbed the path, rang the bell and then hammered for good measure. The door was opened after a moment by a man I guessed was in his early sixties. He wore heavy, horn-rimmed glasses like the ones Michael Cain used to wear back when the world was young, and a gray cardigan like the one his grandfather used to wear before that. He had it buttoned up and I could see a pipe poking out of one of the pockets. He smiled at me and said, with a hint of reproof, "I came as fast as I could. Can I help you?"

I raised an eyebrow. "I hope so. I need an extension."

"Oh, well then, you'd better come in. I'll show you some drawings."

I thanked him and he led me through a spartan, minimalist living room with a stone fireplace, furniture with bare, polished wooden legs, and five cats, to a kitchen in tubular metal and black and yellow Formica. A sixth cat followed us in and I saw six dishes on the floor with cat food in them. Each dish had a name, so I guess the cats could read. He waved a hand in their direction and said, "Don't mind the gang. I was just about to make tea. Will you have some?"

"Thanks. I need to be on my way. I'd rather get down to business if you don't mind."

He gave a small, private smile as he prepared two mugs with tea bags. "How do you know you need to be on your way?" he said, then glanced over his shoulder as he switched on the kettle. "I haven't given you your instructions yet. Sit down."

I sat at the Formica table. He took a large manila envelope from on top of the toaster and dropped it in front of me. From the pocket that did not contain his pipe he took a pair of latex gloves and pulled them on. Then he opened the envelope and extracted an ID card. He handed it to me.

"Do me a favor and get lots of fingerprints on that, would you? Nothing alerts the intelligence agencies like an ID card with just two fingerprints on it. You are Joseph O'Brien. I thought you had a bit of an Irish rogue look about you. You live in Chicago. Your job, address and other details are all in the envelope. None of it will stand up to close background checks, obviously, so try to avoid drawing attention to yourself. Here is your driving permit and a credit card for any expenses you may have to incur as Mr. O'Brien. Give them a good maul too. When you are done with them, burn them thoroughly."

I looked at the two documents and the card, then up at Ernst. "What the hell is this? What do I need these for?"

"Don't shoot me, I'm just the messenger." He said it into the envelope, fishing out a couple of sheets of A4, which he handed me. I looked at them. They were just biographical details that went with the ID documents. He went on, "Now, at twelve noon you will take your car to the SP Parking at First and Colombia. You will go to the very top floor and there you will meet an old friend of yours..."

"Who?"

"I have no idea. All I know is that he will be waiting there for you. He will deliver an uninteresting saloon car to you, and tell you what to do and where to go, so to speak. He will then take your own vehicle back to Boston." He smiled. I didn't. I had decided I didn't like him.

"Who gave you these instructions?"

"Even if I wanted to, I couldn't tell you because I don't know."

The kettle had stopped boiling, but he made no move to make tea. I guess he had decided he disliked me as much as I disliked him. I said, "Are we done?"

He nodded and waited. I took the documents and stood. "Thanks for the tea. Say goodbye to Mr. Tiddles for me."

"Goodbye. Close the door on your way out."

I made my way to my car, aware of him watching me from his window.

It was a short drive along Beacon Avenue and over Holgate Bridge, up to the Waterfront. All the way I was asking myself who the 'old friend' was that was going to meet me at the parking garage. I wondered briefly if it might be Marni or Gibbons, but I was pretty sure they were still in Oxford.

I arrived with a couple of hours to spare, but drove the Zombie to the top floor anyway. There were only a couple of other cars up there, a Ford Focus and a Dodge Charger. I climbed out and was immediately buffeted by the wind coming in off the bay. The view was spectacular and I took a moment to look out over the dark stretch of Puget Sound. When I turned to make my way to the elevators he was standing there behind me. I should have known it would be him. I smiled.

"Kenny."

"Good morning, sir. I have your car. May I say what a pleasure it is to see you?"

I laughed out loud, partly at his old-world formality, and partly at the sheer, unexpected joy of seeing him. "It is a pleasure to see you, too, old friend. It's been a long time, too long."

"Indeed, sir. Almost two years. Rosalia sends her best wishes. You are missed at home..." For a moment I didn't know what to say. I was overwhelmed by feelings that confused me. He must have sensed it because he smiled and held out a key. "It's the Dodge, over there, sir, a nice V8.

Miss Marni said to get something inconspicuous, but I thought you'd like something with a bit of grunt."

"It's a perfect choice." I took the key and handed him the ones to the Zombie. Then I laughed again and slapped him on the shoulder. "Let's go and have coffee, Kenny, and you can tell me about Rosalia and the house... Has it really been two years?"

We rode down in the elevator and walked up to 3rd Avenue, where we found a café with tables in an internal patio. We ordered coffee and I sat watching the man who had been my father's butler for two decades; who had in many ways been more of a father to me than Bob Walker ever had. He was now my butler, though it was hard for me to think of him as such, and since my father's death I had barely set foot in the house. Listening to him now, filling me in on the state of the lawns and the gardens, of the woods, the house and Rosalia's health (Rosalia—my surrogate mother—my cook!), I realized, almost with a sense of panic, that what he and Rosalia wanted most from me was for me to take my place in that house, and bring order back to their world. To fill my father's shoes.

He fell silent and I realized he had finished his coffee and I had barely touched mine. He hesitated a moment, then said, "Miss Marni gave me a message for you, sir."

"Yes," I said. "I had almost forgotten. It has been so good to catch up..." Even as I said it I was aware that it was both true and hypocritical of me. Though I loved Kenny and Rosalia, every fiber of my being wanted to run from my father's legacy, and they were a part of that legacy. And yet, I could have sat all day listening to him and his stories about rosebushes and the falcons that were nesting on the chimney pots.

"The message is, sir, that she wishes you to drive to Spokane, to leave the car in a side street there and to purchase, cash, a ticket on the Empire Builder, which I understand is a train, to Chicago. And, once there, to purchase a ticket to Washington, D.C., in the name of Joseph O'Brien. Again, she advises that the ticket should be bought cash. There is a room reserved for you, in the name of O'Brien, at the Hotel Hive, on F Street. It is a... um... *modest* establishment, but I do not believe you will be staying there very long. Today is Monday. On Wednesday evening, at six, you will be met in the bar by a gentleman. He will ask you how your extension is progressing, and you will inform him that it is a work in progress. He will then take you to meet somebody. I am afraid, sir, that I do not know whom you are to meet."

I nodded for a long time. I was thinking that things wouldn't even get started until Wednesday, but I had told Abi I'd be away a couple of days or a week. It was going to be considerably more than that. I sighed. "Thanks, Kenny." I looked at my watch. "I guess we had better get going."

On the way back to the parking garage Kenny said suddenly, "Sir, may I ask a question? Two, questions, in fact."

"Of course, Kenny. Anything."

"Can we..." He hesitated. "Can we expect you home at some point, sir?"

I smiled. It was a good question, and I wasn't able to answer it until we were stepping out of the elevators onto the roof. I walked him to the Zombie and as he opened the door I said, "It's a question I have been asking myself a lot lately, Kenny, and I'm beginning to think that the answer is yes. I don't know when. Maybe I'll know more after Wednesday."

"That is good news, Rosalia will be very happy."

"What's your other question?"

"Will Miss Marni be with you?" I guess he saw by my face that there was no simple answer to that one, because before I could reply, he said, "Ah, I see, sir. Well, I'd best be getting back then. Perhaps we should leave a few minutes between my departure and yours. We'll be hoping to hear from you in due course. Goodbye, sir."

And with that, he climbed into the car and slipped silently away.

CHAPTER 2

The drive to Spokane should have taken six hours but it didn't. The four wheel drive Dodge, with its V8 growl, is not a car for cruising or looking at the scenery. I hit the I-90, crossed the two bridges, and after Issaquah I was out of the city and burning rubber at 100 MPH, headed east in the afternoon sun. Both me and the Dodge were happy.

I arrived in Spokane at five PM, dropped the Dodge in a side street and, according to Kenny's instructions, bought a one way ticket to Chicago on the Empire Builder. I discovered then that there was only one a day. It departed at twenty-five minutes past one in the morning and arrived in Chicago thirty-six hours later, at three fifty-five in the afternoon. It would have been faster by ten hours to drive, but I guess Marni, or Gibbons, was trying not to leave a trail. At some point, I figured, I might find out why.

Premium was extortionate, but for once in my life I took a leaf out of my father's book and went first class, because I got a room, a bed and food, all of which I was going to need.

I called Abi from a pay phone and told her I was going to be at least a week, maybe two, but that I was more certain than ever that I was coming back. She was quiet, like she was trying to believe me, which made me wonder whether I believed myself. I was pretty sure I did, but I was also in uncharted territory. Family were things I had been running from as long as I could remember. Now, suddenly, I found I wanted to create both.

After I had hung up, I killed eight hours by getting lost in the city, buying a book, having an early dinner at a restaurant and then downing some drinks and watching TV in a late night bar. At one AM I made my way to the station and boarded the train.

The rest of the journey was a kind of interminable blur: the relentless rhythm of the train on the tracks, and the endless spectacular scenery of the north, interspersed with chapters from a futuristic dystopian thriller about a guy fighting an unwinnable war against an all-powerful organization that controlled world governments. I wondered if the author knew how close he was to the truth. But eventually, after thirty-six long hours, we arrived at Chicago, and I shoved the book in my bag.

From the railway station I took a cab direct to O'Hare and managed to get a seat on a flight departing that evening at seven forty-five, arriving at ten thirty. I called the hotel and told them I'd be arriving earlier than expected. I could have booked in at the airport Hilton, stayed the night and caught a morning flight, but it felt like I had been traveling all my life, and getting nowhere. Now I just wanted to arrive, get the job done and go home.

I finally climbed out of the cab at the Hotel Hive at just

before midnight, sixty hours and three thousand miles from where I had started, with still no clear idea of what I was doing there, or when I would be able to go back to Independence, Abi, and the life I was trying to build. I checked in at reception and discovered that Marni had had the good sense to book me a king-sized attic. I rode the elevator up to my room, poured myself a large Bushmills and collapsed on the bed.

I SLEPT in late and had brunch in my room while I showered and shaved, and wondered what the hell I was doing in D.C. So far all the instructions I'd received had been aimed at one single thing, ensuring that nobody followed me. And the only items I had collected had been documents to conceal my identity. Now I was here, in D.C., as Joseph O'Brien, and whoever I was due to meet in the bar would presumably tell me why. But the fact that I was in a hotel in Washington, rather than a dive in the Bronx or a hamlet in the Mid West, could mean only one thing: that Gibbons and Marni were trying some kind of political power play. This clearly involved Gibbons' political 'connections', but what I was struggling with was how it involved me.

As I thought about it I realized there was a second possibility, and that was that I had been duped and I was here to meet Ben. D.C. was Ben's turf, and twice already I had been brought here to his office at the Pentagon. But the last time I'd met him here had resulted in the deaths of several senior members of Omega, and one former president. I was pretty sure that next time I met Ben, he'd be trying to kill me, not talk to me.

It was unlikely, I decided, to be a trap set by Ben, but I was also pretty sure that he would be making an appearance sooner or later.

I spent the afternoon in my room working out and killing time, and at five thirty I went down to the bar. There was a lot of red brick, dark wood and artsy elegance. I ordered a martini very dry and found a table near an open fire. There I sat to wait. My contact arrived at five fifty-nine with a luminous sign on his head that said 'Navy Seal'. All six foot two of him stood in the doorway in his Italian suit and his Ray-Ban shades, assessing his immediate environment and seeking his target. I sighed and looked at the small flames in the hearth. After a moment I heard his large feet cross the floor to my table.

I looked up at him and smiled. "Hello."

He spoke with no inflection at all. "How is your extension progressing?"

I nodded. "Well, you know, it's a work in progress. Sit down and order a drink, will you? And try to stop looking like a damn Navy Seal."

His right eyebrow twitched. "Sarah asked me to hurry. She has the roast on. We can have drinks when we get there."

I shook my head, drained my glass and stood. As I grabbed my coat I asked him, "You ever consider a career in Hollywood? There is something so natural and believable about your delivery."

"You ever consider a career as a comedian? You're funny."

Outside it was getting dark and there was a bite in the

air. He started across the sidewalk and I saw he had a black Grand Cherokee Laredo waiting with its hazards flashing. As he moved around to the driver's door, he said, "In D.C., this is blending in."

I sighed for the second time. Maybe he was right, at that. We spent the next hour driving all over the District of Colombia, as far north as Fort Slocum Park and as far south as Wesley Heights by way of the White House. All the while he seemed to have his eyes fixed more on the mirrors than on the road. I decided he was thorough, and made up in attention to detail for what he lacked in innate intelligence. He was a well-trained gorilla.

Eventually he seemed to relax and we headed, by way of many side streets, toward Trinidad. On Montello Avenue he turned right into Penn Street and stopped outside a slightly dilapidated, double-fronted red brick that looked like it might have been new in the 1890s. The front lawn was running to seed and the Georgian gabled portico was shedding its white paint. He glanced at me. "This low-key enough for you?"

I nodded. "Yeah, your ninety grand Cherokee fits right in here."

"Quit griping. She's waiting."

"Who is?"

"Go and find out, hot shot."

Just for a moment there was hostility in his eyes. Resentment? Hurt pride? I climbed out and made my way across the lawn, along the cracked concrete path toward the front door. I heard the big engine whine and watched the red taillights move away into the dark.

The door was plain wood with peeling varnish. I tried the

bell. It didn't work, so I rapped with my knuckles. After fifteen seconds the door opened. The hall inside was dark, but I could make out the form of a man holding a gun. He said, "Step inside, put your hands on your head and face the wall."

I didn't move. "How about I break your neck instead?"

"I wouldn't do that. You're covered on three sides. Besides, I just want to check you for weapons. Quit being an asshole and step inside."

I went in and put my hands up. He kept his distance, closed the door and snapped on the lights. I was in a dingy hall with a staircase opposite, and a door on either side. There were two men, both with the same Special Ops look: short hair, expressionless eyes and shirts that didn't fit across their chests. The guy holding the gun on me was in his fifties, the other was twenty years younger, with dark hair and dark eyes. He said, "Face the wall."

I gave him the dead eye and said, "No."

He frowned, like the moon had just risen in the west. "Face the fucking wall!"

I spoke to the older guy. "No. Frisk me if you want, but I'm not turning my back on you until I know who you are and why I'm here. And if you try to take my weapon I'll break your arm. Now I came to D.C. because you asked me to, so let's get this fucking circus over with or I'm going to walk out that door and go home."

His frown deepened. "You have a weapon? You came here with a weapon?"

"Sig Sauer p226, I have a knife in my boot. And make no mistake, I'm serious. Touch them and I'll break your arm. I don't know who the hell you are or why you asked me to come here. And frankly, your reception stinks. Start explaining, pal."

The older guy hesitated. He wasn't prepared for the unexpected. Few people ever are. When people hesitate, that's when you take charge. I said, "I gather I am here to meet somebody?"

His face said I was right.

"Keep me covered. Take me to them. If I am satisfied that I am not in danger, I'll put my weapons on the table."

He sighed and jerked his head toward the door behind me. "Through there, and keep your hands where I can see them."

His young pal pulled his Glock and opened the door. I followed him in. The older guy stayed behind me. I was in a long room the stretched from the front of the house to the back. There was a fireplace that was cold and black with ash. A coffee table stood in front of it with a seedy sofa and a couple of threadbare armchairs. Heavy, sage green drapes were drawn across the windows at the front and the rear, and the light, which was dull, was from a couple of old lamps with flyblown shades.

There was a woman sitting in one of the armchairs, watching me. I recognized her. She was younger and more attractive in the flesh than on TV. I guessed she was in her late thirties, with densely curled copper hair and dark blue eyes. Her clothes were expensive, as you'd expect, but understated and elegant.

I nodded. "I should have guessed, Senator Cyndi McFarlane." I turned to the older guy. "I'm going to put my weapons on the table. I'd appreciate it if you holstered yours.

We're friends here."[1]

McFarlane looked at them and nodded. "Major Hawthorn, Lieutenant Garcia, this is Captain Lacklan Walker. He is a friend. I would like you to leave us alone now."

They left reluctantly and she turned back to me. "Please, leave your weapons where they are. The drinks are on the sideboard. Mine is bourbon. May I call you Lacklan?"

I spotted the bottles. As I poured I said, "If I can call you Cyndi."

When I handed her her drink, she was smiling. "Well, as it seems we may be spending some time together, I don't see why not."

I sat and raised an eyebrow at her. "Does it? Are we?"

"Yes indeed. Your instructions are to..."

I was shaking my head and interrupted her. "I'm sorry, Cyndi, there has obviously been a misunderstanding somewhere along the line. I don't work for anybody, and nobody gives me instructions. I was asked to come here by an old friend, and I am here because I am doing her a favor. Let's be clear about that right from the start."

She stared at me for a long moment. Then she raised her eyebrows and stared into her drink. "I see. Well, I stand corrected, but this poses a problem, because now you are privy..."

I shook my head again and interrupted her for a second time. I could see it was getting on her nerves. That was OK with me. "I am privy to nothing so far. I was asked to come and see you by a friend. So I came. I don't know the details

---

1. See *A Harvest of Blood*

and for now nobody has used the magic word. I'd like to keep it that way."

She was staring at me hard now and looked like she might be about to get mad. "I have to say, Captain Walker..."

"Mr."

"*Mr.* Walker, that I am not accustomed to being interrupted constantly *or* being spoken to in this way."

"I can see that, Cyndi, but if you want my help you had better get used to it. Now, how about we start again from the beginning, and this time you tell me what it is you would like my help with. If I agree, then you can make me privy to any details."

Her cheeks had flushed and her eyes were bright. There was an edge to her voice when she said, "Yes, *sir!*" I waited, and after a moment she went on, "Without making you privy to any details: I need to travel to a given destination to meet with your friends. You can imagine what we are going to discuss, so I needn't tell you just how important it is that I get there in one piece. Your friends suggested that you were the man for the job."

I jerked my head at the door. "What about Major Confusion and the Subtle Boys?"

"Do you *have* to be so insulting?"

"Sometimes, yes."

"Your friends, both of them, said that you were the best there was. Professor..."

"Don't!"

She sighed. "He said that my security team were no match for..."

"I hear you. He's right. They may as well go around with neon signs on their heads. The people you are up against are very well funded, well trained and professional. But you know that. You work with them every day."

"Will you help?"

"Do we need to leave the country?"

"No."

"And the meeting is with my friend and the professor?"

"Yes."

"How long will this take?"

"Well, that depends to some extent on you, but I would imagine it will be three or four days. No more than a week."

"OK, I'll do it."

She didn't look overjoyed by the news. After a moment, she said, "About your fee…"

"No fee. I told you, I don't work for anybody. But there are conditions."

"Why am I not surprised?"

"I am in charge of this operation, and you make Major Hawthorn and his boys aware of that. We do things my way or I am out."

"Very well. Anything else?"

"Yes, who else knows about this?"

"Nobody."

"What about your husband?"

"My… Now *come on!*"

"How much does he know, Cyndi?"

"He is my husband! We have no secrets!"

"That changes as of now. People's lives are at stake, not least mine. You tell him nothing until you get back. If that is a problem, we are done here."

"Mr. Walker! I have had just about *enough*…"

I stood. "Thanks for the whiskey."

She was on her feet. "Now you wait just one goddamn minute, mister!"

I shook my head. "No. I am not prepared to have people's blood on my hands simply to pander to some silly notion of the sanctity of marriage. You want to play nice, get out of politics. My father murdered his best friend because they told him that if he didn't they would slaughter his family. When he'd done the job, they promoted him to one of the highest positions in the organization—the organization you are up against. That is the kind of people you're dealing with. If we do this, the operation is hermetically sealed. And that includes your husband." I took a step closer to her and looked her straight in the eye. "Put this operation in the hands of your band of clowns, and you'll all be dead before the end of the week. And that would be a shame, Cyndi, because I have always admired you a great deal. They need you, but they don't need Major Hawthorn—or your husband."

I could tell she really wanted to slap me, but I could also see she knew I was right. After a moment she took a big, deep breath and said, "Mr. Walker, Lacklan, will you *please* sit down."

I sat. She sat. I took a sip of whiskey and pulled a pack of Camels from my pocket. I showed it to her and said, "Do you mind?"

She held out her hand. "I'll join you."

I flipped the Zippo and lit her cigarette, then I lit mine, inhaled deeply and sat back. "Now, make me privy to the details."

She sipped and took a long drag. As she let out the smoke she said, "I need to get to New Mexico, Albuquerque, for a meeting with Marni Gilbert and Professor Philip Gibbons. They both say you know Omega better than anybody, and you have hurt them badly in the past."

I nodded. "They're right. OK, Cyndi. Here is how we are going to do this. You are going to go home, and you tell your husband that you have to go out of town for a few days. If he asks you where, or why, you tell him that it is confidential and you can't discuss it."

"He won't believe me. We have never..."

"That's not important. The only thing that's important is that he knows you are going voluntarily and you don't want to tell him about it. All we need is that he doesn't alert the cops because he thinks you've gone missing."

She spread her hands. "Fine!"

"What is your normal routine in the morning?"

"Oh, um..." She shrugged. "I rise at six, breakfast, work in my study, then at nine Charles, that's Major Hawthorn, drives me to the office..."

"OK, you're going to do that as normal, but tomorrow you are going to take a detour and you're going to go to the public parking garage on 9th Street. Go to the topmost floor. There you get out and you get into my car. I'll be waiting for you. You tell the Major to wait half an hour before leaving. Then he goes on to your office. He goes to the parking garage there. Waits ten minutes and then continues with his usual daily routine. Have you got all of that?"

She nodded. "Yes."

"Repeat it to me."

"*What?*"

"Repeat it to me, Cyndi."

I made her repeat it twelve times until she had it verbatim. Finally I made her tell me her address and stood. "OK, get one of your boys to drop me on Florida Avenue. I'll get a cab from there. And Cyndi? I am serious, you tell Hawthorn the bare minimum that he needs to know. Anybody else you tell absolutely nothing. That includes Marni and Gibbons, and especially your husband."

She stood. Her face flushed red. She'd had about as much of me as she could stomach. "Why *especially* my husband?"

I stepped close to her. "Because if I was out to find you, to assassinate you, the first person I would target would be your husband. If he doesn't know where you are or what you are doing, he may just have a chance of coming out alive."

She went white.

I said, "The people you are going up against are very bad people, Cyndi. You need to have assimilated that by tomorrow morning."

She stared at me for a long moment, her eyes making small, darting movements over my face. She was asking herself if she had made a smart choice or the worst mistake of her life. After a moment, she called, "Charles, come in please." The door opened and the major came in. "Please take the captain to Florida Avenue..."

CHAPTER 3

I<small>T WAS ANOTHER</small> J<small>EEP, PRETTY MUCH LIKE THE ONE</small> I had been brought in. Maybe she'd got a discount on a job lot. We crossed the front lawn under a black, starless sky, climbed in and slammed the doors. As we pulled away, he glanced at me. "So what's the story?"

"No story."

"What does she need you for?"

"That doesn't concern you."

We turned into Montello Avenue. "Everything that affects the Senator's safety is my concern."

I studied his face a moment and decided he was either in love with his boss or working for Omega. I said, "That is an admirable sentiment, Major, but unless you're going to put toothpicks under my nails, forget it. This doesn't concern you. Period."

We didn't speak again till he'd dropped me at the corner of New York Avenue. There, I stopped with the door half open. "Don't share this with anyone, Major. Not your colleagues, not your wife, not even your dog. Do you understand? Don't let her share it with her husband either. Are you hearing me?"

He didn't say anything, but he nodded. I got out. I waited till he'd disappeared from sight, then I crossed the road and hailed a cab. I got it to drop me at the Veteran's Park on G Street, by way of the CVS on K Street, and walked the block to the hotel. I ran up the six steps and pushed into the lobby. There was a young man on reception.

"I need to hire a car for a week or so."

"No problem, sir, we can arrange that for you."

He rattled at the keyboard on his computer and I handed him Joseph O'Brien's ID, driver's permit and credit card.

"For tomorrow morning, sir?"

"Eight AM or sooner."

"Seven thirty?"

"That's fine."

"And will you be dropping the car off here, sir?"

"No, I'm checking out tomorrow at six AM. I'll drop the car off at O'Hare in Chicago, a week from tomorrow, on Thursday 22nd."

"Very good, sir." He tapped in my card details and handed me back my ID and credit card. "It will be out front seven thirty tomorrow morning. Enjoy your evening."

I had a pizza at the hotel pizza restaurant and went up to my room to sleep and prepare for the next day.

———

THE SENATOR LIVED IN AN ELEGANT, understated, five million dollar, red brick house on P Street NW. I was there at eight thirty the next morning, parked in the shade of some elegant plane trees fifty yards from her door, in an anonymous Ford Focus. I was wearing the latex gloves I had bought the night before at the drugstore, and waiting for her to show.

At nine, just as she had said, the Black Jeep rolled up to the door and Major Charles Hawthorn climbed out and rang the bell. Two minutes later, she stepped out of the house and he opened the back door of the Jeep for her. He checked the road, climbed in behind the wheel and took off. I followed them east, staying about seven or eight cars behind them, watching in front of me and behind me to see if they were followed—or if I was being followed.

Eventually they turned onto Pennsylvania and then I Street, and from I Street they turned onto New York Avenue and made for the Technoworld Parking Garage. I closed in, just four or five cars behind them, and followed them through the barrier into the dark maw of the entrance. As we spiraled steadily up toward the top floor, their tires echoed mine in a weird rhythm of sqeals, like wounded pterodactyls chasing each other, screaming in the cavernous half light. We finally came to the top floor. I saw the red lights on the black Jeep up ahead and stopped a few paces behind it. The major got out and I got out to show him it was me. He opened the door for the senator, spoke some urgent words to her. She shook her head and came to the Ford at a half run. He carried her case to the trunk and put it in next to my shoulder bag. As I closed the trunk he eyed me.

"She better come back in one piece, Walker."

I didn't bother to look at him. "Save it for your memoirs, Major. Wait half an hour before you leave." I climbed in behind the wheel and handed her a pair of surgical gloves.

"Put these on, don't take them off until I say you can."

She took them and stared at them. I turned the car around and headed back down the ramp. She was still staring at the gloves, frowning.

I said, "Do it now."

"Is this *totally* necessary?"

"Yes. Do it. Then turn off your cell. The GPS makes it trackable."

She sighed and pulled them on as we came out of the garage and into the morning sunlight. Then she turned off her cell, like it was the most boring thing she had ever done.

We crossed the Potomac via the 14th Street Bridge, as though we were headed south. After Springfield we joined the I-95. I kept one eye fixed on the rearview mirror all the time, drove fast and changed lanes a lot. At one point the senator said, "What are you doing? What's got into you?"

I said, "Don't talk till we get to Montclair."

Her cheeks may have flushed. I wasn't looking.

By the time we reached Montclair I was pretty sure we were not being tailed, or at least not in a car, and I pulled off onto Dumfries Road, headed west. Pretty soon we were in semi-countryside. She gave me what was probably meant to be a withering look and said, "Can I talk now, *sir?*"

I still had one eye on the mirror. "Wait till Manassas."

She didn't talk again until I took Route 15 out of Warrenton, headed toward Culpeper. Then she couldn't contain herself any longer, narrowed her eyes and shook her head and said, "Have you *any* idea where you are going? Are you lost?"

I smiled at her, which made her frown, and said, "Not at all, Cyndi. We are on our way to Charlottesville."

"And in what universe is that on the way to Albuquerque?"

"In the one where you want to get there alive."

"And if possible this year!"

Satellites I couldn't do anything about, except hope Omega didn't know yet that I was Joseph O'Brien, and therefore what car I was driving. There were no choppers above us and I was certain by now that we were not being tailed by a car, so I allowed myself to relax, settled to a steady seventy and said. "You know time is relative, right?"

"*What?*"

"I aim to get you to Albuquerque in three to five days."

"*Three to five days?*"

"But that is going to seem like five years if you don't stop griping." She drew breath but I kept talking. "Tell me something, were you an only child or an older sister?" She turned in her seat and stared at me with wide, angry eyes. I glanced at her and shrugged. "My money is on elder sister. Am I right?"

She turned back to the road. "I do not intend to have this conversation with you. You are rude, boorish and insulting."

I shook my head. "I'm not being insulting. You are a good, caring person who wants to do the right thing and look after people weaker than herself. I think that's admirable, and it is something you often find in elder sisters."

She frowned at me for a while. There was suspicion in her eyes. "You're serious, aren't you?"

"Yeah." I looked at her and smiled. "You're also bossy and certain that you know best all the time."

She sighed.

"Most of the time you probably do. But in this case you don't. I do."

"So were you an older brother or an only child?"

"I was the younger brother. Hated my father and wanted to rebel. It was either sex, drugs and rock'n'roll or the army. I chose the army."

She was quiet for a while. "You don't seem the army type."

"Yeah, well, the Regiment isn't quite like the regular army."

"Your father was in Omega?"

I nodded. "One of the top three."

She considered me for a while. Outside, the world passed in a steady flow of trees, occasional houses and farms, and the steady throb of eastbound vehicles passing on my left.

"You must know a lot about Omega."

"I know more than most people who are not members."

She looked curious. "Why aren't you more involved with Marni Gilbert and Professor Gibbons? Seems to me you could be a real asset."

I shrugged. "It's a long story. They have their way of doing things. It isn't my way." I studied her face a moment. She didn't look away. I said, "They are a bit like you, Cyndi. They believe that they can tackle Omega by following the rules. They believe that Omega is like the Mafia, or a drugs cartel: a problem *within* society, that can be dealt with in the same way as other problems, by applying the usual solutions, and that life, society, the world will just keep right on going." I shrugged. "But it isn't like that."

She gave a lopsided smile that was half humorous and half skeptical. "It isn't? OK, maybe they are more powerful than the Mafia, and the corruption goes to a very high level, but it is still within society, and we still have to deal with it by following our own rules." She shrugged. "That's why it's called the Rule of Law."

I waited a moment, watching the long, straight road ahead, sucking my teeth. Finally, I shook my head. "Cyndi, if you had gone to this meeting with Gibbons by plane, which would have been the logical thing to do, by tonight you, Marni and Gibbons would have been dead. If we had taken the main east-west interstates—the obvious route—by tonight we would have been dead. You are a United States congresswoman, but you are forced to take an elaborate, secret route across America, in a hired car, because Omega is hunting you down. I have been twice to their office—in the Pentagon..."

She leaned forward, frowning. "*What?* They have an office in the *Pentagon?* You cannot be serious!"

I raised an eyebrow at her. "As I recall, the Mafia have no offices in the Pentagon. You have no idea yet what you are up against." I waited a moment, wondering how much to tell her. "You remember the Federal Agent who helped blow the nuclear bomb at the UN about a year ago? They thought at first he was Agent Harrison McLean, then it turned out not to be. In the end they never traced him, right?"

"Of course I remember, it was what started my campaign."

"That was me. I defused that bomb. It was intended to trigger a war with Europe."

"*What?*"

"And as an incidental bonus take out Marni and Gibbons. You kept asking on TV, how could terrorists get hold of a U.S.-made tactical nuclear device? Well, now you know. The terrorists were a front and the bomb was supplied to them by Omega. Omega owns people in Congress, in the military, in the courts and in law enforcement."

She had gone very pale. "Is this true, what you're telling me? I can't believe it. It's science fiction."

"You once described them as a cancer, on TV. They are not a cancer, Cyndi. They are a symptom of a sickness that goes much deeper. When I tell you they have an office at the Pentagon, and that former president Hennessy was a senior member, I am just scratching the surface."

She stared at me for a long time. Then she said, "Hennessy... He was killed, in a bomb blast at the Pentagon, just a few days after..." I glanced at her, but I didn't say anything. She put her hand to her mouth. "That was *you?*"

I shrugged. "Was it?"

"But... *you're a terrorist!*"

"Don't get carried away, Cyndi. Right now I am the guy taking you safely where you need to be. Don't lose your perspective."

"You can't go around just murdering people willy-nilly because you don't agree with their politics!"

I burst out laughing.

"*What* is so funny?"

"Your belief in your system. It is actually refreshing. I

wish you knew how many men, women and children were murdered by the people who died in that office. And not because they disagreed with their politics, simply because it was expedient to kill them. Marni's father was one of them."

"What proof have you got of that?"

It wasn't so much a challenge as a plea. "Proof? Proof I could put before a committee, or a court of law? None. My father told me on his death bed. Gibbons and Marni, they have some proof we have accumulated over time: recordings, video..."

We were quiet for a time as we approached Charlottesville. I turned onto the I-64 and started heading west.

"But if you plan to challenge Omega through the courts or through committees, you better be damn careful about what judges preside, and how those committees are constituted."

She shook her head. "Dear God, I hope I haven't made the biggest mistake of my life here. What will you do to me if I refuse to cooperate with you?"

I considered her for a moment, then sighed. "Nothing, and to be honest, Cyndi, that is the least of your worries. You have been very vocal about your belief in the existence of a government within the government, and Omega must be acutely aware of you as a threat. By now they will have studied you and they will know everything about you and your family, and about your associates and friends. Chances are very high that they know about this meeting."

"How could they?"

"That depends on how careless you have been. Your security team is sloppy, overconfident and arrogant. So are you. There are a number of people they might have got to, and a dozen ways they might have found out. We have to assume they are looking for you right now." I gave a small laugh. "You don't need to be afraid of me. Right now is probably the safest you've been for the last year." I grinned. "I'm like the good Terminator. I won't let anything happen to you, but you do need to trust me."

She didn't look amused or convinced, and we drove on in silence, toward the George Washington national forest.

Scan the QR code below to purchase TO RULE IN HELL. Or go to: righthouse.com/to-rule-in-hell

Printed in Dunstable, United Kingdom